Julie's World

James Alan Conlan

Ireland
First published by Ryehill Publications
2003

987654321

ISBN   1-902136-05-5

Cover by i-catch design
Printed and bound by ColourBooks Ltd. Dublin.

JULIE *The Book*

    I am totally alone. Why should it be so for me, a nineteen-year-old girl? My life is already spent! I look at myself; here in Granada, frozen in time on this unyielding, concrete rooftop with blood on my hands. I did what I had to do in this terrorist world and now there is no one to comfort me. My mind is stunned into an eerie silence. In a daze I watch the uninterrupted light of the full moon mark the vivid details of this Spanish city in slumber. My eyes look up at the great Alhambra, that Arabic fortress of eternal paradise; even this world wonder is paled into insignificance compared to what I have done.

Tonight, this night, silence weaves its unseen cloak. In the background I hear the students, driven by the testosterone of the creative force, packing like sardines into their disco haunts; each one a living frenzy, seeking, frantically seeking without stopping to question what is being sought. I wonder if there is one among them who really knows what I discovered by chance?

But how can they possibly know when all their energy is robotically spent trying to steel-closet themselves from the cold reality?

I look at myself, because now I must look at myself; there is no one else to turn to, not even the mother earth spirit that guided me to now. She is not concerned with the momentary flash of my particular individuality. I sense her indifference as she breathes in and breathes out all forms of life in her unwavering amorality. Now I see the secret of life. It has opened to me and I must pay the terrible price for knowing too soon.

The world is the foray for the individual; time, more time, each moment a race against time before it's too late, each moment spent for self-determination and self-fulfilment. I too have been there and it caused me to fight against all authority imposing upon me. My individuality, my self-determination had been all-important to me. Yes, I have lived intensely and it has led me to this, standing alone on a rooftop in this ageing city looking into total emptiness. All too abruptly life has dumped me on this impartial perch. Here my turbulent mind is obliged to face the unwavering reality of that terrifying aloneness behind existence that few have the courage to face. In a piercing despair my heart is calling to the soul of creation for solace. No answer it gets, only the deafening silence. My body shivers from the surging busts of inner coldness and still the mother earth spirit yawns her indifference.

There can be no more dreams, no hope for me of going on; I am standing alone on the point of existence, at any moment about to be blown into eternal oblivion. Face to face with nothingness, too late, alas, I vividly see I am life in this body, the only life known to me directly in my immediate experience. Up to this moment I have been like all others, endlessly rushing away from the 'now' and into an imagined future for my personal fulfilment. Ironically, the knowledge is mockingly tearing at my chest. All possibility of a future for my personal self and its world has been erased this night. Now I can see what the alchemist meant when he said: "Individuals come, each one making a personal commotion, like Cleopatra or Hitler made their individual commotions, then without exception all are devoured again by the nothingness behind the dust of it all, never more to be seen once the spark of each individuality finally re-settles."

The question looms in my mind; what is really important? The alchemist told me the answer is deep within me, but right at this moment I fail to reach it. The unchanging permanence behind existence keeps flashing through me, one moment illumining all, the next plunging me back into the unwavering darkness. It is clearly telling me I am but a temporary projection from nothing to nothing.

But why should I be cursed with such mind-blowing insight? It is far, far too soon for me, a young woman of nineteen barely awakening to life. Why should my individuality be so cruelly shattered? Please answer me? I'm calling to you, Mother Earth! Is it all a terrible dream? Am I going totally insane? Someone, something ... please answer me.

Nothing! Behind the worldly noise of this city I hear only your unchanging silence. Indifferently, you continue your impartial dance before me, weaving the cloak of your immediate guise in the illusiveness of this ancient place. I cry in pain and still you refuse to answer.

Must I accept your uncompromising truth? My God, there is nothing out there. Even before I was born into this, I am totally alone. I must take hold of myself before this mind explodes, before this nothingness grips me.

"Be calm; breathe in, breathe out, pause, be steady," I sense the voice of a higher intelligence speaking from somewhere within.

Must I attune myself now to this eternal silence behind existence? Is it the end?

Yes, it is; there can be no going back, my life is finished after what I have done this night in Granada; but more so, it now appears, after what I have come to finally realise.

How did it come to this?

Is it because I fought against all resistance to break through to the universal intelligence?

But I needed to know. Nothing was going to distract me. Now I see that life's distractions are the natural shields against knowing before one's time. Once one knows one can never again go back to the place of not knowing. There can be no return to the innocence or the ignorance. This is the price one must pay for going too far too soon.

JULIE

Without consideration I plundered the vast unknown after breaking through the defined parameters of the psyche that keeps humanity bound. Then, without warning, the hidden secrets behind existence unfolded to me at phenomenal speed, a speed that is even faster than being instantaneous, so fast it is already done before it actually begins. Such seeing is impossible to relay in words. I cannot explain it, not even to my pitiful self, hence the silence can be my only solace.

But I still have this body; full of life and vigour! What can it do with the terrible burden of knowledge imposed much too soon on its shoulders? Why must it suffer so?

I look into the shadows of the night and all I see remains tauntingly the same as before. Yet all within me has totally changed because of the speed leading up to this moment.

Oh Mother Earth Spirit, why do you not speak to me now? Just moments ago your womb was pregnant with all life oozing forth like a perpetual fountain of clear waters. Have you not fed me the milk from your breasts of abundance? This night I did what I had to do, did I not? Your knowledge ordained it so. Here in my anguish I call on you to show me the way out of my plight. But there is no reply. The eerie silence forces me to look inside your womb, and now I see it empty and barren.

I sense the life energy pulsing through these veins, this body, the only one known to me. Too late I know that 'I' am life here and now in this body and there can be no other. The alchemist told me I would only realise in my own experience there is none other than 'I' in existence. This primary knowledge I must accept. 'I' am completely alone to face it alone. Now I can see the world of the senses is but a temporary projection of the brain; the mother earth spirit is not even out there. Her silence obliges me to ask myself why should it be otherwise. Indeed, why should I deserve a particular answer?

JULIE

Who is asking the question? Is it not my wretched self at the point of losing forever its personal world?

Life has seen it all repeated so many, many times before. The alchemist pointed out that it speaks directly to me through the reflection of 'I' in all that stands immediately before me. Looking at this ancient city I see it has fostered many ages. It has said an impartial farewell to weeping Arabs, embraced Christian hoards, witnessed the spilling of blood time and again turning its rivers to a crimson red. Unperturbed by all these events where thousands came, lived, made love, suffered and died, the pulse of the creative force lives on in this place, quite unconcerned whether or not it is still entombed in its ancient splendour. It is the pulse of the blood in my veins and it clearly reflects I cannot escape it; nor can I change it, not even with this tumultuous mind, which now I know is the hellish volcano beneath the unspoilt beauty of life unimpeded. I see that 'I', life, am neither past nor future. 'I' am only now, the timeless 'now' as the unending pulse of the timeless.

My individual mind clings to this as the only certainty. There is not even the present for my personal self, for the present is also in the realm of time. Any moment this present can be taken from me, sucked into the past and once more locked away in a psychiatric tomb.

I try to focus again on my breathing, willing myself to reconnect to the pulse of the life in my body. It is all I have left; everything else has gone, my dreams, my hopes of tomorrow, all have been snatched from me through the horror behind this night. There is nowhere to go, nowhere to hide, no possibility of willing it all away. The finality of the looming consequences for what I have done is already breathing its cold, deathly breath upon me. How precious, how sweetly precious is life; how vividly clear it is at the moment of losing it forever.

The city's magical hue mirrors the circle around the moon. Looking at it through these eyes it seems as though the entire creation is mockingly laughing and dancing the unending dance of perpetual life before me. Too much to bear, my individuality further shrivels. The weight of the anguish upon me is muting my individual mind. I must accept it is clearly over for me, the individual person. Shocked into this 'emptied-ness' there is nothing left to impede my vision. My world is destroyed by my own hand and what a cold finality I have brought upon my destructive self.

Could there possibly be a silver lining to this grimacing cloud hanging over my personal world?

Could I have arrived at a point of enlightenment? No, definitely not, there is no enlightenment, no continuity for the person; no grandiose notions can save it.

'What do you now see?' A voice within me asks.

A voice in my head! Is it my imagination? My body twists in acute attention.

'What do you now see?' It speaks again, as clear as day causing the hair to stand on the back of my neck.

A third time it poses the question: What do you now see? The beauty of life at its end, a butterfly pinned to the spider's web, I am obliged to answer.

What do I see? I see the dance of humanity clinging to the crust of the earth amazing itself again and again by its own reflection; I see the tumult of human endeavour rising like a serpent's head from the murky depths of the psyche; I see it having its temporary display, then retreating again back into the psychic swamp; I see the swamp unperturbed by it all, re-settling in humming silence awaiting the next upheaval. There is a shimmering point in the centre I can see! Closer I look! To my amazement it is 'I', unending life, standing in the midst of the repetitive process. I see the individual self being thankful for this terrible night of events. A sudden flash! The unruly mind is silenced; and 'I', whoever I am, transcend it all into the shimmering behind existence. Now I can see; it is warm, beautiful, absolute aloneness, the eternal peace of my soul, a permanent halt from the hell of my bliss-seeking world.

I feel a quiver! The mind is back! Why should it be so? Why must I continue to be stuck in this time warp?

The students have locked themselves into their haunts and the city sleeps beneath me, as indeed the individual sleeps in its programmed pause between the unearthly sounds of its own inner torment. So must it continue, it seems, for the perpetually inert in the breathing in and breathing out of our imaginary worlds.

As I look much, much closer I can see life in all its splendour, uninterrupted, as though smiling to itself behind the unseen madness. It is the love, the pulse and the breath transparent of the cool night air. It is the joy, the pain and the all-embracing dance of 'I' being life in this body. Yes, I can connect to this and I love it deeply.

But there is no individuality in it. Life has taught me to love nothing in particular. 'Tis now I know how naïve I am whenever I try to personify love; now I know when it is much too late for knowing. I see my mind desperately clinging to the guilt as a means for its own survival, pounding the reminder that I have committed the most terrible crime against life itself this night.

Why did it happen? Too late I now know why.

In the alchemist's presence I was awakened from my mind world to a speed of consciousness beyond that of light. Then I foolishly allowed the consciousness to crash again on the particular. It is obvious it would have to end this way. I was given the elixir of life and then I lost it again. Now life is dealing with me hard and direct. It has rocketed me to this perch of the timeless with no other option but to be at one with the cold reality. Here again I am reconnecting to my first awakening. I know in my heart that death does not separate me from him, nor will it separate me from life when I, myself, must inevitably pass through its door, regardless whether or not this mind can understand or accept it.

The initial realisation of this hit me in Dublin, my place of birth. I recall how less than two years ago the wise old man of master consciousness told me of this particular moment. Since then it seems like many lifetimes have passed with all that has so unexpectedly happened.

At the time when I encountered the alchemist's presence I was but a confused child still being terrorized into the mould of this make-believe world. But I must have been sufficiently awake to receive the key, even though the stagnant rituals surrounding my parent's fabricated existence had all but smothered my life essence.

Being an only child can have its advantages in a house filled with love, but the opposite applies in a house filled with pretence that is cloaked in old superstitions. I was the scapegoat burdened with all their un-faced issues. It may not have been their intention, nonetheless, in their unseen ignorance my parents placed all their deceptions upon my innocent shoulders. Rebellion only helped to make matters worse and I could see no way out other than bearing the brunt of their world and the ensuing psychological pain in silence. As a result I went into myself, thus causing the dark clouds of their opinions to close in upon me.

My father, being a psychiatrist, had medically labelled my condition. In his mind-world I was mentally unstable and in continuous need of medical treatment. His unyielding fixation caused me languid periods in psychiatric hospitals with my spirit brutally muted by the force of his conviction. When one is told often enough one is mentally ill, then, sooner or later, one takes it on board. Was he right or wrong? He claimed to be the medical expert.

JULIE

During my time as a patient I saw everything relating to the mind going into slow motion. Whenever a sporadic burst of insight broke to the surface of some other sufferer there was always a medic nearby to douse it with drugs. In such institutions the order of each day is docility, but my little intelligence was sufficiently swift at the time to see through and beyond it.

During one such period a man called Frank befriended me. It happened via his silent attention when I first became aware of my own reflection in the pain he showed in his eyes. I could see he was filled with compassion for me and he made me feel that I was being deeply loved. Gradually we talked a little until he reminded me of the futility of words and this is how he introduced me to the silence. As a matter of fact, he was the first to show me how to let the mind fall still as we sat together in the grounds of Saint Pat's in Dublin.

Frank was in his early thirties and he had excelled in the new exploratory world of biotechnology. The brilliance and phenomenal speed of his brain had attracted the attention of large multinationals. He told me how he had been working on new research in Germany and Holland before he finally snapped. He spoke of the pulse in the atom that is faster than the speed of light. In other words, we are here and not here simultaneously. Such speed of consciousness took him beyond the matchbox world of the scientists where no one could relate to him anymore, least of all his immediate family. When the limited minds of the medical world were faced with his situation they could only diagnose insanity. Their singular treatment for this being drugs, Frank's extraordinary brilliance was soon doped into the tiny pigeonhole of their understanding.

But he was there for me and he became my close friend and guide for one of my lengthy confinements. What I learned from him was the only beneficial thing I received during all those times I had been committed by my father to mental hospitals. Frank was the first glimmer of real intelligence that came my way. He was the precursor of what was about to come in the person of the alchemist who later answered my questions relating to the pulse in matter as described by Frank, something the scientists have not yet fully discovered.

The portal to meeting the alchemist happened when I saw the hand of that wise old man reaching through the crowd in my direction. His words echoed through the hollow drums of my own denials calling on me to wake up. Wake up I did, and what an awakening it was after being in his presence.

Directly afterwards I startled my father with my first real protest at the door of the synagogue in South County Dublin. I had taken him on and I clearly knew what was lying before me. As a child of the earth I could no longer accept the apparent falseness of the world he presented, nor could I anymore accept the age-old superstitions sustaining its falseness. It seemed as though his self-imposed lack of vision was his only shield from reality. He needed to be part of his fold being held together by the ideology of exclusion, the sacred curse that only serves to bring calamity upon itself time and again. His fear shut him off from the universal intelligence of life immediate, whereas, the truth was far too precious to me and, having tasted it once in the alchemist's presence, I would settle for nothing less.

Just like any spirited teenager, I had to fiercely fight against my father to free myself from his grip. My battle centred on breaking down the superstitions holding his make-believe world together. To that world he appeared as a rock solid man and a great psychiatrist where people came to him for assistance. But they were unable to see his insecurity and his desperate need of their support to sustain the image he had of himself. In fear he clung to his beliefs and imaginary god, the same fear, as I can now see, that is the lingering curse humanity has always imposed on itself. The multitudes are born within its confines and they act out their lives according to the repetitive programme. Whenever truth manifests through such all-powerful individuality of a Buddha, a Socrates or even Jesus, the Judaic heretic, to raise the consciousness of all, still it gets overshadowed again by the babbling words of fearful fools and followers.

In the distance I hear the police sirens still rushing to the dreadful scene I have left in my wake. There seems to be no letting up. Why did it happen? It obliges me to re-exam it all from the beginning.

I challenged the entire belief structure and I was accused of being mad. By all means I could question the ideologies of others, but how could I possibly doubt our own great heritage! Were not our ancestors guided by the prophets? How could I be so blasphemous as to challenge the very foundations of our own established order? No one should defy the self-assumed wisdom of the elders; anyone so daring is insidiously shunned and silently excluded. But I had been opened to a greater wisdom before I was sufficiently drugged to breathe in the full extent of their worldly mucus. Now I clearly see all their fixations as nothing more than sheer, pathological madness.

"What do you see?" the voice interrupts.

I see how the seeds of all such beliefs were planted for particular minds way back in the past. Not only have they outlived their usefulness but they have grown into giant size trees and the consciousness of humanity is being stifled by them. Even the bitterness of their fruits surely tells us the time has come to transcend them. In fact, I could see this before I was exposed to the transcendental consciousness of the alchemist. Even at the age of twelve I could see that life was far more expansive than my father's narrow vision. But his unshakable attitude left no way open for me to reason with him.

The truth for him was far too daunting to accept. The belief structure was serving its purpose, he needed it so he had to defend it, even against the fact that this very same structure has created its destroyers in the past. His mind was only capable of digging down to the face of Hitler, then loading the blame on the shoulders of this crazy man. There it must stop; one inch deeper and the cold reality might have to be faced. The easy way out is in giving in to the fear, thus closing off from the greater intelligence coming through the cosmic order of all things.

But I cannot blame my father for that. Is it not so with the masses in general? The whole of humanity seems to be caught up in the repetitive past, like walking backwards through time and totally missing the immediacy of life in the now. I felt the truth of this even before the alchemist explained it in the words:

"In the greater reality there is no past. True, the past is substantive, but it is only substantive in relation to 'now'. A beginning in the past can be no more than a concept of the mind. The truth of this cannot be seen by the scientists simply because their thoughts are locked into the repetitive programme relative to matter and linear progression on the visible side of the pulse in the atom. This is their world, which is mind and not life, imposing itself upon the natural order of the higher intelligence."

He was referring to the speed of consciousness that is faster than the speed of light. Unable to be such intelligence, this world of our fathers needs its belief structures to give substance to its madness, whether it be expressed through wilful acts of terrorism or devout religious practice, both of which I have had to face.

Such is this patriarchal world, and to me my father was the most immediate representation of it. I soon realised that most of his private patients were part of the conscience brigade as they rattled through their grievances, always different yet always more of the same. Gradually I began to see the pattern after hearing it all through the half-closed, consultancy door. It emerged that fear and guilt were the main ingredients behind most of their problems. Time and again I was seeing the ugly head of a jealous and angry god eagerly waiting to discard those wretched souls, if not to the unspoken void of exclusion, then surely to the Christian fires of hell, either here in their world or in some imaginary world hereafter. But none could see how they had been programmed and instilled with such terror in the first place.

Soon I realised that believing in any such things is merely a strategy for expunging the psychological fear of death and is nothing more than a denial, or a falsification of the reality. How pathetic it is for a daughter to see a seemingly intelligent father allowing such fears to wilfully block his vision. But he could not accept it. His holy book, being his solid rock of ignorance, was his one support and the foundation stone for all his patriarchal falseness.

I attended a Catholic school and, excused from religious instructions, I was able to listen from the end of the classroom. This gave me the vantage-point from which I could easily see their belief structure similarly based on the imposition of fear. In fact my childhood was the hell on earth I had in some unknown way called upon myself. Little did I know what I was soon to discover; the real burning of hell is only felt when one decides to escape from it. Logically the burning has to be the way out.

But one has to be courageous, for escaping from hell is actually escaping from the conditioned force of the tribal mind. For me it meant discarding all the beliefs being imposed upon me by my immediate family, society and its historical background spinning back from the timeless now. It meant stepping alone into the void. I too had fear and whenever I gave into it I knew it was holding me back. But I could also feel the wonder of life, alive and vibrant within me and I knew I had to trust it completely as the burning within me commenced.

'What do you see?'

I see how most people think they know while nobody really knows. No matter where I look I meet it again and again; people wanting to believe in some notion or other while refusing to accept that believing in anything is merely a presupposition. It is not possible to be the truth in the now when the mind is consumed with crazy notions regurgitating the past. At times I see it clearly and then the clouds of confusion return again. But the mother earth spirit always has the answer whenever I need her; that is, whenever I am still enough in myself to listen.

Is that why she seems so silent this night? Am I in too much turmoil to receive her message? I know I should be spending this time examining myself, but before I do, I feel compelled to look at this world now crashing upon me and crushing me out of existence.

'What do you see?'

I see ignorance; people everywhere believing in stories and ignoring reality. But reality cannot be ignored forever. Sooner or later a calamity has to occur to explode the falsehood again. Yet, in spite of the greatest sufferings endured, somehow or other the ignoring seems to find continuity. Through the mouths of the living dead it maps a way to slip into other generations where the calamities of the past become revered as part of our great heritage, or atonement to a vindictive god for previous misgivings. Quite obviously, no one really wants to wake up!

JULIE

The masses, it seems, need their beliefs and superstitions. Oddly enough, most religions have been devised by men. Then they are supported by those women who are seeking security of tenure, or some form of permanence for themselves through their sons, while life immediate is screaming the opposite; dust unto dust, as it was, so it is now and it always must be. And what is terrorism but another kind of belief? They make bombs, kill and maim in similar lack of vision. As a child I had come to realise that man has no idea. Quite obviously, it is different for woman. The biological changes occurring in my body at that time spoke louder than any of their repetitive words. But not for every woman, it seems.

I could not reach my mother. She was totally occupied in her efforts moulding herself into being an acceptable part of men's fanatical world. Everywhere I looked I could see women striving for equality with men. But few if any could truly see men's dementedness and why they were striving with their holy books or bombs to force their fixations upon others. Hardly anyone seems to question the ideology behind the ongoing madness. Am I the crazy one? Am I the only one who sees the entire world of men gone mad with the women rushing behind them trying to be equally as mad?

My mother had shut herself off completely from her womanhood, even though she did not seem to realise how she had isolated herself. This left me with no one to turn to for help or true understanding. I was totally alone facing the terror of this patriarchal figure with his litany of rules and regulations about his all-important ideologies.

Had I not suffered enough? Why did I have to go through it again in the open world of terrorists with their ideologies that exploded in my face this night?

Why should it be put on the children to suffer the terrible burden? My God! How long does it take to awaken?

17

JULIE

Yes, indeed, I see it now as I stand here alone looking into the shadows of my short-lived past. I am amazed at how far I have travelled in such a short time since being in the presence of the alchemist.

I was hardly seventeen and aimlessly rambling through Temple Bar when I first spotted the small advertisement in a café window. It was a cold, Friday afternoon in Dublin and I was returning from a dentist appointment. The thought of being locked up at home in preparation for that weekly ritual of the Sabbath was at the forefront of my mind. Reluctant to face it, I was dragging out the evening in the city centre when the poster grabbed my attention.

"The truth shall set you free," the words seemed to shout directly at me from the countenance of the man in the picture that really drew me to it. Although his hair was snow white and his skin was loose on his face, yet there seemed to be an eternal youth sparkling through his deep, penetrating eyes. I knew I was groping, reaching for straws, and I was open to swallow anything with a ring of truth in my desperate attempt to create some meaning to my life. Something told me I had to meet him, but it meant travelling to the city centre on the evenings of the following week.

Four of the five I managed to attend before my father checked with the school on the Friday to confirm if the teachers had really arranged a week of late study for the more diligent pupils. Then I was confined to the house for a month of nights for failing to disclose to him or the school where I had been.

The punishment did not disturb me. In those four evenings my consciousness had been penetrated. For the first time in my life I had met someone who was not only speaking the truth but was living it as well. The alchemist assured me I was not mad, rather I was one of the few sane in a world that is an open-air asylum.

I was open to him and sufficiently innocent at the time to receive his enlightenment without hindrance. During those four evenings an extraordinary shift of consciousness occurred within me. I discovered for the first time that I am completely alone in the actual 'being' of life in my body. This man of master consciousness helped me realise that I am life, totally and absolutely. He not only clarified it through his words, but he led me to the actual realisation of it in my inner being, which has nothing to do with the world of the mind. It was he who awakened me to this fundamental reality that is ever present before the thinking mind infringes upon it and slows it down. In his presence my consciousness speeded up to 'be' the immediacy, or to be the 'now' as he put it. Yes, I transcended the turgidity of the mind world, thanks to this man's cosmic presence and guidance.

In the ensuing clarity I could see life more clearly and I could not help but notice the world around me as that of the living dead with people running frantically from one gush of thoughts to the next, all caught up in some mental time-wave. The ongoing reactions of the masses became more and more predictable to me, and the world laced together with fear-ridden beliefs could no longer hold me, even though I continued to attend the rituals in body until that day when I finally exploded and swore I would never again go into their temples.

Then the Rabbi was called to the house. They came to me and argued against their fears of accepting the truth. I tried to be logical but they did not want to know. They could not listen, nor would they try to listen. In agony I called on them to wake up. Frustration gripped hard on my chest as I realised I was completely alone facing a jabbering crowd. In the midst of the turmoil I heard the alchemist's words repeating within me:

"Without ears to hear they cannot hear; without eyes to see they cannot see. Can you give them ears? Can you give them eyes? Try if you must, but do not forget in the greater reality all is perfect right now, exactly as it is. We perceive in space and time and this is our limitation. See and accept that everything is as it is and know that nothing in space and time has space to happen before its time."

Suddenly, I could see it clearly. These people before me were not my family; they were in a different space and time zone, complete strangers to me, even my mother as she meekly stood in the background lost to her fear of the dark suits and sinister faces imposing their ignorance upon me. I rose from the chair, ran to the bedroom and locked the door from their world where I silently wept deep into the night until restless sleep eventually engulfed me.

That very night was the eve of what was to change my direction completely, even though at the time it all seemed so insurmountable, like being at the end of a dark alley with no way out. But the aloneness then is no comparison to the terrifying aloneness I am now experiencing here in Granada so many, many miles away from Dublin. Now I stand in total isolation, barely holding on, as I look out through these eyes on a cold and indifferent world.

How could life be so cruel to allow it all to conclude in the way it has done?

Why must there be such finality in death?

Who am I asking?

I am asking you! Are you not with me right now?

I trust you will tell me whether or not I am mad. I do not know. Indeed, not knowing is all I truly know. You alone are my God, my judge and my executioner.

Can it be any other way?

Obviously not!

The morning called. I made my way to the small bathroom at the rear of the house. It was seldom used and I needed to be alone. I needed to distance myself from those violently emotional vibes consuming my father's presence. Then my mind started pounding again as similar emotional rage took hold of my body.

On what authority did he have the right to lock me into his emotional world? I could see how he had already muted my mother into a silent existence. She had been a woman of remarkable talent, but now she was reduced by him to a robotic slave. She hardly spoke as she quietly moved through time, each day another day nearer to her one and only apparent escape. Yes, it was more than obvious, I had to somehow escape from his obsessive brutality.

I could not accept him to be my biological father. Should I be carrying his genes in my blood then I would surely have to kill myself. No, I could not accept any connection with him, not even through a piece of haphazard sperm. At least my mother bore me in her womb for nine long, agonizing months, two of which were before the wedding, a fact she completely denied whenever I tried to open the lid of her past.

If only she had courage to go it alone, surely, she could have done. She had the world at her feet before she caved in under the social pressure. She left behind the one real lover in her life when she decided to become the burden bearer of her Jewish heritage. She never spoke of him, but I had pieced it together over the years.

He was a Catholic from the north side of Dublin and he came from a family with little money. Apparently, it was a passionate and turbulent affair that lasted right up to the day of the marriage. That day now appears as the day my mother died with me in her womb. In my foetal state she entombed me in her pain and my presence as a child seemed to be a constant reminder of the hell she had chosen. I was being faced with the brunt of that hell as I entered the kitchen on that final morning.

There was no toothpaste so I needed to go back upstairs. But I heard a stirring above me and I knew he had commenced his daily ritual. I could not face him again and I made do with salt from the kitchen. At that moment I realised I hated him and everything about his world. My eyes fell upon the carving knife on the breadboard. Then I knew I had to get out before real madness griped me. Bringing the Rabbi to the house was the final straw. I had put up with about all I could handle. Five times he had me committed to hospitals for treatment. But his type of treatment was the mutation of the life essence within me. This was his only way of meeting my fiery spirit. Such terrible torture! Is it possible for anyone to understand?

The heavy footsteps descending the stairs sent cold shivers up my spine. My body froze. He was in the doorway, holy book in hand, with black eyes staring at me.

"Sit down young lady right now and listen, this is final," my ears received his words as concrete blocks pounding my brain. Then something exploded within me.

"Final!" I screamed. "'Tis final for you, you demon from hell! You can take your book, your phoney god, and shove them up your ignorant arse".

He grabbed me violently in his anger and I still do not remember how the knife got into my hand, nor do I recall him grabbing it by the blade. But I can recall seeing the blood on the floor and all over the draining board. Then nothing mattered anymore. Obviously, I had been driven too far and I was completely out of control. I truly became aware of my fury when I saw it reflected through the unexpected fear in his eyes. While struggling to wrap the wound with a kitchen towel he cowered out of reach at the far side of the table. Seeing his vulnerability for the first time, the rage consuming my body was driving me to finish him there and then. Having lost control of myself I pushed the table to one side as he cowered between the fridge and the wall. By this time he had clutched a chair to protect himself and, in the ensuing struggle, the knife fell from my hand. Still shouting in anger I grabbed my bag and banged the back door behind me. It was sudden, violent and finished.

Where could I go? What could I do?

Not looking around, I walked from that house still tasting the salt on an empty and heaving stomach, the only clothes I had being those on my back. Deep inside me I knew it was the final blow; such a volcanic eruption had abruptly brought the smothering world of my past to a bitter end. Now there was no going back. But little did I know at the time it was only the beginning of the real hell about to present itself.

Innocently, I felt it was over. Surely nothing could be worse than what had occurred. I had won my freedom in such an unexpected way. For me at that moment, it was truly over, it was finished. Even though I felt sure of this, yet unimaginable fear griped at my feet as I walked in a daze through my tears. But something in my solar plexus, like a tingling sensation on fire, spurned me onward towards the unknown, while deep psychological pain was exploding in fragments inside me. My body convulsed while my feet robotically carried me through the shadows of the early morning. I was not even aware of the other persons on the footpath making their way to work. Aimlessly, I walked and walked. Then, rounding the corner at the end of the long street joining the main road leading to the city centre, the early morning sun broke through the haze and blazed its light and heat directly upon me. Freedom! I could feel its embrace; it was blessed life itself spilling into every part of my body. I knew I had arrived at that point without decision; it had not been schemed nor devised by my mind. As I continued to walk I kept repeating the alchemist's words to myself: "It is as it is, I have to accept it, I have to accept it."

The resonance of his voice in my inner ear responded: "Acceptance is the only contribution the person must make." Somehow I knew whatever was about to happen would be right, as long as I stuck to that voice of truth the man had awakened within me. This alone was my rock that I had discovered by chance.

I remember the young man and his magical flute; how his shaggy hair stuck like a worn-out mat to his head. I spotted him playing for his breakfast as I stepped off the bus close to the railway entrance. He had nothing apparent to give and the little he had he obviously needed for himself. Yet, he was the only one to notice my plight and he instantly stopped when he saw me. Directly looking into my face through his deep, searching eyes he posed the question: "Would you like a hot mug of tea?"

I found myself nodding and going with him. We crossed some disused railways, after which we continued along some lanes. Eventually we came to a makeshift hut located between some derelict buildings. This was his home with a gas ring and kettle. I noticed an old mattress with some covers piled in one corner. Two biscuit tins and three empty jars summed up the rest of his belongings. But he seemed blissfully content with his lot as he slowly poured the boiling water into two waiting mugs.

I recall how I wrapped my hands around that hot mug of tea, the first time having it without milk and how delicious it tasted. It was early May and the morning was not excessively cold, yet I could not stop my body from shivering. He moved without speaking and placed an old blanket around my shoulders as I sat there looking into the empty space before me. Later I noticed him casually rolling a cigarette with no hurry about his action. When he reached out and offered it to me I could feel the anxiety rising within me. I shook my head; having been through so much I had little trust left in humanity. But he sat there motionless with his outstretched hand, unperturbed, until I eventually reached out and took it. Then he rolled another for himself and lit it before offering me the lighter to do whatever I willed.

Gradually I began to warm to his presence. His silence was the most precious gift I could have received that morning. It made me feel as though I was at last in the presence of a true psychiatrist. He did not have the look of a scholar, yet he seemed fully tuned in to life. There was no urgency about him, being completely at ease, yet fully alive to the moment.

It was my first step into the great unknown, that journey of wonderment the alchemist had mentioned during those four evenings in Temple Bar. A surge of great privilege momentarily consumed my body as the thought flashed through my mind. Then fear suddenly gripped me as an unexpected second thought secured a foothold. Soon my father would have the police, the media, indeed everyone out looking for me. I saw the image of his blood on the floor of the kitchen and I started to shiver again.

"I can't go back ... I just can't," I was muttering aloud in a daze when I felt the young man's hand on my shoulder.

"You don't have to do anything you don't want to do," was all that he said.

Then he refilled my mug, thus causing the disturbing thought to gradually fade into the background. When the next thought came I was a little more prepared for the emotional wave accompanying it. The alchemist had spoken about such emotions and he had opened my eyes to see them for what they are. He had said that once I would clearly see and understand their source they would lose their power over me for good. Now I could see how the pleasant, idle thoughts open the door in the mind for the unpleasant ones to enter and this is how the emotions are triggered. Little did I realise I would be experiencing the truth of his words so soon.

Obviously, it was my time, even though I was so very young. But awakening to life has nothing to do with age. In the phenomenal speed of events it all appears as being part of the same moment, sitting in front of the alchemist for four special evenings, then sitting in the hut with that silent young man, and now being here alone with you as my only listener. Such, I was shown, is the natural speed of consciousness when not impaired by the particular.

Back to the hut; the flute player rose to his feet, told me to rest and to make it my home; he had some busking to do and he would later return with food. Then he was gone.

I curled myself up in the blankets at the corner of the hut and before I knew it I had fallen into a dreamless sleep. Strange as it may seem, it was the best sleep of my life up to that moment. I eventually awakened to the heat of the evening sun as it caught my face after edging through the half-open doorway. The silence was amazing, not just the silence around me, but the deep silence within me as well. I remember sitting there in the stillness, enraptured in the moment as time itself appeared to be frozen. It was my first real taste of freedom from the turmoil of my mind and its terrible world.

Then he returned with fresh bread, cheese and milk and I could feel each cell in my body light up with delight. At that moment it was a natural feast; my taste buds were ecstatic as I savoured each mouthful. Soon my belly was full and it helped my voice to return. But I found I had nothing to say except to thank him for the food and to let him know I needed a toilet.

"Take a walk in any direction," he replied in a manner of natural helpfulness. I took him at his word and found a place to relieve myself behind a burnt out car.

Little was spoken after that. I just sat and watched the moon appear through a few scattered clouds in the night sky over Dublin as I savoured the extraordinary ease in his presence. There were no questions about who I was or where I had come from. Although his vocabulary was limited, nonetheless, I could sense nothing rising in him, no wants, not even expectations; he seemed to be fully content just being in the moment taking in the strange beauty of the derelict buildings silhouetting the city night.

It all seemed so unreal that I began to question myself as to what was real and what was not. I could clearly see that the world of my father was not real. He even disallowed me to have a boyfriend and I wondered why. What could have been his problem? There I was, for the first time alone with a young man and I could see nothing harmful in it. So what could have been my father's fear?

Like a flash of lightening it struck me. His fear was of himself. He only knew man as he was himself. In his ignorance he was a psychological abuser without even knowing it. Not only that, but he had abused his own intellect by misusing it to cloak his ignorance. He even abused woman through his approach. I could see it in the way he belittled my mother. He inflicted me with his abuse in the form of the huge restrictions he caused me to suffer and then defended his actions by trying to tell me he was protecting me from the evils of the world. But from whose world was he really trying to protect me?

I knew I had seen this before, or at least I had psychically felt it, but that night in the hut while alone with my thoughts I could see it all the more clearly. His enclosed way of thinking and his mind-made world were the source of all my problems and mental traumas. This is surely what drove me away.

In the medical field he was an acclaimed expert and an acknowledged lecturer by budding, student psychiatrists. But all his expertise did not match up to the fact that in practical terms he knew absolutely nothing about life. If this was the best the world had to offer then logically something had to be seriously lacking in the world. I knew it then but I did not listen, for again I partook in their world and re-entangled myself in its web. Now I see it when it is much too late, as I stand here stripped of it all speaking to the cold wind bearing down from the Sierra Nevada mountains.

"Stilling the mind is one's only escape from the repetitive process," the alchemist advised.

But it is easier said than done, is it not? He had told me that entertaining thoughts without applying them to action is a waste of energy and time. In the hut with my gypsy friend was the first time in my life being in a clear space. Before then it was either my father or some hospital staff who had been appointing themselves as the organisers of what I should and should not think. I felt I had to use the time at hand to work things out. I needed to know who and what I really was in the sense of what I had heard the alchemist say.

The barrage of thoughts did not disturb the serenity of my new-found friend. He sat there totally unconcerned while focusing his undivided attention on carving a flute from a piece of wood. Looking at him I realised I was in the presence of real intelligence. I tried to match it up to what the alchemist had said about real intelligence and the pseudo intelligence of the transient world. Then another dialogue took root in my restless mind.

Is this young man the real intelligence? I silently questioned myself.

"Real intelligence is formless; it is the ability to see things as they are with no person in it," the alchemist's reply instantly flashed from the void within.

"The young man beside you is merely the silence through which the real intelligence is being reflected upon," the resonance of his voice continued.

But, if it's reflected intelligence then where is its source? I tried to reason with myself.

The answer was suddenly clear, but I could not accept it. Everything is being projected by the human brain and existence, as each one sees it, is the screen on which it is being projected. This could only mean that the source of all life is coming from some place within the body; my father, my diagnosed madness, the horror behind this night here in Granada, all are being projected as my particular world through my particular brain; no brain then no projection, just formless life pulsating from the source of real intelligence. As a corollary to this, 'I' in the body have to be the source. Logically it has to be so.

"No, it cannot be me," I shouted aloud, not realising I had broken the silence.

The young man slowly turned his head, frowned a little with a look of puzzlement on his face and asked;

"What is your name?"

"Julie, Julie Steinheart."

"Mine is José María," he replied in an air of repose without adding anything further.

Again the silence returned and filled the hut with its presence. For some time I just sat there wondering what else to say. It was a strange sensation, like waking from sleep and finding something awesome from some other dimension standing by your bed.

"José María! With a name like that you must be Italian or Spanish?" I intrusively questioned, being unable in myself to reconnect to the finer vibration of the natural silence.

"Yes, I'm Spanish," he replied, as he put down the piece of wood he was carving, excused himself and disappeared down the laneway.

I sat there alone trying to regain the silence in myself, trying to return to that less troublesome state I felt I had just exploded. But my mind was again in turmoil, like a speeding train out of control and fast running out of track.

"No, I cannot be the source," I kept repeating to myself.

If I were the source of real intelligence then I would have to be the source of all life and such would be impossible. I began to fear I was on the borders of insanity as the waves of thinking and trying to reason it out kept spinning through my head. In the psychiatric hospitals they had been trying to convince me through their looks and assumptions that I was insane. There I had the reflection in their many faces, but in the hut I had nothing to image my reflection upon apart from my mind. Now I was beginning to doubt my sanity and this in turn was bringing on further panic attacks. The gloom was too heavy to bear when I began to realise I was the one projecting it all. Again the alchemist's words flashed from the void:

"You can only increase your intelligence by giving up your negativity."

The young man returned. As I looked up at the outline of his body in the darkness I suddenly realised the moon had gone. Even the distant sound of traffic had all but faded into the stillness of the night. He motioned it was time to sleep by giving me a blanket and wrapping himself up in another after rolling out the mattress. I sat there for some time looking into the blackness behind the shadows, hoping the confusion would ease in my mind. Eventually it did, but with jagged edges. One moment a wave of panic rose to such a crescendo I feared my head would explode, the next moment I could feel a wave of stillness sweeping through my entire body. Then the panic would return, building and building to a higher pitch than before, but only to recede again. So it continued well into the night, each time stronger than before, to another point of exploding my head. I was thankful for the presence of my silent friend; it was comforting to know there was someone nearby to save me from my madness.

But I could not stop the panic attacks being fuelled by the mind. I thought about Frank and our times of meditation together before they had taken him away. I waited for his calming influence to enter me, but nothing would come. My body would not stop trembling as the emotional discharges continued to pound my brain like tidal waves crashing against unstable cliffs. I tried to recall what the alchemist had said in relation to such a situation, but nothing would come. Then, out of the blue, his answer to a question relating to reality edged into focus.

"What is reality, you ask me! But you only ask when you are in the pits of your misery. Why are you miserable? I will tell you why. You are miserable because you are not getting your way! Instead of accepting life as it is, you are stuck in your head and what you imagine you try to force into existence. You foolishly convince yourself that your imaginings are part of your natural fulfilment. Then life in its goodness delivers an awakening blow. You feel the sudden pain of it, just like banging your head off the wall! You come to me for an immediate cure. I tell you to stop imagining, to stop banging your head off the wall. You thank me, of course! But it will not be long before you start doing it all over again. Once more you stagger before me, seeking another fix, another cure. What is reality, you ask! I say, see it as it is, accept it as it is, 'be' it as it is. This is the one and only reality."

He was right of course. It is exactly as he said; but try putting that to a mind in emotional turmoil, there is hardly a chance! Yet, his words did help me dissolve some of the emotions when I started to recognise the pattern. Instead of trying to fight the panic attacks I sunk deeper into my being from where I could simply be the observer. From there I began to see the climacteric of each attack getting weaker and weaker. Gradually they lost their potency, no longer being able to feed from my life energy when I stopped myself fighting against them. Within a couple of hours a relative calm had returned, enabling me to lay down beside José María and re-enter his peace.

How far I have travelled since then. Right now I look into myself and I see there are no more panic attacks. The emotions no longer bind me, and for this I am eternally grateful. Now I know I can never again be catapulted back to that courser plain of living death. Pure sensation is only present, shapeless and formless behind the senses dissolving all probability of emotional fear re-captivating my being. Yes, it is the affirmation that I have passed through the emotional world, never again to be trapped within its confines. This space is clear at last with nothing other than ice-cold acceptance impartially awaiting the Spanish dawn.

JULIE

It was a strange relationship with José María that lasted for most of a week. It gave me the necessary space to explore into my own subconscious. I had to transcend my own contribution to the ignorance sustaining the world. My gypsy friend never interrupted, as he came, went, mostly in silence and shared with me his food.

We spoke very little except for the few stories he told me about the magic embracing this place of his birth called Granada. Apparently, he had lived in this city with his mother during his childhood years and their home for much of that time was one of the caves overlooking the Darro valley. But she died when he was barely fourteen and from then on he was left to fend for himself. I never questioned as to how he came to be in Dublin nor did he volunteer to tell me. We had an unspoken mutual respect for each other's privacy and neither of us pried anything more than was freely offered. Having found my peace with him I was beginning to cherish the clear space to explore myself and the deeper reality of life within me.

Then, without warning, the dreaded moment arrived. It was sometime before dawn when we were suddenly awakened by strange voices and the glare of torchlight. Panic gripped me like a savage hand squeezing my throat when I suddenly awoke to two uniformed figures at the doorway of the little hut. In a country accent one of them spoke my name; "Julie ... Julie Steinheart?"

I did not answer. Then in the light of the second torch I saw they had a photograph of me. One of them was still talking on his two-way radio when two others, an older man and a woman, appeared out of nowhere and ruthlessly entered our private domain. Then everything happened so swiftly. I recall being grabbed by the arms and marched down the alleyway with José María cursing in Spanish being forced along on my heels. No more questions were asked, as we were frog-marched to a waiting police van with wire mesh on the windows. They had no interest whatsoever in any civil rights we may have had at the time. "You are being taken in for questioning," was the sole reply to my feeble demands.

The menacing sight of the van caused me to freeze even further in terror. I tried to wrench myself free from their grip and we both ended up being handcuffed, while they still refused to give us a reason for their actions. We were bundled inside, taken to the police station, then locked into separate cells, and that was the last I saw of my friend in Dublin. My brief interlude for reflection, the first in my life, had been violently shattered. I coiled myself in a corner trying to disappear into the old jacket and jeans that José María had found for me during our little time together. But I could find no comfort after the interlude of peace with him had been so brutally savaged. The panic attacks were back with all their might. In the mental institutions I was usually given drugs for these attacks, which I rarely took, but I would have taken them then if they had been offered. It was the most terrible panic I had ever experienced in my life.

In less than an hour my father was there; my greatest dread had materialized. My mind flashed back to the incident in the kitchen and the fear I had witnessed that morning in his bloodshot eyes. Now I was the one exposed and completely vulnerable to his revenge. I could not stop from wetting myself when I overheard him being asked to sign some papers. Then I listened to the heavy footsteps coming down the corridor and, to my horror, he was at the door of the cell with a policeman. A key entered the lock and indescribable terror gripped me.

"No! I'm not going back, I'm not going back," I screamed as I clung to the steel bars fencing the little window at the rear of the cell. Knowing I had totally lost control of the situation I endeavoured to use my feet to kick them away as they steadily approached me. The policeman forcefully unlocked my grip while my father grabbed the old jacket with his uninjured hand. I was still kicking and screaming as they forced me across the concrete floor. I remember clinging to the frame of the door as they tried to drag me through, and the more they tried to force me the louder I kicked and screamed. More gardaí arrived on the scene. Then a senior officer ordered that I be left alone and my father, protesting loudly, was taken to another room.

I could not stop myself from shaking all over. Even my teeth were in pain from rattling. My tongue was bleeding and my entire body went into convulsions as I tried to curl up and physically disappear in the corner. A lady officer came into the cell and she tried to come close, but my terrified appearance must have cautioned her. She sat down on the bench and, as best she could, she tried to talk comforting words. But there was no comforting me then, for I could still feel the deathly vibes coming through the concrete walls. I was again trapped in his world, this time much worse than before, and I knew he was using all his power of control to direct the situation.

Next, a doctor arrived and started asking me all sorts of questions. "Have you ever been abused at home?" was the most repeated one.

Of course I had been abused, the worst type of abuse imaginable, but I knew that such psychological abuse could not be explained to the medical profession. Physical abuse through body or intent was their self-imposed limitation. Not only that, I had lost all confidence in the medical world. I had well experienced how the doctors in general have no understanding of this far more serious type of abuse. Even in my terrible panic I could still see their mental limitations. It was an impossible situation. I could only bring myself to answer his question with another. "Do you even know what abuse is?" I found myself trying to mutter in a trembling voice that had dropped several octaves due to the shock.

The questions went on and on as he tried to medically fit me into his limited mind against my protestations.

"Please ... please leave me alone," was all I could eventually plead.

Three times he came and went. Then food arrived, cheese and salad sandwiches, but I could not eat a thing. The sight of the food made my stomach heave and I actually got sick in the corner. I completely lost track of time, but it seemed like an eternity being trapped in a nightmare. Such extreme anguish could not possibly be real; soon I'll wake up, I tried in vain to imagine. Then the alchemist's words re-echoed through my grief and jerked me back to reality.

"It is as it is. No matter how terrible or how beautiful the mind might try to concoct the situation, nonetheless, the fact remains the fact. There can be no escape through the imaginary mind. Accepting your life as it is in the here and now is the only way out, the only way of transcending the plain in which you are trapped."

I knew I was trapped in that plain and there was nothing I could do to change it. The waves of emotion continued to batter my brain when two female nurses materialized before me with an open straightjacket. Their images seemed grossly distorted as their outstretched hands approached me in the corner, each grabbing one of my arms, then roughly forcing my body into the harness. How could anyone be normal again after such an experience! It was not my body anymore, just a lump of flesh and bones being taken away for disposal. Then, with my feet hardly touching the ground, I was forced outside to be finally bundled into a waiting ambulance.

After much twisting and turning through the congested streets and the periodic use of the siren it eventually came to a halt. I knew exactly where I was, even though I did not wish to know. It had come to a stop outside the mental asylum, a place of high security for the criminally insane, and I could hear the gates being slowly opened. The ambulance edged forward and stopped again, waiting for the exterior gates to close behind it. Through a slit in the frosted glass I caught a glimpse of the inner gate, more than five metres in height, as it slowly rolled back. There and then an intense realisation gripped me; I was being taken inside this mental prison to be locked away where there could be no escape. Instinctually I knew it was all my father's doing. This place of horrors was the pinnacle of his world and his acclaimed profession. Here he would have all the help he needed to shape me into a thing that would be seen by his world as a normal person.

The ambulance and its contents were now safely confined within the grounds and I was being moved forward again to the final halt. Moments later the doors opened from the outside and two stern male warders appeared in my vision. Without a word being spoken one of the nurses tucked a folder of papers under her arm, sprung from her seat and scurried away towards a distant building. The warders, with the help of the second nurse, hauled me in through a door that sharply closed on my heels. My mind was numbed in shock as my body was dragged along to the heavy sound of their boots breaking the deathly silence. I was taken down some narrow corridors, then into a room and laid on a wooden bench. I remember the straightjacket being slightly raised and someone briefly examining my lower body. Then I was rolled over and a skinny man in a white coat tried to inject me with something in the rump. But I kicked against it and the needle fell from his hand. He cursed and muttered that I could suffer without it. Again I was hauled along another corridor to the sound of human moaning and lamenting coming from behind

JULIE

closed doors. I had entered hell. But instead of fire and burning, everything happening around me seemed to be cold, heartless and clinically clean.

I arrived at a cell where I was finally brought to a halt. The woman stepped inside with me, took off the straightjacket and stripped me naked, as the two men looked on from outside and my last sense of dignity was shattered. Then someone produced underwear and a shift for me to put on. That was it. There was no sense of caring or gentleness about the way they roughly handled my body as they left me there and locked the door behind them.

It seemed as though I was observing it all from some other dimension as the padded door sharply disappeared into the walls with similar padding. When I tried to focus my eyes I eventually noticed something that resembled a window that was well out of reach and close to the ceiling. Still engulfed in terror with a crippling pain in my chest everything quite abruptly went silent. But the noise of it all continued in the back of my brain, the shrill sound of the ambulance siren, the pounding of boots re-echoing down the corridors, the pitiful moans coming from the world's discarded and the protesting voice of my father being pushed away by the senior policeman who had stepped in between us.

Suddenly, in the middle of my grief-stricken state, for a second time, the unexpected happened. An enormous wave of unimaginable calmness burst through from somewhere deep within me. I was suddenly aware of its presence as it slowly but surely started to permeate every cell of my numbed body. This had happened only once before on the third evening of the seminars given by the alchemist in Temple Bar. But this time the happening was far more profound. Like before, I had no control over it. Instinctually I knew I had to surrender myself to it completely. From somewhere deep in my subconscious I could sense that the alchemist was still with me and guiding me through. He had opened the door to the cosmic order of all things for me to see and enter and in a few short moments the terrible nightmare was inexplicably transformed into a natural state of total acceptance. His assuring words again re-echoed to me from the void:

"Know that all is perfect. It is exactly as it is. Acceptance is the only contribution the person must make. You wish to unravel the elixir of life. Now you are being given the key, but it can only be realised in your own, direct experience."

Then everything began to clear. The padded cell was my physical prison, but it was also my immediate home. My body was confined, yet I somehow knew my spirit was freer than it had ever previously been. My body re-straightened from the foetus position and it sat erect on the edge of the bed as my eyes naturally closed. I found myself sinking into a deep meditation. Perhaps, meditation is the wrong word as I was not meditating on anything in particular. It was more like a natural state of absolute freedom where I was not present in the normal sense of being present. Even though I was completely alone, yet I was fully aware that I was not separate from anything around me. There were no feelings involved, nor were there any thoughts arising in my head as I became completely engulfed in that indescribable state of being the expansiveness of boundless life in my body.

All during that time while I sat there in the uninterrupted stillness I was vaguely aware of the door being opened and closed periodically. But, strangely, no one entered the cell. It appeared as though a protective mantle had been placed around me and, without knowing why, the medics were obliged by a higher power not to disturb me. Deeper and deeper my consciousness descended until it was absorbed by the cosmic intelligence rising from a point to meet it.

So it remained for the rest of that evening and well into the night. Eventually I became aware of the presence of someone sitting beside me. My eyes opened of their own accord as my head gradually turned to one side. To my surprise, a young nurse was gazing at me through her tears. My hand slowly moved without I willing it to move and it gently touched her cheek. Then both our faces broke into a smile. She was the first to speak.

"Your name is Julie. Mine is Ruth."

The softness in her voice spoke more than the words. She was looking directly into my eyes and I knew she could see right into their depths. At that moment she appeared as an angel from the heavens beyond having come to be with me. I immediately noticed how her fair hair gently touched her white uniform in a way that seemed like a golden aura of love. Instinctually I knew this was my second step into the great unknown and a sensation of deep privilege swept through me. I could sense the energy of the words "thank you, thank you, thank you" deep inside me, without needing to know who or what I was really thanking. I had been through hell and I had survived, but only because I had been exposed to the cosmic order of all things through the reflected presence of the enlightened alchemist. This, I now know in my own experience, is the greatest privilege that life can bestow upon anyone.

Ruth became my confidant and she devoted most of her free time to me. Her gentle nature enticed me to eat again and, unlike the others, she never stood over me when the medicine was being administered.

The days turned into weeks and I refused point blank to accept any visitors. Gradually I was allowed a little more freedom. First it was the exercise room, then an open assembly area with a large lounge and television for those who needed it. When the house doctors considered it was safe enough I was transferred to a less restrictive part of the prison hospital. This did not deter Ruth from keeping in daily contact. We talked about many things, but mainly about what I had realised through my brief encounter with the alchemist. I cautioned her not to believe anything I was saying, but to see if it was true in her own experience. I needed to know. It was the only way I could be sure that I was not insane like the world around me was seeing me. My knowledge amazed her at times, but I reminded her that I did not really know very much; it was something else. In the alchemist's presence I had been exposed to cosmic consciousness and the world is not part of it; for such intelligence is beyond the world's comprehension, and it opened me to take action against what I could not accept in my life. Then the world demanded its price, and this is why I was locked away, simply because the world could neither understand nor accept it.

The doctors continued to perform in their usual, predictable way and I had no problem being the perfect patient. I had been through it all so many times before and repetition, for better or worse, creates expertise. I won their confidence and they agreed it would be medically unethical to allow my father to intervene in the treatment process. I was assured of this, that I was in safe hands and my rights would be fully respected.

Then my mother arrived in the visitor's lounge. A warder argued with me that a mother should not be denied the right to see her child. Reluctantly, I agreed to meet her and I was escorted to an outer wing of the hospital. As I was walked through the exterior door of my own section I realised it was my first time in the open air since my incarceration. The sight of the green grass and the trees in the grounds invigorated my body. But when I looked up at the blue sky and pockets of white clouds so far above my head the sudden feeling of spaciousness made me feel dizzy. I realised how quickly I had forgotten. The warder sensed my dislocation and he purposely took the longest way round the grounds to give me time to readjust myself.

When I entered the room and saw my mother standing there in her usual posture the emotions hit me like a damn bursting open. But somehow I managed to hold my control in the long pause before we embraced. The void between us swiftly forced us apart again and we stood for a moment at arm length looking at each other without any words being spoken. Then, with great effort, we embraced again and both of us cried.

When I looked in her eyes I instantly saw her vision of me as a mentally ill and very disturbed and unwanted child. Such was the speed of consciousness instilled in me by the master. I just could not accept her self-imposed limitation and I shook her by the shoulders while telling her it was not true. But no matter how I tried I could not break through to her. She was still locking me out, just like she had locked everything out that resembled the truth during all my childhood years. I felt that I had to break through to her, I had to break down her barriers. Somehow I had to make her understand the truth of my situation.

"Mother, the world is sick but I am not sick," I found myself trying to explain.

"I know, I know," she replied in that platonic tone that spoke for itself.

I was not getting through. How could I get through to her? She was married to a psychiatrist who would have told her many times how mentally ill people usually think they are okay while the world is not. Her stubbornness infuriated me further and before I knew it I found myself challenging her as to why she had married him.

"I married your father because it was the right and proper thing to do," she replied in defense.

I could not listen to her denials any longer. Indeed, in this neutral ground I had no obligation to listen. I was no longer part of her life or her home and I clearly knew I would never be part of that scene again. Her unyielding pretence caused me to openly explode upon her.

"He is NOT my father and well you know it! How can you go on and on lying like this to yourself?" I so demanded without giving her further space to avoid an issue so important any longer.

"What do you mean he is not your father?" she feebly stammered.

"You know he is not. You abandoned my real father to marry him; and why? I will tell you why! You could not escape from your bloody religious past."

I had said it at last without even realising I had. Up to then I had only sensed it as a comforting truth because I hated him so much. She appeared to be completely taken off guard and this must have been the last thing she expected coming from the daughter she had completely ignored. But I could instantly see the truth of it all in her eyes. She could not deny it any further, even though she had tried to bury her secret so deep she would never have to truly face it. Little did she know there can never be secrets. Like the alchemist had said; "By the way of things, sooner or later everything hidden is flushed to the surface."

Ever since my conscious perception had been sharpened by him I could see the dark secrets on people's faces, the masks they were continuously wearing, their postures, the way they would speak and the words they would use, even the chosen friends and the social standing being served, I had come to realise were all part of their unrecognized hedging from the reality of their own condition. I could see through the entire masquerade and my mother was struck with the cold reality of this in my sudden attack.

It had not been too difficult for her to fool the man she had married. He was merely a male who had succumbed to his own limitations, thinking and acting like males usually do, totally predictable, and being a psychiatrist made little or no difference. All my anger and frustration up to that time had been pitted against him. But now I was suddenly seeing it was more so my mother's fault that I had been committed to that mental institution, her unexpected visit having flushed it out in the open. As she stood there before me she instinctually knew I was seeing right through her.

Her colour started to change, first to white as the blood slowly drained from her face, then to crimson red swiftly rising from her neck and lower jaws. I could see the anger twisting her mouth as she spoke.

"What should I have done? she demanded. "Do you think I should have changed my religion?"

For a moment I was shocked into silence. Was this the extent of her defense? Was she still hiding behind such pretentiousness and using it as an excuse for what she had done? Was she such a stranger to me by further insulting my intelligence? It caused me to explode even further.

"For fuck sake, fuck religion! Can you not see the insanity behind all such nonsensical beliefs? Your ongoing rituals and so-called Passover are all a mask, an excuse for failing to be what you are. How can you further insult me by hiding behind such a flimsy excuse! I'm not stupid! Indeed, far from it, right now I can see everything going on in your head!"

I had broken through to her core, or I must have hit on a nerve, because I could hardly believe what was happening as she physically attacked me. It was the last thing I had expected from her. She didn't have an aggressive nature and I never had seen her like this before.

"How dare you talk to me like that about our culture and roots; how dare you, how dare you," she continued to shout as a security guard entered the scene.

He came between us and tried to calm the situation. But something had been triggered inside me and I could no longer hold myself back. All the pent-up frustration still gripping my body further exploded in her face. I had to spill everything out and the moment was at hand to do it.

"Lie to me if you must, but please stop lying to yourself. You know in your heart you never gave a damn about such stupid beliefs. You went along with them to please that fool you married. But what about me? Did you give me any consideration? No, you didn't! You abandoned me when you abandoned my real father. Then you almost smothered the life out of me before I was born, trying to hold on to me in your womb for as long as you could for appearance sake. That's right! Is it not? The only thing you have ever cared about is your own appearance!"

She stood there behind the security guard's outstretched arm with a stunned look on her face, unable to deny the truth she was hearing.

"How can you call yourself a mother when you never gave a damn about me! All you can ever think about is your own misery! You never set out to know me, nor could you see how that screwed-up excuse you married abused me so much and ruined my childhood."

I could sense the relief in my body as I unloaded my bottled-up feelings relating to the hellish existence she had given me. Her bottom jaw dropped and the energy was rising in her to respond, but still I continued to spill everything out in the open;

"This was the childhood you gave me and now you dare come in here and accuse me with your sanctimonious looks of I being the one who is mad! You have done this to me. You are the one who has put me in here. Are you unable to see it? Or are you so stupid? Can you not see what you have done to your own daughter? You married him for your own convenience. But I am the one who must suffer for you. Do you give a shit? Look at me! I am an innocent child. Can you not see what you have done?"

JULIE

The truth of it all was far too sudden for her to bear. All through those years she had fed the demon sustaining her denials and now the demon within her was cornered. Its ultimate response is always expressed through violence. It broke through the uniformed human barrier and physically attacked me again while screaming; "How dare you, how dare you speak to me like that."

At this point the security guard must have been calling for assistance, for two matronly nurses appeared on the scene. They grabbed my mother by the arms and were in the process of ushering her into the hospital before the security man managed to convince them of their mistake. She was then taken outside to the main foyer and in the commotion of it all I was left alone to find my own way back to the cellblock.

In a daze I walked out the wrong door without realising what I was doing. Then I saw the car parked by the trees in front of the main offices. A shift of perception occurred at that moment within me as the thought immediately flashed through my mind of escaping there and then with my mother. Although I hated her for her stupidity, still I loved her and I desperately wanted to break through to her. I felt it was vital to conclude what had just begun. This now was the one priority.

I made my way to the car to wait for her escape from the commotion she still seemed to be causing inside and I was almost upon it before I noticed him in the driver's seat. It was the bandaged hand holding the mobile phone to his ear that first caught my attention, sending shivers through me. It never had dawned on me that he could have been with her. The sudden sight of him caused my body to freeze to the ground. If he moved his head an inch I would have been right in his vision. Panic grabbed my chest and I had to will my feet to slowly edge backwards. My shoulders gripped in a spasm, but I somehow managed to

46

make it to an open doorway without being spotted or arousing suspicion. Once inside I rushed along a corridor away from the sight of him and his bandaged hand, not knowing where I was heading or what might happen next. After spotting a door leading to toilets I went inside and locked myself in. Gradually I returned to my senses and looking around I noticed I was in the nurses changing room. There were some clothes on hangers and more neatly folded on shelves. At that moment it seemed as though the mother earth spirit was guiding me through. There was a navy jacket just my size and I soon found a white blouse and black skirt that matched. A small suitcase revealed a cosmetic kit. Before I knew what I had done I could hardly believe it was me I was seeing in the mirror pinned to the back of the door. All I needed were shoes and it took some time before I eventually found a pair that fitted. Then, as I readied myself to leave, I noticed a jar filled with coins on one of the shelves. After burying a fistful in my pocket I braved the world and dared to venture outside once again to the car park.

Thankfully, they had left. As I approached the parking lot a young man with a briefcase, who had the appearance of a visiting doctor, was about to get into his car. It was my chance to escape if only I could build up my courage. After taking some deep breaths I steadied myself and, walking over to him with the strongest smile exuding all those bewitching wiles I could muster, I asked;

"Are you going towards the city centre? I've missed my usual lift."

His face lit up as he replied; "I'm not going all the way, but I could drop you at a bus stop if that would be okay."

I gladly accepted and got into the car beside him.

He introduced himself as Charles Boland while remarking that Ruth, which I used, was a lovely name. I could not help but notice the strain in his eyes taking in the shape of my legs as he spoke. He was in full flight spilling his life story as we passed the high security wing and eventually approached the inner gate of the hospital perimeter. Panic gripped me like an iron fist behind the frozen smile on my face as the security guard on duty glared at us both through expressionless eyes. It seemed like an eternity being stopped at that spot as he fumbled through papers and passwords to ascertain clearance for us. I could see he was not sure of himself, but luckily for me he allowed us the benefit of the doubt and pressed the button that triggered the inner gate to slowly roll back. We moved forward into the outer enclosure and we had to sit there for what seemed like another eternity waiting for the gate to slowly close again behind us. Now we were facing the outer gates with a sterner guard staring at both of us. I had made it this far with the panic attacks like a volcano about to erupt any moment. The security guard directly behind us was still going through the pile of papers trying to clear up his confusion. It was a nerve-wrecking moment. But I managed to bury myself into the young doctor's story, so much so that the outer gates eventually opened and suddenly we were moving in traffic. I was back in the world and I could hardly believe what was happening.

"Where exactly are you heading?" the young doctor asked. "Anywhere near Rathmines will do," I replied, with the intention in mind of finding the flat that Ruth was sharing with others.

To my surprise he took me all the way. The last thing I had expected was to be chatted up. He gave me his phone number and made me promise I would call him before he finally allowed me my freedom. But there was nothing compassionate about him. His one intention was sprawled all over his face and being a doctor did not excuse him. To me at that moment he was no different to the majority of men I have encountered, brain-dead through the mutilating force of the testosterone. Nonetheless, he had well served his purpose and his phone number went into the first litter bin I met on the street.

I called the hospital from a public phone box and told them I had left with my mother. Then I managed to get through to my mother and I told her what I had done. But I went on to remind her that I was her one and only child and this was her one and only chance to redeem herself. At first she sounded shocked. Then she agreed to meet me and she promised she would come alone. But it was still too soon to trust her.

We had arranged to meet in the public foyer of a large hotel close to the canal. When I arrived there I noticed there was a coach parked on the roadway outside, quite obviously waiting for a group of visiting tourists. I slipped inside without being seen, curled myself up on a seat and patiently waited. I needed to make absolutely sure I would not get caught again. Indeed, I would kill myself rather than face back to that mental asylum. If my mother was not prepared to help me then I was ready to die if I had to, or remain a fugitive for the rest of my life.

I watched the steady flow of people as cars and taxies came and went. Finally a white taxi pulled up outside the main entrance and out she stepped. From what I could see she was alone. But I had to be certain. I could not take any more chances, so I followed her inside and watched her for some time as she looked around. Twice she looked directly my way but she failed to recognise me. When I felt it was safe I stepped forward and brazenly said;

"Mother, do you fail to see your own flesh and blood?"

At first she looked totally stunned. Then her face filled with amazement. Her expression told me she could hardly believe what she was seeing.

"My God, Julie! Is it really you?"

"Yes Mum, 'tis I," I replied in an air of tense delight.

"But you look so different, so grown up! And where did you get the lovely clothes?"

"Mother, I stole them!"

"What! You stole them!" she exclaimed, appearing shocked for a moment. Then her face softened a little and she exploded into hysterical laughter. Miraculously, the icc had been broken between us. We sat down together at a table by the far corner of the foyer where we talked and listened for the very first time.

"I'm glad he had left for the airport just moments before you called," she explained. "He has gone to London for two days and from there he's going on to some medical conference in Geneva and I don't expect him back for at least a week."

She shed tears of relief and I was amazed when she actually thanked me for bringing her back to her senses. Although the confrontation had at first shattered her totally, she was thanking me for helping to redeem that innocent girl in love she once had been. She went on to explain, that was before she had allowed her love to be so brutally destroyed by the world that had taken hold of her essence. But she wasn't blaming the world. She confessed it was all her own doing.

She mentioned how the hospital had contacted her almost immediately after I had phoned her.

"They were very anxious about the situation and were insistent that we return there immediately," she said.

She went on to tell me how she had to be forceful with them, even to the point of threatening them with a major lawsuit. I was being detained with the criminally insane, even though I had never been charged with a criminal offence. It was her lawful right as a mother to rescue me, seeing that I should never have been there in the first place. Apparently, this calmed matters down a little and she assured them she would go in the following day with her lawyer to sign the obligatory papers if necessary.

I asked her to tell me about my real father, but she was finding it difficult to speak anything about him. I would not let go and I had to insist.

"For goodness sake, I need to know, Mum," I implored. "Surely you can understand that."

After some hesitation she settled herself in the chair and I waited. She twisted and turned several times looking for another escape as I continued to wait while holding the silence. Eventually she started to speak.

"We were together for seven years. It all started when I was still in my teens. As a matter of fact I had just turned sixteen when we first met on a school outing to Kilkenny. You could say it was love at first sight."

She had to stop, as she fought to hold back her tears when the waitress arrived with the silver tray. She was a stocky woman in her mid-thirties with dyed, blond hair and what seemed like a permanent smile. I noticed her sensitivity as she gently placed the china on the table, then the silver teapot and the plate of assorted cakes.

"Mum, what is his name?" I eagerly demanded.

"John ... John O'Brien," she slowly relented.

"Where is he now?"

"I honestly don't know. I haven't seen him since the day I got married. When I turned around after the service had finished he was standing alone by the doorway. I still remember how our eyes had met. There was a huge question-mark of 'why' on his face before he turned and walked away without looking back."

"Did he know you were pregnant with his child?" I asked.

"No, he had no idea," she replied.

"Mum! Why didn't you tell him?"

"Julie! How could I? He had crisis enough in his life at that particular time."

"Please be honest with me," I further pressed. "We have made it this far, so tell me! Was that the real reason?"

"You are right. It was not the real reason. You know, I loved him dearly, Julie. Every moment we had in those early years together was heaven. All through our college years our love survived. He was in Cork; and me, as you know, I went to Trinity. But we still managed to be together on most weekends. For two summers we worked in England, one in a hotel in Devon and the other in London where we shared a little bed-sit for three months. Then something happened in Cork and he was expelled from College. I never knew exactly what it was. But I think it had something to do with a professor who had written an article condemning the IRA. John was accused of being part of the gang who had beaten him up for writing the article. This really shattered him at the time. He came back to Dublin and started working in a bar somewhere close to O'Connell Street. But something about him had changed. He started drinking more and more and no matter how I tried to hold our relationship together he still seemed to be slipping away."

"Mum, did you try to find out what was troubling him?"

"He had become very secretive, Julie. No matter how I tried I just could not get through to him. He had shut me out completely, and it seemed he had done so purposely."

"So you decided to leave him?"

" No, it was not like that. Your father … I am sorry Julie, you know who I mean … Jonathan entered the picture. He was much older and already well established in his career. I was able to bring him home and introduce him to my parents, a thing I could never have done with your father."

"Oh Mum! If only you had, things would have been different," I pleaded.

Indeed, things would have been very different. I was sure that my life would not have been the hell I endured. Then she was the one reminding me to be real, just like the alchemist in Temple Bar had done.

"Julie! Surely you know there is no reality in 'ifs' and 'maybes'. I know now how I was totally caught up in appearances. You have made yourself perfectly clear and all I can say is, I am sorry, Julie. Oh Lord! I am so sorry from the bottom of my heart for all I have failed to do."

She was crying again, this time really genuine tears of remorse. But somehow there was no emotion rising in me to meet her. It must have been a huge ordeal for her, but my scars were far too deep and emotion was no longer part of my presence. Through my own traumas, and more significantly, having been in the enlightened presence of the alchemist, such feelings of emotion had been all but severed. He had made it clear that real love is not an emotion. I sat there, knowing that I loved her, while at the same time being aware of the ice-coldness of this love. It seemed as though I was one of the ancients patiently listening to the past demeanours of a child as she again started blaming herself for taking on the ignorance of the world, thus entrapping herself during those wasted years of her life. It became too much for her to endure. She excused herself and went to the bathroom.

As I sat there alone I could see myself looking on at the entire scene of mother and daughter clearing up their past misgivings. It was the strangest sensation. I found myself being the heart of both while simultaneously being neither one nor the other. It seemed as though it was merely a play being acted out before me. Without knowing it I had slipped back into that place of deep nothingness that had been opened to me by the alchemist. The sound of his voice again flashed through my brain in an instant relating to the ignorance of the world my mother had mentioned.

"First you enter the nothingness and then the nothingness enters you. Soon you realise the only consistency is the

JULIE

nothingness from which all things apparent arise. Do not be moved by any of it. Just stay observing, even without the attention of there being an observer. This will take you deeper and deeper until eventually you will break through the threshold. Once the threshold is broken there is no turning back. But up to the point of the threshold there is much turning back. This you will find in the organized religions and schools of philosophy in general. Here the dawning of truth in the mind loses its potency as it becomes re-intellectualized and is turned into some other acceptable dogma. The clingers might even elect a leader or an upholder of their newly found dogma from among themselves. But the elected ones are usually those with least vision. It has to be this way, for ignorance can only be led by ignorance. Do not be fooled by any of it. It is merely the outer pulse of existence psychically vibrating as the mass ignorance of human consciousness. Know that such ignorance is the unending endeavour trying to escape from the inescapable nothingness."

It seemed quite strange to me that my mother had turned the appropriate key in my brain before she went to the bathroom and, once opened, his words continued to flow from the depths of my own subconscious.

"The world arises within the fragility of the pulse and it imprints on itself an assumed permanence, which is the human mind. Next the belief structures as the many gods of humanity take psychological form to sustain the pseudo permanence of the projected world. Then the social structures take root as protection against the simmering fear of being faced with the piercing truth. No other form of life knows of such fear. It enters only through the human mind. This is how the world arises from the psyche and comes into the emotional play in the way we know it. It is real, but it is only real unto its own unreality, and love is not part of it. It is the world, an imposition, but it is not life, nor can it ever be life."

It amazed me how clearly his voice re-echoed on the screen of my brain whenever I was astutely alert, such as being with my mother at that time while she was clearing her past. I was meeting the full understanding of the alchemist's wisdom, not through my mind, but through my experiential being. It was like sitting at the edge of a pool of universal intelligence and not having to retain anything in particular, for anything I needed to know was making itself instantly available as the events of my life unfolded.

"What do you want to do, Julie?" my mother's voice penetrated the long silence, not realising she had returned.

"To do, Mum? What do I have to do?"

"I mean right now, Julie. Why not come back home with me tonight?"

"You know I can't. What's between you and him is your business, Mum. You know I can never again be anywhere close to his presence."

"Yes, I can truly understand how you see him. But at least come home with me tonight. We can have most of a week together. It will be just you and I, just the two of us with time on our hands to work things out."

There was little else I could do, having failed to find where Ruth lived in Rathmines, so I nodded in agreement. She paid the waitress and then checked her change, making sure it was correct. Unknown to her, I took some of the larger coins from my pocket and placed them quietly on the table as a 'thank you' gesture to the lady for the space she allowed us.

Then together we went outside arm in arm into the cool, afternoon air of Dublin. She was about to call a taxi when I suggested we should get the bus instead, explaining it would be a new experience for her. I told her I wished to treat her, that I would pay the fares.

"But Julie, you have no money?" she questioned in an air of expressing my dependency upon her purse.

"Oh yes I have," I coolly replied, as I took the fistful of coins from the pocket of the navy blue jacket.

"Where did you get so many coins?" she exclaimed in open dismay.

"Mum, I stole them, of course! Surely you know by now a girl has to do what a girl has to do in order to survive in this hostile world!"

Again she was shocked. Stealing clothes may have been an almost forgivable thing in her eyes, but the thought of stealing money seemed to be totally out of the question. Why was she shocked over a few harmless coins? Perhaps, there was something I was failing to see as she lectured me about the importance of money for most of the journey on the bus. I recall what the alchemist had said relating to the type of energy being transported in money, that one should be aware of it as it changes hands, and also of its role in the reincarnation of the ignorance perpetuating the world.

But what has all this to do with the present moment?

Why does it still trouble me as I stand here alone awaiting my final hour of judgement?

Obviously, there is so much more I need to realise about myself and my particular contribution to perpetuating the ignorance.

"When one clearly sees it then it automatically ceases," the alchemist said.

JULIE

It was a kind summer's evening as we got off the bus at the top of the avenue leading down to Dublin Bay and Blackrock village. I had been down that avenue many times before but I felt I was then seeing it for the very first time. The trees were vividly green against the contrasting backdrop of the water-blue sky mingling in the distance with the blue-grey colour of the sea. Birds were chirping and bees were humming in the hedges, all busy at work in nature's own way unperturbed.

My mother's joy showed in the lightness of her footsteps as we walked briskly without being in any real hurry. Soon we rounded the corner leading to the small estate of semi-detached houses. I was aware of a nervousness in my stomach, but there was no real anxiety present like there had been in the past. It amazed me how insignificant the house appeared as it came into sight. It had always presented itself as a sinister barracks but now it seemed totally denuded. The rooms, previously foreboding and huge, now were small and unimportant as we entered. I went up to my bedroom facing the landing and slowly walked around it. Again I was surprised that it held absolutely nothing for me. I could hardly imagine having spent most of my years within its confines. Now it was no more than a lingering imprint of some bad dream.

I came back downstairs and went into the kitchen where mother was trying to make herself busy in her usual way. I sat on a high stool with my elbows on the breakfast counter and my face cupped in my hands. Eventually she stopped whatever she was doing, looked straight in my eyes and immediately received the entire picture I was seeing of her.

"I know, I know," she said. "I can see what you are seeing. But it's all I have got. It's all I have to show for all these wasted years."

"Surely Mum, you don't have to waste the rest of your life just polishing again and again over polish?"

"But where can I go? What else can I do with my life?" she pleaded.

"There's many things you can do, teaching for example; after all, you are qualified. Why not return to college for a refresher course? My friends at school have told me how their mothers have returned to work."

"But you know how your … I mean, how he thinks. He would not let it be seen that his wife has to go out of the house to work."

"For God sake, Mother! Will you come out of the dark ages! He has never considered you. He does not give a shit about anything other than his own appearance. He has made a rag out of you for all these years. It is time you grabbed hold of yourself and left him for good."

"It's no use talking like this. I have made my bed, now I must lie in it."

"Yes, you must I suppose, for as long as you keep lying to yourself," I replied with a touch of sarcasm on the pun.

She responded with a long sigh, clearly knowing it was fruitless to argue with me any further. She could see I was too flippant with words. Not only that, but she had faced more than enough for one day.

"Let's have some supper," she suggested after disengaging herself. "I'll put on the pasta while you go and settle yourself in."

I decided to take a shower and then go through my clothes. But again I had difficulty trying to identify with anything I was finding in the wardrobe and cupboards. It felt as though I was in the bedroom of a complete stranger. There was definitely no sense of belonging and it made me wonder if there ever had been such a sense. The unexpected confrontation with that strange feeling caused me to ask; where is my home?

Nowhere being the immediate reply, the sudden realisation of it sent a shiver through my body. Being alone with nowhere to be and nowhere to go can be quite a shock to the system. But I knew I had to move on and I stuffed a rucksack with the few things I considered I might need for the journey. I was packing for nowhere, not having the slightest idea what the next step might bring. Not only was I being emptied of my past but it appeared as though I was being emptied of my future as well.

The alchemist had talked about this emptiness, but he had referred to it as 'emptied-ness', which is totally different. It means being emptied out completely and having nothing left in the cup of the self. It seemed as though I had been hurdled into that state without having any preconceived intentions of such a thing happening to me. I had listened to his words and now I was receiving their meaning.

"Before you can receive the new drink of life your cup must be emptied of the old," he had said. "If your cup is already full with the old then you cannot receive the new. You are not ready to receive it. You will continue drinking from the old and the older it gets the more poisonous it has to become. Nor can you mix the new with the old. Should you try to do so then the new becomes contaminated by the old. It instantly becomes more of the old and again the new will be missed. You must be 'emptied' of the old before you can transcend your condition."

My mother called me for supper and soon we settled down together to a night talking about everything and anything, but nothing in particular until we eventually braved the subject of the man she had married.

"Well, at least he doesn't know he is not your real father and that has made my life a bit easier to endure," she tried to explain.

"That may seem so on the surface, Mum. He may not know it in his mind, but he is fully aware of it in his psyche and this is his problem. There are many levels of knowing in the body, but the majority of people never surpass the mental plane, particularly those who think they are intelligent. This is how they become blocked with their congealing beliefs and opinions, and end up contaminating everyone and everything they touch."

My mother seemed bewildered and I found it impossible to explain anything relating to the higher intelligence immediate to us beneath the surface world. Nor could she grasp the obvious, how he was going through an internal war. In his mental world he could see himself as my father, but to sustain this mental impression he had to deny the truth pushing through his psyche. Some people refer to it as a sixth sense, or intuition, but it is much more direct than that when one empties oneself of one's tiny, mental way of seeing things. His head was full to capacity thus causing his mental disease, and I, being the external object of his disease, was thus obliged to endure the ongoing hell he was creating within himself.

Although she seemed unable to follow me into the next level of knowing that is available to us, nonetheless she did seem to get the gist of what I was trying to explain and I was aware of a shift occurring in her consciousness. Obviously, this shift would have huge results for the better in her life.

The following morning she called a taxi and made her way to the hospital to sign the necessary papers. While she was gone I unpacked, went through the things once more and re-packed them all over again. The day passed quickly and our second night was more or less the same as the first. We talked a lot about what I might do with my life and her suggestions were both logical and sensible. She had me almost convinced that I should return to school to do my final exams. I could stay with her parents in Killiney and she was edging to phone them to make the arrangements.

Then the unexpected happened. It was about ten o'clock and we were so engrossed neither of us heard the car pull into the driveway. The door opened and there he was with his case in hand and his mouth wide open. Terror instantly gripped me. Without even saying hello he demanded how I got out of the hospital.

"I signed her out and she should never have been there in the first place," my mother responded as she jumped to her feet in defense.

His face reddened with rage.

"You signed her out! Are you trying to tell me you know more about her condition than I do?"

He was towering over her tiny frame and his fists were tightly clinched. When my eyes became fixed on the whites of his knuckles a gush of fear exploded in my stomach and I couldn't stop from wetting myself.

"Yes I am, and so do the doctors at the hospital," my mother replied. "I have signed the necessary papers and they have agreed there is no reason she should be there any longer. As a matter of fact she should never have been there in the first place."

He reddened further as the rage consumed his entire body and his shouting edged close to the brink of physical violence. I sat there frozen to the seat until my courage and vision unexpectedly returned. Suddenly I could see how sick he was in the head and the seriousness of his problem. Without realising what I was doing, I found myself entering the battle. In a single breath I demanded; "Why do you want me locked away? What is your fear? What are you afraid of facing?"

For a moment he was stunned. Up to then I had been merely the object of the conflict, without a mouth and without a brain. I must have touched on some delicate spot for he immediately lost control of his posture. His voice changed as he turned on me with his fury.

"I'm warning you; another sound out of you, you crazy little bitch and I'll…"

Cutting him off in mid-sentence, in an uncontrollable surge of emotion I jumped in front of him to be met with the stale smell of alcohol from his breath.

"You'll what? Go on! Tell me! You'll what? You'll try to have me locked up again? Is that it? Next time you're the one who's going to be locked up. I've told the doctors in the hospital all about you. They're fully aware of your problem. Ask any of them? They know how sick you are in the head."

I had hit him where it really hurt, right in the centre of his world of assumed importance. It was the first time in my life that I heard him using such language as he exploded back into my face.

"I said, one more word out of you, you deranged little bitch and I'll cripple you right where you're standing!"

My mother jumped in between us. She was pushing me away from him when he flung her hard against the couch. I glimpsed the pain in her face and at that moment I totally lost it; not even knowing or considering what I was doing I had grabbed the iron poker in my hand. All I could see was red as I literally flew at him, screaming in rage with words something to the effect; "This time I'm going to split you open, you ignorant bastard."

He had raised his arm to protect himself as the poker hit hard on his elbow. I heard the crack of the bone as he fell to his knees, his body wrenching in agony. Without even thinking of the consequences I had hit him again on his opposite shoulder, using all the energy and weight of my body. He yelled and rolled over on one side from the force of the blow. My mother was just in time to grab my arm before the poker came crashing down on his head with a blow that would have surely killed him. She ushered me into the hallway and ordered me to get my bag. I was up and down the stairs in a matter of seconds. To my great surprise she was waiting for me with both our coats she had grabbed from the hallstand.

"This time I'm coming with you," she said.

At that moment he had struggled to the doorway of the sitting room, his face snow white and his body half paralyzed. I felt no compassion or remorse. As a matter of fact the fire was still in my veins. My mother held against my body as the urge took hold of me to attack him again. He called to her as she was trying to open the door with her trembling hands while holding me back.

"Natalie, I'm in agony; please get me to the hospital; my arm is broken; I think my collarbone is shattered."

She stopped on the outside step and turning for a moment, in an ice-cold voice she said; "To be quite frank, I don't give a damn anymore."

With that last remark we were gone. This time our steps were hurried as we made our way in silence. She hailed down a taxi and asked the driver to take us to Killiney. We were both still trembling after she had got through to her mother on the mobile phone. I was awash with alternating feelings of panic, relief and dismay at what I had done. One moment my blood was boiling, the next my body was freezing cold. While travelling over the hill of Killiney something suddenly snapped inside me and I unexpectedly broke into uncontrollable laughter. My mother looking at me in shocked dismay demanded; "What is the matter with you? What on earth can be funny?"

"Mum, you didn't say the line correctly."

"What line? What are you talking about?"

I tried to explain. "You know, Mum, that famous line from the movie, 'Gone with the Wind'. When we were leaving you looked at him and said: 'To be quite frank I don't give a damn any more.' You almost got it right. If you had said,

'Frankly my dear, I don't give a damn', then it would have been the perfect ending!"

With that the tension exploded and we both broke into tears of hysterical laughter.

The taxi driver in his broad Dublin slang intruded from another world; "Are you's cumin' from a party or wha?"

The lights were on in my grandparents house and their anxiety met us on the roadway as we rounded the corner.

"Are you all right? Is there something the matter?" Granny anxiously inquired before we had time to get out of the taxi while my grandfather was opening the door.

"Yes Mamma, there is," my mother's voice trembled. "Please do not be upset with me; I just cannot take any more. I have left him for good. I had to do it before he would have me locked away in a mental asylum as well."

"Oh, my poor child. Please come inside out of the cold. And Julie? Are you okay after your long ordeal in that hospital?" Granny fussed.

"Don't worry. I'm fine, Granny, as long as Mum is okay," I tried to reply. But I was far from fine with myself. Deep within I was shocked with what I had done. It was the second time it had happened. On that first explosion with the carving knife in the kitchen it was more of an accident in the way it had occurred. But this one was seriously different. I was being driven by something enormous bursting through from the depths of my psyche to kill him. Even my mother had difficulty getting the poker out of my hand and again when pushing me out the door. The alchemist warned that one should never vacate one's house, such as being carried away by the emotional world, and this is exactly what I had allowed happen. Now I was meeting the shock waves of the monster receding back into the pool of the psyche after finding release to perform its damage. Like a bolt of lightening it struck me that I am capable of being anything, even one of the worst hounds performing for Hitler, once I allow the flood gates to be opened by vacating my house. Indeed, there is no such thing as being good or bad at the deeper level of one's being when one is being truly conscious; but what an enormous responsibility one has to the world asleep when one has awakened.

We were taken into the back kitchen and the teapot was immediately summoned. This is Granny's natural cure for everything; tea is her remedy for disemboweling any monstrous crisis. The gory details had to be thrashed out in full and I allowed my mother to do all the talking. I just sat there quietly disengaged at the end of the table going further into myself.

My grandfather was quick to notice. He got up and gently taking me by the hand he said; "Come with me Julie. I've something interesting to show you."

In childish excitement I was led into the back scullery and then towards a basket with a lid in the corner. I was well aware of my grandfather's tricks. He usually enjoyed hitting me with things by surprise. So naturally, I was being rather cautious. As I opened the lid to look into the basket, to my amazement out jumped a snow-white puppy, not much bigger than a kitten.

"His name is Rambo and he's the new addition to the family." Granddad informed me.

At this stage it was up in my arms like a fluffy ball of tingling sensation licking me all over my face and lips.

"Rambo!" I exclaimed. "How could you give it such a macho name? It's much too fluffy, much too beautiful to be called Rambo."

"Well," he replied, "With all the break-ins in the street, we decided we needed a guard dog. The ones we saw seemed a little bit too temperamental. It was Esther who spotted this little fellow and that was it. But a guard dog needs a guard dog's name, does it not? So Rambo it is!"

"Granddad, you're crazy! I love him, I love him," I could only manage to reply as I became completely engulfed in its sensational presence.

That was it. It was impossible for me to part with him and, with a little persuasion, Granny agreed he could sleep at the end of my bed for the night. Strange as it seems, it gave me an extraordinary sense of belonging. The absolute naturalness of it and the feel of its tiny heartbeat against my body wiped everything clear from my mind.

Innocence, it is so preciously sweet! Oh, to be able to return there again. But how can I ever return. The injuries I inflicted upon that man are trivial compared to what I've done in Granada this night. But tonight I had not vacated my house; there were no emotions at play. I did what I had to do, being true to the situation. Now there can be no return to anything resembling a natural order. I cannot expect the world to understand by allowing me to continue my life unimpeded. But I must not forget the alchemist. He did advise me to be prepared for huge and sudden change in my life once I had openly accepted his cosmic challenge. I now know that whatever is about to happen must be equally faced in the spirit of the moment.

JULIE

Shortly after six o'clock the following morning all hell broke loose without warning. I was awakened by the commotion at the front door. After racing to the window I saw a police car stopped outside. I could hear my mother's voice above the others: "It is not true ... it is not true ... he came into the house and attacked us both."

There was a lot of arguing, and then I could hear my grandfather speaking sternly: "Officers, quite obviously this is a case of serious domestic violence."

"We are just doing our job," a voice replied, "a complaint of serious assault has been made and we are obliged to follow it up. The girl has done it before; we have it on record she previously assaulted her father with a knife. Also, it appears from our inquiries that she got released from psychiatric care in a very unusual way."

"I must insist; you are failing to understand the situation," my grandfather's voice again intervened.

"I'm sorry if it appears harsh, but we have to take the girl back to the station. She will be given the opportunity there to state her reasons for what she's done."

No, I could not go back. There was no way I could cope with that all over again. I would kill myself rather than allow them to take me. My grandmother came into the room as the arguing continued and I flew into her arms for protection.

"Granny, I have to get out of her. I have to get away before they see me. You know how he hates me and he's doing everything in his power to drive me insane."

She looked at me for a moment with a questioning look on her face as I continued to plead: "Granny you know I'm not mad; please Granny, I am your grandchild; don't let it happen again; please help me."

Her response was immediate as she straightened her back and it took me completely by surprise.

"Come with me, child. Leave the pup where he is. We'll use the back door."

I could hardly believe it was happening. My grandmother who had always been so strict, who had always been drilling me that I must respect authority, was now helping me to escape from the police!

We managed to get down the stairs unnoticed. Thankfully my grandparent's house is terraced and there is no access from the front to the back. She led me through the laneway leading from the tiny rear garden, then we crossed a road and down another laneway almost closed in with bushes. Within moments we were at the back door of a house that was obviously familiar to Granny. An elderly lady came out to greet us. She had snow-white hair neatly tucked into a bun at the back of her head. I noticed how she was already elegantly dressed, despite the fact it was still so early in the morning. It appeared as though she was leaving for some important engagement. Her face lit up with delight when she saw us.

"Esther, come in, come in. And this must be Natalie's daughter. Julie, isn't it? Come in, come in. Oh! What a lovely surprise."

"We were out for a morning stroll and I just had to call in to show off my favourite grandchild," Granny replied without blinking an eyelid.

"Oh! This calls for a nice cup of tea. Let me put the kettle on. I was just about to do some toast with marmalade. You will join me?"

"Yes, of course we will," Granny replied. "That would be lovely, Maggie. By the way, before I forget, can I use your phone for a moment? I feel we may have left the front door open at home. We have a new puppy and we don't want him to get lost."

"Esther, honey, no need to ask. You know where it is in the hallway."

This was another side of my grandmother I had not seen before. Obviously, the personal affairs of the family are very private with her, much too private to even share with her friend. Behind the singing noise of the kettle I heard her whisper; "I'm over at Maggie's house. Julie is with me. We're both safe and sound. But we're not coming back until the coast is clear." Then in a loud voice she continued; "Don't forget to keep the front door closed. We don't want Rambo to get lost!"

Her cool and efficient manner without the slightest trace of disturbance in her voice amazed me. Like a true matriarch she returned to the kitchen and sat down beside me. Then squeezing my hand she whispered into my ear: "Sweetie, this is a piece of cake compared to the things I had to endure when I was your age." With that she giggled like a mischievous teenager.

Yes, indeed, Granny had seen the worst of it when she was a girl. It is something she never mentioned, but I did learn from my mother how she had to be smuggled out of Nazi Germany. Her parents and brothers were not so fortunate. They were never found and the records relating to those events had been destroyed before Germany was freed from that terrible grip.

Maggie returned from the scullery with the tray of tea and toast and that's when the real chatter commenced. While I was deeply anxious to find out what was going to happen to me they were admiring the shape of my nose, my mouth, my ears and trying to figure out which member of the family I took after.

Eventually my mother arrived and, while apologizing for interrupting, she reminded us we had a busy morning ahead. My grandfather was waiting outside in the car. After saying our goodbyes I was bundled in and taken directly to the airport. On the way my mother explained how she had been to the police station and filed a formal

JULIE

complaint of abuse and violence against him in order to
counter his challenge. But the police were still insisting
that I should make an appearance.
"You can if you want, but I'm not going to force it upon
you," she told me. "I know you don't want to, so I've
made arrangements for you to stay with a friend in London
until the heat of it all blows over."
She gave me an envelope of sterling notes, telling me to be
very careful with it. Her speed and efficiency amazed me.
I could hardly believe she had done so much within a
couple of hours and it being so early in the morning. I
couldn't thank her enough for being such a wonderful
mother and friend. Granny added; "We must stick close
together my girl! We must always be ready to help our
own. And we must never forget who we are."
The traffic was unusually light in Dublin that morning and
it wasn't long before we made it to the airport car park.
When my grandfather opened the boot I didn't recognise
the suitcase. It was one of their own they used on their
trips abroad.
"Don't worry," my mother assured me, "I've packed all
your own things neatly inside with a few little extras of
my own I thought you might need."
She had also managed to bring me fresh clothes for the
journey and in a matter of seconds I changed. Everything
was happening so fast my head was beginning to spin.
Soon we arrived at the check-in desk and my mother
produced the booking reference.
"Did you pack the suitcase yourself?" the attendant
inquired.
"Yes, she did. As a matter of fact we packed it together,"
my mother intervened.
I can hardly describe how I felt. The thought of London
was exciting while at the same time I was saddened to part
with my mother when I was just getting to know her. My

eyes were filling with tears until I remembered the alchemist's puzzling words;

"No need to cry about change. The only consistency is inconsistency. The only permanence is change itself. Hold on to nothing and allow nothing to take care of you. Don't worry about it; don't even think about it. Forget what I have just said. When it is happening to you, then you will know it in your own experience."

I could see again how everything he had said in those four evenings were rapidly unfolding in the events of my life. An extraordinary feeling of great privilege swept through every bone in my body and again I found myself uttering the words, "thank you, thank you, thank you" to nothing in particular.

"Thank the good Lord," Granny interrupted.

I must have looked directly at her with that piercing look in my eyes. Any mention of religion, the Lord, or anything relating to such was an instant reminder to me of my tyrant father and being subjugated to his particular beliefs. The unexpected kiss on my cheek from my mother stopped me from saying what I might have later regretted.

It was time to part. In sadness we walked to the departure gate together. My mother embraced me warmly and whispered in my ear; "You will be all right. I have the greatest confidence in you, Julie. My friend, Maura, will meet you. I know you will love her. Stay in contact with me on my mobile and if you need anything, anything at all, please let me know right away."

Granny hugged me tightly while trying to fight back the tears in her eyes as she advised; "Be brave in the face of adversity. Never discard your roots and the Lord will take care of you."

Then Gramps hugged me and, as he shook my hand, I could feel the paper money enter my palm.

"I'm sure the Lord will look out for you, Julie, but a little help won't go astray," he tried to laugh.

I loved them dearly and with heavy heart I walked through the gate. Deep within me I knew I was saying goodbye to that part of my life forever. I looked back only once and saw them standing there, looking and waving. That final image of the three of them pouring out such abundant love to me has frozen in my memory for all time to come. That is, if it's still possible for me to have more time after what I've done in Granada this night.

I really didn't want to leave them. It was cruel, I thought, being dragged away from such incredible love just moments after discovering it. Quite aimlessly I wandered through the shopping areas, not looking at anything in particular, while waiting for my flight to be called.

Why must I leave when I want so much to stay? I was seriously asking myself. Instantly my vagueness was sharply interrupted when I heard my name being called over the intercom;

"Would Julie Steinheart please pick up the nearest red telephone?"

My heart pounded. The police have located me was my only thought. A picture of them formed in my mind with the ambulance, the nurses and the straightjacket waiting to take me back to the mental asylum. I could not move in any direction. I found myself muttering aloud in a manner of prayerful petition.

"Oh Lord God! Please … oh, please don't let it happen to me again."

In a cold, mechanical manner the voice repeated itself. It felt like steel nails being hammered into my head.

"Would Julie Steinheart, who is travelling to Gatwick, please pick up the nearest red telephone."

I looked around and immediately I spotted a red telephone close by. It seemed as though it was jeering at me and tauntingly waiting to deliver me to my doom. I could hardly stop my legs from trembling as I walked over to it, feeling as though I was walking to my death. Picking it up I waited for the terrible news. Then I heard the voice;

"Yes, can I help you?"

"I … I'm Julie Steinheart," I managed to stammer.

"Ah! Miss Steinheart. Your passport and boarding pass are here at the information desk. Can you come and collect them please."

What an unimaginable relief! I hadn't even realised I had dropped them. Nor did I realise how inattentive I'd been as I moped around the exit lounge. But now I knew why I had to go and why there was no turning back. I could hardly get over the incredible coincidence of such a thing happening to me in immediate response to the feelings of not wanting to leave. Then I remembered something the alchemist said in relation to coincidences.

"Never fret. Life will guide you through. Be alert at all times and you will see the signs. What will seem like coincidences may inexplicably appear. Do not try to reason them away, as reason is but an instrument of time. Coincidences are signs occurring in the vortex of existence as your consciousness moves nearer to the point. When these occur, know in your heart you are now moving closer to the point of transcendence. Be calm. Be assured and fully trust. The assurances are always there whenever they are needed. You are on the pilgrim's path, your path that is your own divinity in the here and now. Trust it completely and be assured that all is well."

I had sat in his presence and listened to him speak these words just like the others had sat and listened. Yet, it was only when they re-echoed through the actual experiencing of them in my own situation did I finally begin to get the message. It helped me understand all things happening in my life are absolutely necessary when seen in the context of the larger picture. Nothing can be excluded.

But where is the larger picture right now? I ask myself. Even that seems to have been diminished behind the magnitude of what I have done this night in Granada.

Again I'm confused, I fail to find a connection between this night and the alchemist's wisdom. Surely, there must be more to see and to learn. I feel the shadow of gloom is forcing its way upon me, but I must not be tempted to end it all. I must be patient and trust his words completely. Many times I have faced the impossible since my first awakening and I am still here in body surmounting the insurmountable. Even on my first arrival to London, did I not get through that bizarre occurrence of being abducted? It could only have happened to me, yet somehow an escape presented itself. So I must not flinch from this moment. Whatever is about to happen when I face the world in the morning cannot be anything greater than what I can endure in body and spirit. It is the natural law in the cosmic order of all things in which I am but a minute part while not being apart or separate.

The plane to Gatwick landed ahead of schedule and everything seemed to go smoothly. I was beginning to relax and I found my way through the terminal with remarkable ease after collecting my suitcase and putting my passport into its inside pocket so I would not lose it again. Within moments I was on the train to Victoria and accustoming myself to the new feeling of freedom. It seemed as though I was being carried away from my past on the crest of speed and it was good.

The city suburbs appeared to be endless as the train wound its way through intersections for the final miles of the journey. Eventually it came to a stop and everyone jumped from their seats. People were rushing and scrambling as though London were a spaceship about to leave the planet for good! It was my first journey alone to England and I had no idea Victoria station could be so enormous. The prearranged meeting place with Maura was to be at the paper kiosk by the main exit. When I took stock of my new surroundings everything seemed to be the other way round. In Ireland I had been the one filled with anxiety while everyone else seemed to be at ease in themselves. Here I was the one at ease while those about me seemed to be filled with anxiety. In the confusion of it all I circled the station several times trying to figure out which was the main exit. Eventually I found it, but I was still not quite sure of my position as I stood there feeling completely out of the picture. I had noticed there were more newspaper kiosks than one in the station, something they had not realised. The one I chose was closest to the exit and I trusted this was the place. I was there for a while wondering which stranger would eventually turn up as Maura. All types of people passed by and all looked sharply away whenever they caught me looking into their faces. I started getting flashbacks of the mental asylum and those female nurses with large biceps who had packed me into the straightjacket. The familiar panic began to rise again in my chest. I knew I had to wait where I was, but something inside kept urging me to run. I needed to keep on moving. I had escaped to another country, yet it felt as though my past was about to catch up and possess my body again should I remain standing in the one spot.

The alchemist had talked about this. From what I understood him say, we attract people and situations that are necessary for us to prolong our particulars plays. Apparently, each of us create our own scripts for living according to our lights. We waste a lot of effort trying to change the circumstances of our lives without realising the real necessity for change should be in ourselves. I had not realised before then the profound truth of his words.

I must have been frantically looking into every woman's face hoping she would be Maura. Finally, a youngish looking woman with blonde hair cautiously approached me and said, "you are waiting for me?" with a beaming smile on her face.

"Yes, yes," I replied. "You must be Maura?"

"Sure, that's me, honey. And you must be…?"

"Julie ... Julie Steinheart in person!" I answered before she could finish.

"Of course, of course, Julie; 'tis wonderful to meet you at last. I've been hearing so much about you. Come with me, come with me, my dear. Let me help you with your case. The driver is waiting for us just around the corner."

I took everything at face value. Indeed, my mind was so preoccupied with my world of personal traumas, even if Hitler had appeared at that moment and introduced himself as Maura, in all probability I would have docilely accepted it without question.

The woman grabbed my case and linked me by the arm across some streets and finally to a waiting car that looked quite shabby and old. As we approached it the driver jumped out and opened the boot to greet us. I noticed a scar on his face and a tattoo of a red and blue dagger on the back of his left hand. His rough appearance unnerved me, but the woman was quick to pick up the vibes.

"Oh don't be scared of Geordie, sweetie, he looks fierce but he's really a little lamb."

With that I was packed into the back seat while the two sat in front and never stopped talking to me about the wonders of London and all the amazing and exciting things I was about to experience. It all seemed so strangely new. They did not allow me a free moment to consider the situation, never mind to ask any questions. They gave me some chocolate to eat, the most expensive chocolate in London they told me, manufactured especially for the queen's special guests. It tasted strangely delicious and in my nervousness I swallowed it as fast as they fed it to me.

They possessed a similar urgency to the people I observed in the station. But I was on the move again, being whisked further away from my past without realising I was still recreating more of this past each moment. I began to feel light and dizzy in my head with things starting to fade and reappear as the car sped from one set of lights to the next. I had no idea I was being abducted. My one concern at the time was trying to fit in with this new and strange environment. Eventually they pulled up in a street of terraced houses and I was ushered inside a shabby, blue door. I suddenly remembered my mother had told me that Maura lived in a detached house with large gardens in Ealing. This certainly could not have been it; nor could the woman be a friend of my mother, I began to realise, when I started to examine her appearance more closely. Her perfume was cheap and excessive, as was the makeup on her face. Her dyed, blonde hair failed to hide the dark roots and blotchy skin underneath. But it was too late. The sweetness of the woman's voice had turned to bitterness as she forcefully pushed me into a room. I had no idea what was happening, or why it was happening. Then everything seemed to be spinning as I struggled to hold my balance, still not realising I had been drugged.

"Don't give me trouble sweetie and I'll give you none," the woman spouted as she snatched my handbag and left me with nothing.

The key turn sharply in the door while I was still trying to balance myself. I looked around me and, to my horror, there was not even a window on any wall of the smelly room. The light went out and I was immediately plunged into darkness. My mouth opened to scream, but nothing would come. It has to be a nightmare, I tried to imagine. My hands felt my face, my head, and my torso as I desperately tried to hold onto the only reality I had known. The confusion intensified. I could not distinguish whether I was in the hands feeling the body or in the body being felt by the hands. There was nothing external to reflect my senses upon and nothing made sense any more.

I must have blacked out, for the next I remember I was half awake in a strange room with some glaring lights and naked people around me. My body felt very weird, as if it was not my body at all. There was a strange taste in my mouth and I could vaguely recollect having being forced to drink some liquid substance. I had no idea what was happening to me until a faint voice inside my head started calling on me to wake up. It got louder and louder. Then I recognized it as the voice of my mother. The experience was something like becoming partly conscious in the middle of a terrible dream. You know how it is when you have to collect all the available energy and force it towards that part of the brain that awakens you out of your sleep in such times of acute apprehension. As I began to return to my senses I could feel strange hands groping my torso. Then my hearing picked up the words; "For fuck sake, will you get the little bitch switched on!"

Terror gripped me. I suddenly realised I was being coerced into a seriously bad situation. I closed my eyes tightly, focusing all my attention on that point in the blackness the alchemist had mentioned. Instantly I was experiencing it, the pure energy behind existence. Without warning it was like a volcano erupting from deep within me and a surge of incredible fire filled my entire body. Not knowing what I was doing, the energetic force caused me to instinctually spring to my feet. I remember diving between two glaring lights and there was the sound of crashing objects, breaking glass and voices swearing. I recall how I twisted and turned while trying to untangle myself from electric cables that felt like snakes clinging to my body. Then I was at the door and the blonde woman was blocking my path. The next I remember she was cursing while falling backwards with blood all over her face. Within a moment I was out on the narrow street, while still not realising I was naked. Geordie got out of the car with his eyes and mouth wide open at the sudden appearance of my naked body. But the energetic force possessing me was far more powerful that anything relative to myself. My foot had sunk into his crutch without I realising what I had done and he fell in a heap on the pavement, cursing and screaming. It did not stop the speed of occurrences. In an instant I was behind the wheel of the car and, turning the keys, it moved forward in surges. I had no experience of driving, apart from the few lessons I had received from a school friend. But I managed to manoeuvre away from that place through different streets until I brought the car to an awkward halt close to some trees.

My suitcase! I thought. I jumped out and almost smashed into an old man who was walking by with a dog on a lead. He looked the other way pretending not to notice my nakedness. I could not stop my hands from shaking as I fumbled through the big ring of keys until I eventually managed to open the boot. To my great relief my suitcase was there and I dug out my jeans, a sweater and runners. My head was still spinning as I tried to regain myself. Looking up I saw the trees looming over me in a strange, vivid greenness. Then I noticed the colours everywhere were grossly exaggerated. Was it real or imaginary? I was not sure, still battling against the drugs in my system.

I stood there taking deep breaths until my pulse rate slowed down. Then I noticed some boxes of pornographic pictures in the open boot and it caused me to explore further. I uncovered a small, black briefcase and, prising it open, I came upon some documents and two bundles of money. I had no idea how much was in it. But she had stolen my handbag with all my money and personal things. Bizarrely, events were unfolding in a way completely outside my control. It was not to be argued. I unfolded two twenty-pound notes, slipped them into a pocket in my jeans and put the rest of the money deep inside my suitcase. Then I locked the car where it was, threw the keys into a hedge and cautiously walked back to the main street where I hailed down a London taxi and asked him to take me to Victoria station.

Six hours had passed since my first arrival. There was no point in looking any further for Maura so I made my way to a phone and called my mother. She was out of her mind with worry, but I couldn't tell her what had happened. Apart from being so stupid not to have read the situation at the outset, I was thankful to have escaped so quickly and seemingly unharmed. It was far too much to explain and, still unsure of my mental state, I needed time to reflect before I could dare mention it to anyone. This may be hard to comprehend for anyone who has not experienced a childhood such as mine with a parent daily pounding the view that I myself am the sole cause of everything being wrong about me. To a point without knowing it he was actually right, but not through the source of his own enslavement. I told her I had lost my way and I apologized for being such a nuisance.

"Maura is very distraught," she informed me. "She was late getting to the station due to unexpected traffic, and after three hours waiting she had to return to Ealing to collect her son from school. I will phone her right away and tell her you are on the way by taxi."

"Please make sure it is an official London cab," a little too late she warned.

What had happened was not my mother's fault. Yet my mind was eager to engage in the thought that it was. My life had been nothing but misfortune in relation to mostly everything she had placed before me up to that point in time; the man she had chosen to be my father, for example, was the greatest misfortune I could have been given. But the wisdom of the alchemist's words was present within me to instantly disperse such thinking. It was my own play, my own karmic recurrence; through me the play continued to reconstruct itself. I knew when the consciousness within would be sufficiently swift there would be no more referring to the past and therefore no more repetition of it. But I had still some worldly distance before me, it appeared.

When I asked my mother for Maura's address, while making the excuse that I could not seem to find it in my bag, I could hear the relief in her voice as she told me to call her again immediately I had safely arrived. The taxi driver was very friendly and he tried to strike up a conversation as we travelled through the streets of London. But I was not very responsive as I was eagerly focusing my attention on the road signs and checking them against the street map I had bought at the paper stand in Victoria on my second time round. We might be living in a world of endless probabilities, but this time I was leaving absolutely nothing to chance.

Eventually we arrived in the borough of Ealing. Unlike where I'd been, it seemed to be filled with trees in blossom and the feeling of spaciousness was everywhere. Within moments he pulled up outside a large, detached house hosting a front garden filled to capacity with roses of every colour. Before I could pay him Maura was on the scene with the fare in her hand. She hugged me furiously. Then she stood me at arm length and looking me all over she could hardly stop herself from talking.

"My God, Julie, it's like taking a trip down memory lane. You are exactly like your mother was when we were teenagers. I'm so excited you are here. Forgive me for not being able to wait at the station. I stayed for as long as I could. After three hours I had to return to collect Damian from the nursery. I phoned all the neighbours for help but none of them were home. I was so worried that we might lose you. London is very big and there's a lot of funny people out there, we can never be too careful."

I was still trying to regain my focus as I stood there staring at her. My head started to feel light again and I could feel myself swaying as her excitement continued, apparently oblivious of my condition. I needed water and I knew I had to lie down quickly before my body would collapse. At last she became aware of my state.

"Enough of my babbling. You must be exhausted after the long trip. I'll take your case and show you to the room we have specially prepared for your coming."

The perfume from the roses filled the late evening air as we walked up the paved footpath leading to the doorway.

"The first thing we must do is phone your mother," she was saying as she opened the door into the huge hallway.

I was literally gob-smacked by the spaciousness unfolding before my eyes. My mother's sitting room and kitchen in Dublin could have easily fitted into the enormous, oval-shaped space. Then Maura was through on the phone.

"Natalie! Great news, Julie has arrived. It's so amazing. She's almost your double ..."

Allowing her voice to fade into the background I peeked through an open doorway into a living room with a deep red carpet and gold-studded furniture. At the other end I noticed a series of archways spanning the entire width of the room and coming down to rest on four white, ornate pillars. Beyond the archways I could see a large rosewood table with matching chairs and a huge rosewood cabinet taking up the space of an entire sidewall. Glazed patio doors led to a conservatory of hanging plants in full blossom with purple, white and deep pink flowers.

My head was still in a spin, hardly able to keep up with the incredible speed of rapid events occurring. It was like being swung on the end of a great pendulum. Literally moments before I had experienced hell on earth, now I was stepping into what I could only describe as paradise. It brought the alchemist to mind and how one evening I had challenged him with my little knowledge of life. I ran off a litany of words relating to reality while more or less accusing him of nonsensically talking through his hat. His loving smile infuriated me further. Apparently, there was nothing I could say that would have offended him and the harsher I got the more lovingly he smiled directly into my eyes. When I eventually ran out of steam he asked me if I was ready to face the universe.

"That's what I'm doing," in exasperation I replied.

"But everything is moving a little too slowly for your impatience, Julie! Am I correct?" he gently queried.

"Yes, yes! It seems as though the whole world is asleep, not knowing that it's spinning in circles."

"Julie, be patient just for this moment. Allow yourself to listen. The world you are seeing is rising directly out of you. In fact it is rising out of each and every one of you here present. It is your creation. I know you might say you have not created the wars and the hunger, and rightly so. The wars and the hunger are part of the world, but in your immediate experience, in your body here now, all life is rising out of a source that is within you. I am asking you to look at life as it is in your experience. Your consciousness needs to be extraordinarily swift in order to outpace your limitations. You live in the mind. You see the world through the mind. You get caught up in the slow and cumbersome 'cause and effect' of the mind-world, thus missing life completely. But do not just believe what I am saying. Please check it out it in your own experience. This is the only way you can be sure whether it is true or not.

JULIE

Ask yourself right now where is life? Before you answer you must first re-connect with the sensation of life in your body at this moment. Doing this you will realise 'you' are life. The things you can see, feel, smell, taste, hear and sense are merely forms of life. But these things are not 'actual' life in the inner sensation of your own immediate experience. They merely reflect the 'actual' life that you are in your body. You are either sufficiently awake to hear what is being said or you are not. If you do not hear it in the deeper sense of hearing, then so be it; a tree goes on being a tree, a fish goes on being a fish, a cat goes on being a cat, and a rock goes on being a rock. If you are connecting with the sensation that the words reflect then you are on the threshold. The door is opening to you and all you can do is trust. This is the only way to transcend the limited known. That first great step you have to make it alone. I am merely a voice coming from the void to guide you some of the way. You see me as someone separate from you, but the essence of me is not outside you. I am just a mirror reflecting that which is already within you. From where you are standing it may appear impossible to take the initial step. Why? It would mean letting go of everything. I mean absolutely everything you see as your visible world around you."

Then he turned his piercing eyes directly into mine and challenged me openly with the words;

"Are you ready to take that step, Julie? Are you ready to relinquish your world in its totality? All you need do is be still, be silent, and allow the response to rise right now from your heart. But I have to warn you; you must be prepared to fully accept it. There is no in-between ground in what is being opened to you."

"Yes, I am ready," was my instant response without even considering the consequences I had at that moment drawn upon myself.

"Then do not be amazed at the phenomenal speed of consciousness you are about to encounter," he warned.

"Do not be amazed by the bizarre events you may have to pass through. Do not be amazed," he slowly repeated as he turned to the others and continued;

"The world you know is a vortex in time and everything within the vortex is spinning and spinning. This is how everything seems to be repeated in one form or another. As you begin to re-connect with the source of life within, you will find yourself moving down the vortex, moving in from the outer circles where most things are forgotten by the time they are encountered again. As you come closer to the point or the source within you in your experience, the circles of reoccurrence become smaller and smaller. But do not be unduly concerned; you will be sufficiently aware to read the signs. These may appear as coincidences happening around you. The coincidences are merely a sign that you are getting closer and the circle of reoccurrence is getting swifter. Do not allow the mind to dissect or divide. Know that all things are interconnected, interrelated and interdependent. When you reach the point of the vortex you will re-cognize it, then you will know that the cognition is always immediate. It is from where I am speaking to you now.

"As I speak metaphorically I can tell you these things. You can hear me intellectually, but it still remains unknown to you. It has to be so, for you cannot know it without the realisation of it in your own direct experience in that body listening to these words. This is why you are here, going round and round in the vortex of time. The transcendental realisation is the actual passing through the point, passing through the eye of the needle, or the eye of the vortex, so to speak."

"Julie! Julie! Your mother wants to speak with you," Maura's voice interrupted.

I hadn't realised I had plunged so deeply into my subconscious. I spent time talking with my mother and thanking her for handing me over to her good friend. Maura excused herself and went upstairs to check on her son who was still sleeping. It gave me the time alone that I needed to absorb my new surroundings when I eventually got off the phone.

I recall the warm feeling of security that moment as I sat there in the huge hallway taking in the fresh smells around me and observing the shadows being created by the late evening sun. How wonderful it was, that new beginning. Even after so much trouble I had received and possibly caused, life was still openly generous to me.

Why did I have to destroy it? What possessed me to re-indulge in my past?

The cold reality sweeps through me like the harsh wind from the snow-capped Sierra Nevada. There is no way back for me now. There can be no return to the security and warmth. Life is so very precious, every moment of it. Now I know as I face the certainty of losing it for good. Whatever is to be my fate after this terrible night, all I can do is accept it.

JULIE

My room was off the first landing with a huge window looking out over the rear garden of flowers and fruit trees. It had a built-in wardrobe neatly fitted behind the door and a narrow archway leading to a small bathroom with a shower. A bed took up the middle of the floor, large enough to sleep an entire family.

"I'll leave you to get settled in," Maura said as she introduced it to me. "You will meet Damian later; he's fast asleep at the moment after his morning at the nursery. By the way, what would you like for supper?" she added.

Oh, anything that's going. I'm not very fussy," I replied.

"But I don't want to force something upon you that might be against your beliefs," she remarked.

"My beliefs!" I exclaimed indignantly.

I could never abide by religious customs such as sticking to a particular diet according to some crazy rules of a bygone age, nor could I understand how seemingly intelligent people could be so easily doped through their psychological fear of some mind-made patriarchal god. I felt I had earned my freedom from all such nonsense.

"Would fish be suitable?" Maura proposed apologetically.

"Yes, fish would be fine," I said, while trying to remove the unexpected harshness from my voice.

"Well," she replied in relief, "I've got lovely fresh trout from the early market this morning. Paul will be home in an hour and we can all eat together. But you might like a little snack to keep you going until then. You've been on the go for most of the day and you must be starving."

"No, I'll be fine. I would prefer to wait; anyway, it will take me at least an hour to get unpacked."

I needed to shower. I felt I could not wash myself enough to get rid of the feeling still lingering from that dreadful experience. I began to wonder if I had been sexually abused. How would I know? Using the hand mirror I carefully examined every inch of my body. But all I could find was a bruise mark on my left arm and a swelling on one of my toes that throbbed.

The shower brought me back to life and all thought of taking a rest soon disappeared. I allowed my hair to dry naturally as I took in the cool evening air by the window. When I looked outside I noticed the sun beginning to disappear behind the taller trees at the back of the garden. The picture was gently serene and it exuded peace and tranquillity. I tried to take it all in.

What a strange day it had been up to that moment, from early morning being awakened by the police in Killiney, then making my flight to London and then being abducted. I began to realise how lucky I had been to survive through it all. Being much too fast to comprehend I could still feel the pounding going on in my head. As I sat there on the window ledge I noticed how the life presence in my body seemed very fragile and vulnerable. I was aware how my thought process was inconsistent and there were moments when I wondered if I was imagining it all.

I decided to unpack and hang up my clothes in the solid oak wardrobe. To my surprise, some were new and I did not recognise them. Then I remembered my mother had been to her friend's boutique before she picked me up at Maggie's house early that morning and a gush of love passed through me for her. As I was taking out the larger garments from the bottom of the suitcase I was stunned when the two bundles of money scattered all over the bed. I started gathering up the notes, putting the fifties, the twenties and the tens in respective piles and to my surprise there were thirty-three fivers left over. After counting it all I could hardly believe it amounted to three thousand four hundred and fifty five pounds. This did not include the two twenty pound notes I had previously put in my pocket. I was astounded, not knowing what to do being in possession of such a large sum of money. I sat there in utter amazement at what the day had unfolded, then I remembered something else the alchemist had said;

"Whenever you find yourself in a situation and you don't know what is the proper thing to do, then do absolutely nothing. Stay looking from that place of silent looking where there is no mind stuff involved. The answer will come when the mind is not doing its spinning in circles and blocking it."

But I must return it, I thought to myself. The money is not mine to keep. It is wrong to have it. Yet, how could I return it when I didn't even know where I had been? But surely, I must be guilty of theft, my conscience tried to argue. Then the intelligence behind his voice spoke again in my head;

"Don't get entangled in conscience. See it for what it truly represents. Conscience is nothing more than a moral code being created according to the convenience norms of the masses. It is put there by the priests and used as their lever of power over you. Your consciousness cannot speed up sufficiently to 'be' the truth until you break free from all such nonsense. Note that conscience and judgement are of the same ilk. Don't judge the situation. Let this be your only mantra in life. Trust me, it will be more than enough to get you through."

But grabbing a fistful of coins from the nurses' money jar in the hospital was petty compared to the amount I had now in my hands. Still neither was more significant than the other. This I could see when I looked at the situation without applying a pre-coded programme of conscience or judgement to it. The fact was the fact and the money had come my way without any preconceived scheming on my part, just like all the other precarious events had come my way that day. I packed the money into two socks and put them into the suitcase together with the heavy clothes that

I knew I would not be wearing for some time. After that I managed to put the case on the top shelf of the wardrobe, out of sight, out of mind, and that was it.

Maura knocked on the door, telling me supper was ready whenever I was set to join them. I came down with her and she first introduced me to her husband Paul, then to little Damian who was shy for a moment. But I was hardly seated before his shyness disappeared and he started climbing all over me. He became over-amorous and I felt rather awkward and embarrassed when he started kissing me on the lips.

"They do it in the movies," he exclaimed lovingly as he fought against my resistance.

His father was laughing at the funny side of it. But, much to my relief, Maura grabbed hold of him sternly and seated him at the far end of the table from where he continued to absorb their full attention.

"You'll have to forgive him," his father interrupted, "he's just not used to having such a beautiful young woman in the house for supper."

Indeed, beauty was the last thing on my mind after going through one of the most tumultuous days of my life. But I could see it in Damian's eyes, the way he was looking at me, it was obvious he was receiving me as being very beautiful and he was eagerly determined to express it. Behind my embarrassment I found it refreshing to receive such adoration coming from his unspoilt innocence. It was enough to outweigh that lecherous look on the driver's face earlier that day. As Maura and Paul became totally absorbed with their son trying to keep him in order I could barely comprehend how everything was so turbulently fast, being tossed from the worst scenario to the best, all in a matter of hours. I felt that life was dealing me a rapid course of enlightenment. But the alchemist did warn me when he said;

"There is no in-between ground in this course. Once the initial step has been taken into the unknown there is no turning back. When the unknown enters the realm of the known it cannot be unknown again, there can be no return as the bridges of past inevitably dissolve. Even the new quickly passes into the old and it too disappears. But the personal self with all its personal baggage is built upon the accumulative past and it is totally dependent on it. You are not what you think you are, because whatever you think is the personal self, the waster of your true essence. I am here to awaken you to your true essence, therefore, there is no escape for the personal self once the initial step has been taken. Don't be moved to act upon any of it. Don't try to perfect, to chop or to change; just stay calm and hold the resonance. Sit quietly and watch it all fade away, while you, the silent watcher, remain. By so doing you are ridding yourself of the personal self and all its baggage. In other words, you are clearing the way towards realising the immortality of your true essence."

I was by now fully aware that the path I had innocently embarked upon was not for the faint-hearted. I was also aware that the speed of events occurring in my life since my encounter with his cosmic essence was directly linked to the challenge I had made to him.

"Know that nothing is separate in the greater reality; all things interrelate, interconnect, and are interdependent," he had said many times. "Your awakening from the sleep of the living dead is part of the awakening of all humanity. In all appearance you are individually separate. But, even though you carry the stamp of your own uniqueness, yet, universally speaking, you *are* the whole. Yes, you are the whole of life."

What an extraordinary statement, I thought. But I could not deny the truth in it. I looked upon Paul and Maura with their adorable son Damian as the perfect family. Yet, I could also see, even in the presence of such perfection, how temporary it all is in the greater universal play. They were certainly an example to humanity, and so was my mother, having expressed the courage to face the truth of her own situation. I began to realise that everything is perfect just as it is, even my abductors who had caused me such pain, confusion and grief. I was beginning to see that it was all being presented as the necessary fuel for the speeding up of my consciousness. The alchemist brought this to light when he challenged; "Are you ready to face the universe, Julie?"

He warned me about the rapidity of events about to occur in my life, but not to be too worried about anything, not to be overly concerned. Now I was realising that the power behind his words had carried me safely through the bizarre happenings I had since encountered. Not only that, but I had been carried through without a stain. I was aware of an incredible freedom after being in his presence. It was freedom from the mental process, the circular occurrence of the mind that the psychiatrists have no real knowledge of yet. But I still had not fully come to realise that I am the whole of life. Then again, he had also made it clear that nothing can happen before its time. I felt the sensation of great privilege shivering through my body.

"Thank you, thank you, thank you," I was once more saying aloud without realising it.

"No need to thank us, Julie." Maura's voice interrupted the flow. "It's our privilege to have you with us. Isn't that right Paul?"

"Yes, sure it is, Maura. It's great to have you with us, Julie. Why, little Damian is already in love with you."

I could feel the blood rushing to my cheeks. For all I knew, I could have been talking it all aloud. How often we hear an oblivious person talking to himself in the street. Even the alchemist had warned that our thoughts can be clearly intercepted by anyone with a little training. For the rest of the time at the table I made sure to keep myself fully present. But strange as it appears, I had been more or less present all the time, in spite of the fact that the alchemist's words kept flashing through my brain at incredible speed.

After saying our goodnights I retired to the huge bed and relished the cool, sensuous sheets next to my skin. My body was still peculiarly reacting to the drugs and sexual stimulants that I had been given by my abductors that day. Yes, life was still bursting through in all its wonder; this very same life I will surely have to relinquish should I fail to fully reconnect before dawn. The personal self is so utterly weak, the more tired the body becomes the stronger it urges me to jump.

That first morning in Ealing broke to the sound of rapturous birdsong. I drew back the heavy tapestry curtains and opened the window. The magical hue shimmering around the trees in the sharp light of the rising sun transfixed my gaze. Next I noticed how the cobwebs sparkled as they haphazardly stretched above the ground between the varieties of shrubs. As my vision expanded further I noticed the tiny footprints of little animals on the blanket of dew softly caressing the neatly cut grass.

The more I gazed upon the beauty before me the more alive it became. It seemed as though its intensity was actually exuding from my own expanding appreciation of it; so much so that I became totally enraptured in the timelessness of the moment. Then quite unexpectedly, a huge sensational wave engulfed my body at the sudden realisation of there being no distance between the beauty I was seeing with my eyes and the beauty I was feeling in my body. It is almost impossible to put into words. My presence did not seem to stop at being just my body; it was as though I was all of it, the dew upon the grass, the cobwebs, the trees, even the shadow of the house casting itself over a third of the lawn. The sensory vibration of the huge wave seemed to go outwards and outwards, beyond the trees at the far end of the garden, even engulfing a plane in the distant sky. At that moment there was nothing separate. I could feel it! Yes! I was sure I could feel it.

Wow! I was overcome by the sheer ecstasy of that sparkling experience. The alchemist could see it all. He knew all of this as I had sat there in the front row of seats questioning and challenging him at those meetings in Temple Bar. What have I done to be deserving of this? I pondered. "But you are it, you are all of it!" his voice echoed through my inner ear. "You are the whole of life," he had said, "and you do not have to believe me, for sooner of later you will realise it in your own experience."

Then Paul appeared in his boxer shorts on the patio close to the steps leading down to the fishpond. As he stretched his limbs I became aware of the sensuality tingling inside me at the unexpected sight of his body. There was a sense of great freedom about him that suddenly intrigued me. He instinctually turned around and his face broke into a broad smile showing off his sparkling teeth as he gave me a wave before disappearing again out of sight.

Next a black cat appeared over the fence and it slowly swaggered across the lawn as though it was on a routine inspection of its own private domain. A blackbird scurried out of its path, flying low without actually leaving the ground. I could see that a certain courtesy existed between them in the manner of their mutual acknowledgement for each other's presence. Yes, all appeared to be in beautiful harmony as I lingered for some time just gazing at it and filling my body through my senses. It was time to face into the activities of the new day and the shower in the room was most refreshing. Within moments I was down the stairs in my summer shorts and t-shirt, not being in the habit of wearing a bra as I felt the size of my breasts did not yet warrant one. Paul re-appeared in light grey slacks that were neatly cupping his buttocks, with a light blue shirt and a flowery tie he was still fixing as he plugged in the kettle.

"You'll have cereal, Julie? Or perhaps some fruit? Please help yourself. You know you are part of the family."

I felt a little embarrassed as I was sure he could sense my aroused attraction towards him. Then Maura appeared in her nightgown and quickly showed me the run of the kitchen. Within moments Damian came crashing through the door and in total confidence flung himself straight into my arms. Breakfast was a stand-up affair, except for Damian who was eventually seated in front of his special cereal bowl. Paul dashed in and out several times collecting the things he needed for the day, and finally he was gone, throwing me a wink as he left.

I helped Maura with the morning chores and then the three of us packed into the car and headed for the nursery. On the way back Maura needed to do some shopping for groceries at her local mall and when we had finished she took me to one of her favourite cafés for morning coffee. On the way she bought me a navy shoulder bag my eye had caught as we were passing some stalls. We chatted for ages about everything under the sun, except of course, my own personal world. As we were leaving I asked her if she knew of a place where I could have access to the Internet.

"Yes, of course," she eagerly offered. "There's an Internet café on Ealing Broadway. It's right at the end of our road. I can drop you off on our way back home. Then you can have as long as you like. It's less than five minutes walk from the house."

I had to assure her again and again that I didn't need money. But she insisted I take the sunglasses I had been wearing in the car. Soon I was surfing the web and, after much searching, I began to realise the web is not the most efficient place for finding a job. Two hours had passed before I realised I was wasting my time. Surfing the web was part of my past. It was my way of temporary escape from the miserable existence I had to endure. It dawned on me that I didn't need it anymore, and what a relief to be free at last to leave it behind. On leaving the café I felt I would never need to return there again. Feeling the new life opening to me, wearing the sunglasses and my new shoulder bag I swaggered onto the street.

But trouble still found a way to harass me. I was crossing at the green light without a care in the world when I suddenly noticed the car from the corner of my eye and instantly I recognized it. As a matter of fact it was the only dirty-white Ford Granada with a black vinyl roof that I had seen in London. I was already on the pedestrian crossing and I had stepped right in front of the bonnet. Geordie was behind the wheel and the woman had a map on the dashboard while pointing to the street sign at the corner. I kept walking while forcing myself not to run or look back, hoping they did not recognise me. After crossing, instead of walking towards the house I went the other way and I looked back just in time to see the tail end of the car disappearing into Maura's street.

My temporary haven was shattered and no answer would come what to do. I continued walking down the main street gripped again in that all too familiar panic. What would the alchemist tell me to do? I tried to imagine. Quite obviously he would tell me to take action. A red phone boot loomed into my path. There and then I decided to phone the police. A voice answered, asking for my name and the nature of my problem. Using broken English and a feigned, foreign accent I replied in the type of vernacular that my friend José María would have used.

"My name! María ... I'm Spanish. I have fourteen years only. Please help me. I've been kidnapped by an English man and woman. They have been forcing me to have sex while they took pictures and videos of me. I've just escaped from their car and they are running up and down the street looking for me. I don't know what to do."

"Where exactly are you right now?" The male voice of the policeman at the other end of the line inquired in a tone of controlled urgency.

"Ealing ... Ealing Broadway, I think ... yes ... it is Ealing Broadway. I can see the name of the road where they are parked. It is a big white car with a black roof."

Then I went on to spell out the name of the street and finished by saying I had to go quickly as I could see the woman coming towards me. I made my way back to the Internet café and took a seat where I had a view of the entire length of Maura's street. Within minutes a police van appeared at the upper end and it travelled slowly in my direction. Before it reached Maura's house the white Ford pulled away. Then a blue police car screeched around the corner right in front of the café and came to a halt blocking off the street completely. Geordie and the woman were trapped. At first there was talking involved. Then their car boot was opened and after that I could see them both being handcuffed and put into the police van. In moments all were gone, including their car, having been driven away by a policeman.

When the coast was clear I swiftly returned to Maura's house, telling myself I would never venture outside again. I was hardly settled in when the doorbell rang. Maura went to answer it, while looking through the curtains I could see a police car parked outside. I escaped to my room and sat there shivering on the bed as I listened to the voices on the doorstep. They talked for a while and then they quietly left. Maura knocked on my door before she entered and immediately saw I was in a state of shock. She hugged me tightly, assuring me that all was well.

"This is not Dublin and they are not looking for you here. As a matter of fact, nobody back home apart from your mother and grandparents know you are in London. The police only wanted to know if I had a Spanish girl living in the house. Apparently, a piece of paper with my address had been found on some people they have just arrested in relation to child abduction."

I couldn't bring myself to tell her it was still directly connected with me.

"I'm on my way to the boutique to check on the new deliveries before I collect Damian from the nursery. Why don't you come with me," Maura suggested.

I felt so very safe in her presence I was more than relieved to go anywhere with her. The boutique was a twenty-minute drive away and it afforded me the necessary time and distraction I needed to get over the delayed shock of the close encounter.

The lady in charge of the shop seemed very relieved when we entered. "I was just about to call you," she said to Maura. "I've had to dismiss the new girl. I caught her red-handed, giving free clothes to her friends."

It was Maura's boutique and she did the hiring and firing as she had been telling me in the car. But instead of being annoyed with the manageress for taking matters into her own hands without consulting her first, Maura turned to me and said;

"Julie! It looks like you have a new job. That is, of course, if you accept."

"Of course I accept," I replied, as I flew into her arms and hugged her.

That was it. That was how I commenced in the rag trade. I loved the job and it didn't take me too long to win the favour of the manageress, seeing that I was a personal friend of the boss. I was eager to learn everything about the business, from reading future fashion trends to finding a market for the out-of-fashion garments.

As the weeks turned into months Maura and myself got on like a house on fire. We soon became close personal friends and she shared with me her experiences and knowledge of the esoteric, in particular about energy fields relating to nature, plants and flowers. Colours were very important to her. She taught me many new things, in particular the importance of balance not only in colours but also in everything I do in the course of my life.

She was amazed at my vision and much of what I had to say astounded her. But she was always able to relate to it and she showed great interest in all I had received through my attendance at the seminars in Temple Bar. She even went as far as checking out the name of the alchemist and she discovered he would be making a visit to London later in the fall. Needless to say, I was ecstatic with the thought of being in his presence again and I could hardly retain the explosiveness of my enthusiasm. But then I remembered he had said;

"Don't waste an ounce of your energy looking forward to any event in the future. Know that all expectations are part of the mind-weed that grows in your garden to suffocate the vines. Looking forward to anything steals you away from the immediacy and spontaneity of life in the moment and it slows down your consciousness."

But still I could not help it. My entire body was tingling with excitement while entertaining the thought of being with him again. Maura had made application for two places. Seemingly, it had to be pre-booked in London and I found this rather strange. In Temple Bar the room had never been more than half full and most of those present were from different countries. I found it quite amazing that, unlike Ireland, there were a number of people living in England who would have awakened from what I had classed as the sleep of the living dead. I was even more excited with the idea of meeting some others like myself. It felt as though I was about to be reunited with my real family and I could hardly wait for November to arrive, as I so much wanted to share my own experiences with them.

Then a letter of apology came in the post with a refund of Maura's donation. It read:

"With deep regret we inform you that the forthcoming talks and all future talks have been cancelled. The Master has quietly passed away."

When Maura read me the letter I exploded in grief. She could not console me. I had no idea how I had become so attached to him and how he had become my rock, all that was life to me. I crumbled like a puppet into her arms. The indescribable grief went on for days and there was no letting up. Paul tried but could not understand what was happening to me, nor could Maura explain it to him. She had to brush him away by saying it was a woman thing.

Then, in the middle of a night as I lay awake with the grief in my bed a picture inexplicably fell off the wall. The sudden bang momentarily jerked me away from my personal pain. Stillness permeated the room and silence, total silence consumed my body. Out of the silence his voice arose with the words he had spoken in Temple Bar when I had been in his physical presence:

"You are but a child of the universe and always are so. I am but a voice within you and always am so. I am always with you, for I am as you are. Please do not try to intellectualize what is being said. Please do not take it on as additional information. Let the words rest deep within the stillness of your being. Put your trust in the stillness. Know that stillness is the way to true understanding. Information is but the fodder of the mind, whereas understanding is the food of consciousness. Know that 'I' am always with you. There is no place other than you where 'I' am. There is but one 'I' and it is in your body listening to these words. You call yourself 'I', do you not? So please do not put your 'I' onto me the speaker. Do not attach yourself to my physical presence. I am but a mirror to you, a reflection only, of the 'I' within you. In truth, my physical presence is not even a shadow of all that you are. All life projects from 'I' through the brain that is the projector. Know this in your direct experience and you have found the elixir of life."

Then he snapped his fingers and as he did so a picture fell off the wall. At the time I brushed it aside as being nothing of particular significance, even when he said;

"Take this as a sign that 'I' am always with you; 'I' am never apart from you. How can 'I' be apart from you when there is but one 'I' and you are it! There are billions of the 'you' but the 'I' is the only reality. This is the primary knowledge immediate to you in the universality or oneness that 'I' am."

The penny finally dropped. No wonder I was unable to antagonize him with all my personal challenges! As a matter of fact, the more I had confronted him the greater the love that permeated his response. The picture falling from the wall in my room that night may have been a coincidence, but he had reminded me that coincidences in this instance are the sign that one is getting closer to the source of all life within one's being. Now I could see how the source is 'I', whoever or whatever 'I' am and it is right here within me. It can be nowhere else. The unexpected explosiveness of such a realisation at that moment made everything crystal clear. I could even see what he meant when he told us how the entire direction of scientific exploration is on a false footing. This false footing includes everything being taken for granted in relation to the world of technology. But he also reminded us that the false is equally necessary. Apparently, it must work its course in order to come to the end of itself.

I eagerly waited for morning to discuss it with Maura. She was so thrilled to see me bubbling again that she clean forgot to get Damian prepared for nursery school. When I explained it in the way it had happened for me she could understand it as well.

"Yes, of course, of course! It all makes sense," she said. "Even Jesus has stated, 'I am the way, the life and the truth.' Surely, this has to be the 'I' he was referring to, does it not?"

"Yes, yes, what else could it be?" the enthusiasm within me agreed.

We went on to indulge our curiosities and Maura teased out that the secret message is obviously in every religion for the privileged few who have awakened to see it.

Now I was beginning to see that everything I had suffered in my life up to that point in time was absolutely necessary for my own partial awakening. Even the consuming hatred I had held for my psychologist father had served its purpose and was now being replaced by compassion. I was finding the change in my consciousness phenomenal, having been given the space in Maura's presence for its continued expansion. It made me realise how privileged I was to have escaped the mediocre.

Looking back on it now I clearly see that nothing can be excluded, not even the grim finality I will surely have to face in the morning.

My mother called. In two days she was coming to visit us and Maura was ecstatic with excitement. For me, although I was happy in one sense, yet I felt somewhat apprehensive. Maura had grown to be my best friend and confidant in many things. For example, she had introduced me to a very friendly and normal doctor, a young woman fresh from medical college who helped me regulate my period and she explained to me in detail what happens to the body as it passes through puberty.

Back in Dublin I was having my periods for almost a year before any of the others in my class and I suffered them in silence not really knowing what exactly was occurring to my body. These things can appear very confusing and frightening to a child. At that time my mother had set up such a wall around herself she was not there in any sense of the word. The psychologist father was even further removed. According to him everything in the world has to be rigidly kept under control by the use of rules and regulations. At the time I felt he would have seen any infliction upon the body as being part of God's justice scheme, my entire being had been so polluted with such destructive beliefs that left me ridden with guilt. Any discussion on such matters was taboo in the house.

Is it not quite ridiculous, when you think about it? Period! What a stupid name for something that is so important! Indeed, I was more than familiar with the word and many times I had heard it being used by adults. I'd never really stopped to figure it out to mean anything more than someone going through a difficult period of time. No one had ever sat me down to tell me. Then again, I was so forward and fiercely independent in myself I was seldom prepared to listen to anyone, and particularly not to those whom I considered to be stupid. Like many teenagers, that meant mostly everyone I had encountered during my early adolescence. So I was thankful to Maura for introducing me to Nuria, the doctor in the nearby clinic who skillfully maneuvered me through my self-created barriers. Soon I opened to absorb the relevant knowledge relating to womanhood in a clear, uncontaminated sense. It was so refreshing and even exciting that I found myself indulging in medical journals and library books at the medical college in the city I had started to frequent during my free time; and all this had happened in a couple of months.

But the thought of my mother arriving felt as though I was being forced backwards again. Paul noticed it at breakfast when he remarked;

"Don't be concerned about Dublin. London is your home now, Julie. You've moved on in life. We all do, sooner or later, and good for you it is sooner. Life moves too fast to be hanging around when it's time to move on."

His remark was very important. It gave me the feeling of being hugged by someone clearly understanding what was troubling me and why I needed to be hugged. Apparently, that is what parents are for. But some parents fail to realize it when they become too preoccupied with their beliefs and notions; when they become too contaminated by their worlds to even notice they have strayed so far from reality. No wonder the child has to be rebellious, to fight against the ignorance engulfing the parents before it becomes engulfed itself.

I swore it would not happen to me. I told myself if I ever had a child who was complacent and not rebellious against me as a parent I would act so outrageously that she would have to rebel. Perhaps that was the situation with my mother. Maybe that was the role she had undertaken with me, without even realizing it herself. It might even be an inherent process in the evolution of human consciousness. But, in relation to meeting my mother again, the same apprehension remained. I could see that my childhood groove had been cut too deep and it still overshadowed the brief interlude of togetherness we had shared during those final days in Dublin. I could not expect the previous past to have fully dissolved in a few short months.

Thankfully it was a Thursday when mother was arriving and it happened to be one of the busy days at the boutique. So I had the perfect excuse not to be around. She was coming into Heathrow instead of Gatwick, so Maura was able to drive to the airport to meet her. The manageress of the boutique had to leave early that day and she had given me the responsibility of closing the shop. I hung on for at least an extra hour making absolutely sure everything was in order. But in truth I was delighted with the opportunity of not having to go home at my usual time. I even lingered in the street, purposely missing my regular bus that I normally enjoyed catching each evening. I had grown to love observing the buildings, the people and the busyness of life from the upper deck. But this Thursday I decided to take the underground instead. I suppose I must have been identifying with the gloom as I descended the steps into the bowels of the earth.

I could never really take to the underground, not even to the ornate metro in Moscow that I saw on a television documentary where some of the stations were displayed as a work of art with sculptures and paintings decorating the platforms and walls. Such decor I could enjoy, but it still would not change the fact that the underground to me, whether later in Paris or there at that moment in London, still represented little more than the moving tomb of humanity's gloom rushing from nowhere to nowhere.

I packed myself into a carriage as one of the many expressionless faces and allowed my body to be whisked along through the long, narrow tunnels filled with stale, hot air and lingering smells of previous passages. Slowly I dissolved into the hypnotic rhythm of the iron wheels banging over the joints of the track and the other clattering sounds coming from steel expressing its pain. The sullen orchestral concerto became amplified as the train passed through intersecting tunnels, then exploding into a sudden crescendo whenever another train sped by in the opposite direction. All of this with screeching brakes and grinding steel presented itself as a grim reflection of my turbulent, childhood years.

"All is interconnected, interrelated," the alchemist had said, according to the way I had heard him and I could acknowledge that and fully accept it. Nonetheless, the underground all too vividly demonstrated to me the cold hard facts of life.

I was jolted awake as the train eventually pulled up at Ealing Broadway. It was my stop and the inescapable time to meet my mother for the first time in my new world. Slowly I dragged myself up the steps to finally meet up with the cool evening air. Wow! It was so refreshing. I could feel the colour returning to my cheeks as I walked up the street. When I turned the key in the door, to my surprise I was met with the emptiness of the house. It was strangely eerie. I went in and out of every room and there was not a soul to be seen. Then I stopped in the middle of the sitting room floor and asked my wilful mind: "What the hell are you doing to yourself, Julie?"

I had wasted an entire day stuck in the thought of having to meet my mother. Now the moment had arrived and my mother was not even there to affirm my gloom. I had unnecessarily caused myself to sink into depression.

"Soon I'll be in need of a bloody psychiatrist!" I verbally reminded myself, the sudden thought of it entering my brain sending a shudder up my spine.

I decided to take a power shower in the main bathroom as I needed to wash off all my self-inflicted rubbish sucking my vitality away. The force of the water pounding my skin helped to diminish the troublesome mind as I gradually reconnected to the natural sensations of my body. I had just stepped out and was reaching for a towel when my mother suddenly appeared through the doorway in a rush to the toilet. We were both stunned. She was wearing tight fitting jeans and a t-shirt, appearing so petite and delicately beautiful in a way I had never seen her before. It was the first time she had seen me fully naked as a woman and in the embarrassment of the moment we could neither retreat nor advance.

Suddenly she flew through the air with the towel in her hand and embraced me tightly, then she spun me round and round while vigorously wiping my body. I have no idea what we said to each other. I can only remember her mentioning she was about to burst and then she was sitting on the loo while still telling me how good it was to be with me again. Apparently, she had spent the entire day in the West End shopping with Maura and now it was our special quality time together in the bathroom.

It was such a joy to see her, completely the opposite to what I had expected. But I had only myself to blame for the previous gloom. At that moment I promised myself never to listen to the mind-weed again. The alchemist had transcended it all and from his transcendental realization I had been given my wings to fly above and beyond its wilful nature. But still it seemed to elude me; my wings were fragile and many times I was crashed to the ground by the unexpected. He had clearly explained that one should be vigilant not to entertain unnecessary thinking. I heard him say that one should only think in relation to taking action. All thought outside of that is a wilful waste of one's energy. Life is moving at such a phenomenal speed it is being continuously missed when the mind is not being used rightly, but that is another story for the earnest seeker of truth to discover, and no matter how much one tries yet nothing happens before its time.

My mother stayed for a week and each day was better than the next until she found the money in my suitcase.

"I haven't been going through your things," she explained in defense. "I was hoping to use the suitcase for my return trip, seeing I had bought so much in the past few days and that's how I came across it. I know you could not have possibly earned such money in the little time you've been here. Be honest with me Julie. Where did it come from?"

I could not tell her and not alone that, I felt I had no duty to tell her. She was merely a visitor in the house where I was now living and paying my way from my salary. She was a guest in my territory, had entered my bedroom and gone through my belongings. Then she went into her guessing games, even challenging me of prostituting myself and that's when the situation got nasty.

"If there is a prostitute in this room it cannot be me because I know I am still a virgin," I blurted at her.

I knew I had gone too far when I went on to accuse her of living the life of a prostitute for all those years with that excuse for a man whom she called her husband. Again my real father came into the confrontation when I accused her of abandoning him when he was most in need of her help.

For the second time she slapped me on the face, but unlike our first real confrontation in the mental hospital, this time she pulled herself back after the first blow. She was shaking all over while fighting against herself as she said; "You always turn it around and fill me with guilt for your own misgivings."

She was right and the realization of it filled my heart with compassion. Looking at me directly through her watery eyes she queried;

"Are you really my daughter? Why do I feel so strange in your presence? What is happening to me?"

"Mum, it's to me things are happening," I tried to explain. "I've been having strange insights and everything is moving too fast. It's not your fault. I can only assure you that I have done nothing wrong or harmful to anyone."

"But tell me about the money, Julie; surely, it didn't just appear out of nowhere?"

I felt it was so irrelevant compared to the vastness of it all as demonstrated to me by the alchemist. This is what I had wished to discuss with her, but obviously there was far too much distance between us. I exploded again in frustration; "Give me a break, Mother! Can you not shake off your obsession about the money! I had completely forgotten it was there and not only that, I have no need of it. You keep it and do whatever you like with it."

"I don't want anything to do with it. I just want to know where you got it," again she demanded.

She was not going to give up and eventually I had to swallow my stubbornness.

"Okay! I will tell you. When I arrived at Victoria station I was robbed, but as fortune would have it, before the day was out I succeeded in robbing the robbers without even realizing what I had done. Please do not ask me for the gory details. I have chosen to put the entire episode behind me for good. I know I have done nothing wrong."

"My poor child," she responded in dismay, "that's why you missed Maura and you have told no one about it."

The air had cleared again between us and I was thankful she did not insist on the gory details. She could well see I was all right after the ordeal and she was content with my assurance that I had done nothing harmful to others. But she did insist;

"Julie, will you stop calling me Mother! What's wrong with Mum, Natalie, anything you wish, but please, not Mother! The tone in your voice is very cutting whenever you use that word. I feel I deserve a little better."

The heat of the moment blew over and we both had survived it. As a matter of fact the episode had brought us closer together. But the question of what to do with the money remained unresolved when I explained to her there was no avenue open to me to return it other than going to the police, an action neither of us wished to do because of the delicate situation in Dublin. A suggestion of giving it to some charity was mentioned, but neither of us seemed prepared to take the initiative to actually do it. I had managed to keep it completely from my mind until she had uncovered it by chance. Eventually I had to say;

"Look Mum, you have the suitcase and I will take care of the money in my own way."

"Julie, I don't know what to say," she replied, "but I am delighted to see how wonderfully you have flowered since you came to London."

We swapped cases and I put the two socks of money together with my winter clothes into the smaller one. Then I put it up on the top shelf of the wardrobe where the other had been and that was that, again out of sight out of mind. I wanted to know more about my real father and I felt the opportunity had been opened to probe a little further. At first she was reluctant to tell me anything relating to his whereabouts, but my insistence was equally as strong as hers had been relating to the origins of the money. Eventually she relented a little and she sat down on the bed asking me to sit beside her.

"Julie, he is in prison. He has been there for at least five years. He got involved with the IRA and he was sentenced to fourteen years for some bombings in Manchester."

At first the news was electric. The idea of my father being a revolutionary initially sent shivers of excitement through my body. Like me, he was not one of the mediocre. From him I had inherited my fire and his revolutionary blood was flowing through my veins. But my mother instantly threw freezing water on my bubbling excitement.

"Look, Julie, will you lose your romantic notions. An innocent child was killed by a bomb that prematurely exploded. There's nothing romantic or heroic about killing anyone and in particular, an innocent child."

But I had to meet him and this she could understand. She promised to find out what prison he was in and to try to arrange a visit for both of us. She felt it was her duty to introduce us as father and daughter, seeing she was the most relevant link between us. At that moment it became the most important focus of my life.

Maura gently knocked on the door and told us dinner was prepared whenever we were ready to join them. Paul was off his seat in an instant as we entered the dining room and, in true gentlemanly fashion, he pulled back the chair for my mother. I could see that Mum was lapping it up as she wriggled her petite femininity teasingly onto the seat. Maura showed a slight displeasure, which I caught in her eyes and I helped dissolve for her with a wink. She smiled through a blush on her cheek and then she winked back reaffirming to me that she and I were still on the same wavelength.

The following day was a Friday, the day of mother's return to Dublin, and Paul offered to take the morning off to drive her to the airport. But Maura was adamant that she was doing it. "Natalie is my best friend," she insisted, "we want to have as much time as possible together."

I could plainly see that Mum was getting a little too fond of Paul's personal attention and she was slowly but surely drawing him to her. She was showing her colours as being a dangerous woman for Maura to have too close to her man. To my surprise Maura called into the boutique to share a coffee with me after dropping her at the airport. I could see the relief on her face and I could also hear it in her voice. Indeed, we were both relieved, then it was back to business as usual. Maura remained at the boutique and spent the rest of the day teaching me more about fashion and future planning.

"What about Damian," I inquired when it came close to the time for collecting him.

"Oh, don't worry about Damian. I have arranged for Paul to collect him. He did mention he could take time off today to drop Natalie to the airport, so now he can utilize that free time to be with his son instead."

Maura is not just a good business manager, she is fully in charge of her life. Even her friend, the young doctor Nuria pointed this out to me when she told me I was in the best of hands. If I had focused on her as my role model perhaps I would not be here tonight suffering this biting wind coming down from Sierra Nevada and the agony of facing the dawn. Then again, everyone's path is different. We are here to discover and fulfill life's purpose in accordance with our particular lights. Who am I to know at this moment whether or not the purpose of my life has been already fulfilled. I may have been born solely for the action of this night, so now it comes to its end.

But it is obviously more than that. The alchemist did advise that 'now' is not only the end without a beginning but it is also the beginning without an end. It makes me realize how little I really know in relation to the greater purpose behind this existence.

JULIE

Autumn in London can be quite spectacular in colours. The leaves on some varieties of trees were changing to a rustic red and yellow with tinges of brown in between while others were persistently holding onto their green. More were already boldly expressing their beauty in their naked barks.

Maura was working on the idea of opening a second boutique in the West End, close to Regent Street. She was hoping that I would be ready enough to act as assistant to the new manageress she would need to appoint. Although I was thrilled with the idea, yet the thought of having to travel by tube every day did not over-excite me. I enjoyed where I was, with my short journeys to and from work on the top deck of the bus, being able to see the people, the buildings and particularly the colourful trees.

Also, Roger had arrived on the scene. He was three years older than me and he was tall, blond and beautifully handsome. One evening at the bus stop it had happened. He was suddenly there and when our eyes first met, I immediately felt we were part of each other's destinies.

But he just smiled and then shyly looked away. He was still on the bus when it came to my stop and again our eyes met with another smile as I purposely brushed my body against his shoulder while making my way to the exit. The following evening it happened again. But I must confess I let the first bus go when he hadn't shown up and waited an extra fifteen minutes for the next in the hope that he would re-appear. Sure enough he did and with another smile followed by his shyness.

This went on for some days and I had no idea what I could do to break through the barrier separating us. One would think that a simple hello would be sufficient, but my unexpected need to be the girl in his life not only blocked all reason but my vocal cords as well. After supper one evening I talked to Maura about it and her advice was electric. Quoting one of Oscar Wilde's famous sayings, 'the man chooses the woman who chooses the man,' she explained now that I had chosen, all I needed to do was to initiate action for him.

"Let him see your exuberance, then he will surely respond. Why not talk to him about the colours of the trees? You are forever telling me how beautiful they are! See his response and then whatever is correct will surely happen."

I hugged her with delight and then spent the rest of the night trying to cope with the excitement of hearing him speak for the first time when we would meet again the following evening.

"Be in the present" were the words of the alchemist prodding my mind. I knew what I was doing to myself, but I just could not be in the present with the all-consuming thoughts relating to a future relationship with this man. I remembered what I had been told about desires, which is really just a fancy word for 'wants'.

"Desires have to be fulfilled," the alchemist said. "This is the only true way to transcend them."

But I did not want to transcend this juicy desire. I knew I was about to take a trip into unreality and I was already blinding myself, even before any real romance had begun. The alchemist talked about energy. Several times he reminded the group that the only way to have more energy is to stop wasting it on idle thought.

"You might be worried about something and the nature of the worry keeps churning in the mind," he had said. "Or you might be bubbling with excitement about some future event, and again the mind keeps churning, devising, scheming and arranging how the future should happen. It is so how you build your imaginary worlds. This is how energy is constantly spent and without the necessary energy it is not possible to transcend your condition. Right thought demands one must be true to the situation. In other words, one must be honest with oneself. But should one look deep enough one might realize one is being totally dishonest even when one thinks one is being honest."

I could clearly see this at the time. I knew nothing about this new man entering my life, yet, all through that night I could not stop fantasizing about him. So I decided to go the other way by indulging the desire in my mind, thus, I hoped, allowing it to burn itself out.

But indulging the mind with fantasy is no different to indulging it with worry. Fantasizing is being dangled from one end of the pendulum while worrying is being dangled from the other, and both are equally removed from the center, or the equilibrium, where life actually is in the moment. According to the alchemist, the equilibrium is constantly missed when the mind is emotionally swinging like a pendulum from one gush of thoughts to the next.

I spent most of the night tossing and turning in bed. At first the thoughts were very enjoyable indulgence, but after much repetition they gradually started to dull. It was time to sleep, still the thinking would not slow down. The craziness of the mental spin had driven all possibility of sleep away. I tried every trick I could think of that might enable me to switch off, but all to no avail. The birds started their morning chorus and I still had not slept. It was madness, utter madness, and worst of all, I knew it.

Soon it was time to get up. I had to fight against the exhaustion of my poor body as I dragged it towards the shower. I could feel the weight on my legs as I heaved my way to the bus stop. The day was a long drag and nothing really went right. The manageress suggested I should go home early and get some sleep. Still I insisted on hanging on until evening.

On my way to the bus stop I bought a can of coke hoping it would give me a lift. It may have been psychological, nonetheless, it seemed to awaken me somewhat. To my delight he was there and immediately I remarked on the autumn colours of the trees.

"Yeah! They are quite cheerful," he replied in a rather sophisticated Oxford accent.

"My name is Julie," I found myself saying in the sweetest tone I could muster.

"Oh! I'm Roger ... Roger Crawford. I am pleased to meet you, Julie."

That's how it all commenced. We got on the bus together. I sat in an empty seat and quite awkwardly he asked permission to sit beside me, with the silly comment, "seeing we are going in the same direction."

Jesus! I thought I was bad, but he was worse. He could not have honestly said, 'I would like to sit beside you, now that we have finally broken the ice.' I sat there in silence not knowing what to say next. The tiredness overwhelmed me and before I knew it I was out like a light with my mouth wide open and my head rolling from side to side to the sway of the bus. Vaguely I became aware of a strange hand on my shoulder and a male voice calling my name.

"Julie! Julie! The bus is approaching your stop. You had better wake up."

I was immediately aware of my mouth being dry and my tonsils being swollen. I could hardly believe what had happened. Not alone had I fallen asleep but I must have been snoring as well. I could hardly speak as I gathered myself back together, got my bag off the floor and hastily said something like, "see you tomorrow Roger."

"Yeah! See you tomorrow Julie," I heard him reply as I jostled my way to the exit.

I cursed my stupidity all the more so because I understood clearly what the alchemist had told me relating to losing my energy. The incident also showed I had not reached that higher state of consciousness where the foolishness of indulging my daydreams would naturally stop. I could have made more effort, but I had failed to do so. My mind was at it again, this time judging myself!

I had so wished to create the perfect impression, then I had fallen asleep in the worst possible manner imaginable. Not only that, but I had no excuse for my behaviour. After all, I had attentively listened to the alchemist's words so I was not suffering from ignorance like most of the world. I knew I was using up the energy by indulging the psychic entity to its imaginary world rising within me to feast itself on my essence. Obviously, the price had to be paid, as the price always has to be paid for foolishness. I crashed into bed that evening and slept the sleep of the living dead. Not once did my body move before morning. Maura was very consoling at the breakfast table when I explained to her what had happened.

"Well, at least you have broken the ice," she said.

She told me to be observant of the look on his face when we would meet again that evening. I was glad of having her for a friend; she was mature enough to see these things more clearly than I could possibly understand them. Even though I felt nervous and ashamed, yet I was still in control of the situation. I was first at the bus stop and it thrilled me to see his face light up with delight as he approached me. Yes! In spite of my drastic performance the previous evening I could see that the ice had been truly broken and I was on my way to my first whirlwind romance. The following evening we had coffee together in Ealing and he kissed me on the cheek as he got on his bus for home. Then on the Saturday night we went to a Greek restaurant in Chelsea where there was music and a place to dance. We caught the last tube home, which I did not find the least romantic. But the stroll up Maura's street hand in hand beneath a full moon more than compensated for it. We talked for some time, as we still felt a little awkward.

Then, out of the blue it happened. I was looking up at him and the moon seemed to be like a halo sitting on top of his head. In that instant I felt I was looking up at a god. Our lips slowly met and we literally melted into each other in one of the most wondrous moments of my life.

As I dashed inside I noticed Maura sitting in the lounge with a smile on her face. It was so obvious to her, but still I just had to tell her and she shared my joy with the same enthusiasm I was feeling.

"You must invite him to dinner," she urged, "but not too soon, even though I can hardly wait to meet him."

Roger was working for an accountancy firm while also studying for his final exams. He usually started at nine whereas the boutique did not open until ten. But we shared most evenings after that on our journeys home together. Sometimes he would get off at my stop and walk me up the street where again we would passionately kiss. To me it was sweet, innocent and beautiful.

Then one night he invited me to a rave-up with his college friends in the country. He had borrowed his father's car for the occasion as the event was taking place in a village in the direction of Reading. Six in all travelled in the car, two more couples who were Roger's age, or maybe a year or so older. I was clearly out of my depth.

A joint was rolled by one of the girls and passed around as we travelled. Roger did not refuse when it was given to him. After taking a deep pull he handed it to me and, not wanting to be rejected by the group, I put it to my lips before passing it on. I was very conscious of my age. Three years can be a huge difference to a teenager and I did not want to be seen as childish or immature to Roger's friends. The conversation got around to vulgar expressions relating to sex and the two girls were the worst of them all. I could hardly believe what I was seeing when one of them started aggressively massaging her boyfriend's genitals while the other exposed one of her breasts and flashed it in the mirror to Roger. I felt a lump in my throat as I noticed the lecherous look appear for a moment in his eyes. It was like the look I had seen on Geordie's face when he saw me naked as I was making my escape from that dreadful situation after first arriving in London. I tried to brush it aside by reminding Roger to keep his attention on the road and, for all our sakes, to be careful with his driving.

Eventually we arrived and we all piled out in the driveway of a country house surrounded by trees and high, neatly clipped hedges. The party was in full swing. People were drinking and smoking pot in the grounds and also in the house which was even bigger than Maura's. I didn't know how I felt, but I knew I was out of place, especially when more of Roger's male friends gathered round me after the word got around that Roger had arrived with a 'fresher'.

I needed support from my man but as the night progressed I could feel the wall of difference getting bigger and bigger between us. A stranger was replacing the Roger with whom I thought I had fallen in love. It became more and more obvious that first and foremost he was there to entertain his friends and I was just part of that entertainment. I tried to get through to him, but he had left me completely as he became more absorbed as one of the drug-crazed crowd. I needed to escape, but I could not find one person who was not indulging in drugs and alcohol.

After standing in a corner by a hedgerow for some time in total isolation, out of the blue Roger approached me and, taking my hand, he led me to the car. For a moment I felt he had woken up and realized what he was doing. He opened the door for me like a gentleman and then he went around and got in on the driver's side. I felt very much relieved, but before I knew what was happening he had fully reclined the seat and he was on top of me, forcing his mouth on mine. Pushing him away I pleaded with him; "What has got into you Roger? What are you doing?"

"It's time we got it together, honey, you're dying for it," he muttered in the drunken voice of a stranger.

"Dying for what Roger?" I demanded to know.

"You know! A lick of the relic! Tonight's the night babe!" He had unbuckled his belt and had slipped down his jeans when I became aware of the chorus outside. His drunken friends had encircled the car chanting; "Go on boy, give it to her Rodgie!"

With one hand he tore off my panties as he wedged his half-naked body between my legs. There was no way to stop him, I was at the point of being raped and my head went into a spin. Trying to scream, nothing would come and it seemed as though I was again trapped in a horrible nightmare. While I struggled against him something the alchemist had said flashed through my mind; "If you really want to come out on top of a grim situation you should never put force against force."

Something came over me and I heard myself pleading; "Wait Roger! Let me suck it first!"

Instantly, he slipped his naked crutch up to my face, purposely exposing my vagina to the mob peering in through the windscreen. I took his penis in my hand and the size of it shocked me as I had never been that close to an erect penis before. Without even thinking I sunk my teeth into it as fiercely and deeply as I could. As blood gushed through my mouth and all over my face and hands he screamed in agony and his head crashed against the roof of the car.

My stomach heaved from the taste of the blood while I desperately struggled to find the door handle. There and then I puked all over the dashboard and I was still puking as I fought my way out. I remember struggling to my feet and running into the house covered in blood and vomit. It was like running through hell with all the drugged faces staring at me through bloodshot eyes and gaping mouths. I searched for a phone, needing to know where I was. First I asked a girl nearby, and then I caught hold of her by the shoulders, shook her and screamed; "What is the fucking address of this place?"

She stared at me blankly. I screamed again and someone else answered. I managed to get through to Maura on her mobile and told her that I urgently needed her help. After that I found a toilet facing the driveway and securely locked myself in. Unable to stop from shaking I knew I had to get hold of myself. I could not let Maura see me in such a state. What would she say? What would she do? Obviously, she would call the police and have Roger arrested and I would probably end up being sent back to Dublin. No! I could not let that happen. This was my problem and mine alone to put right. I washed out my mouth with the hose of the shower. Then I took off my dress and washed off the blood and the vomit with soap and shampoo. It was still wet when the car eventually pulled into the driveway. I put it back on and dashed out of the house before Maura had a chance to switch off the ignition. Jumping in beside her I pleaded; "Maura, get me out of here as fast as you can. These people are crazed with drugs. I will explain to you later."

Without question she spun the car around in the driveway, sending stones flying in all directions. She screeched onto the main road and raced through all the gears until we were safely on the motorway heading towards home.

"How am I doing, Julie? Am I up to your standards?" she said with a glint of glee in her eyes. But I could only manage a faint smile in response as my body was still trembling from the terrible experience. Maura picked up the vibes that something was seriously wrong. Bringing the car to a halt on the hard shoulder and turning to me directly she cautiously inquired: "Dare I ask how was the party?"

I managed to reply; "As you can well see Maura, my legs are bruised, my dress is soaking, I might have even lost my knickers, but I have not lost my virginity!"

She seemed disturbed at the sound of my voice and her expression changed to seriousness. Looking directly into my eyes she further probed; "Is there anything you need to tell me?"

"No, Maura, there is not. I am out of there now and that is all that matters."

"I take it Roger was not up to expectations?"

"No, certainly not. I have learned my lesson, it is over and done with for good. Thank you for getting me away so quickly. You are truly an angel.

"Julie, you may be disappointed with him, but in another way you are very fortunate. Life only has to show you once and you get the message. Most people fail to see it. They need the same lessons to be repeated over and over again. Then they complain about life being hard!"

Little did she realize the terrible lesson I had just received and how lucky I was to have survived it. But I dared not mention it and I could only reply; "Maura, where I am truly fortunate is having you for my best friend."

She smiled and I was glad to get home to my shower. Needless to say, that was the last I saw of Roger Crawford on my regular bus route before Maura finally transferred me to the new boutique in the West End.

The alchemist had more than compensated for the lack of a father in my life. I am sure it was his presence coming from within that helped me take the necessary action. But was it his influence that caused me to do what I did this night in Granada? All I can hear is the silence behind the noise of the city. Silence, deathly silence; there is no answer for the turbulent mind.

The alchemist did warn me relating to the speed of events about to happen in my life once I had openly accepted his challenge. I trusted I would have sufficient stamina to cope. It takes enormous energy to sustain the speed of a rocket blasting away from the gradational pull of the earth, but it takes even greater energy to sustain the speed of consciousness transcending the pull of the world. It means outdistancing the psychic web entombing the mother earth spirit all the way out to the moon's orbit.

In less than three weeks after the party experience my mother was on her way back to London. She had done her research and located the high security prison where my father was held. The prisoners in his section were very restricted with minimum visiting rights, nonetheless, she had somehow managed to secure a date for the following Thursday afternoon.

I had been transferred to the new boutique just days before she arrived and this is where we had arranged to meet. It was a flying visit for her, coming into Stanstead on an early flight, catching the train to Liverpool Street and then the tube to Oxford Circus. She was at the boutique before ten in the morning. Without a moment to spare we made our way to the train station and caught a city express to Wakefield. Although the journey took hours, yet it seemed to be sudden and full of momentum. Speed echoed the towns as the train shot through on that overcast day. Everything was dull and grey and at times it appeared as though we were rushing full speed to a certain meeting with death.

I can hardly describe how I felt. I was on my way to see my real father for the first time in my life and I was totally blank inside. There were no emotions, no turbulence of any kind present. But I cannot say the same for my mother. As we came closer to Wakefield she started biting her nails and I had to reach out to stop her ruining her neatly manicured hands.

"I cannot help it, Julie," she insisted, "I have not met your father for years. He does not even know we are coming. Believe me, this is one of the hardest days of my life. I did not sleep a wink last night and I have to do it this way, fast and furious, otherwise I would never be able to do it."

I could well understand what she meant from what I had learned through the alchemist. Something he said;

"If there is an unpleasant issue facing you in life and it is causing you great disturbance, do not get caught up in feeding the disturbance with thought; rather, take action; even if it means throwing yourself into the centre of it and scattering it in all directions. Action purifies the mental process in one way or another."

Action? Tonight in Spain the only real action I can take is to wait for the dawn. I have no idea how the world is going to react. I might even have to die. But is death to be feared?

"What action can I take?" a woman diagnosed with cancer had asked him.

"Are you dying from cancer right now?" he inquired.

"No, I am not dying right now, but it has been diagnosed and I have been told it is only a matter of months," the young woman broke off in sobs.

He was most sympathetic towards her and after speaking some comforting words he went on to say;

"Feel the goodness right now in your body. Connect with that. Be the goodness. Know that everything is all right now. You are in your body, you are breathing okay and you are feeling no pain. Right now it is good. Stay with the good. Should there be pain in the body be conscious of it. Once you are clearly focused then you can use the pain to assist you in letting go of the mind. As death gradually appears to take hold of the body, know what is happening.

Be fully conscious. Watch it from a distance within you. You might be amazed to discover that death is only a concept of the mind. It becomes clear as the body drops away, once you are consciously present to see it."

I recall him telling us we need to rise above the limitations of the thinking programme and we can only do this by truly understanding the nature of death. But he warned;

"Don't cave in to the mind, for the mind is finished, it has no place to go. At the point of death it all becomes crystal clear if the consciousness is fully present to see it."

He went on to emphasize reality by making it clear that the body is merely a spacesuit in the realm of space and time. We must threat our spacesuits with respect, but we must not become over-attached to them. The spacesuits come and go in this space we call existence, but we should never lose sight of the fact that we are perpetual life in the deeper sense of our being. Then someone inquired about the notion of reincarnation.

"Look into yourself, right now," the alchemist replied. "See who is posing the question. Is it you in your essence? Or is it the spacesuit?"

The questioner fell silent and the alchemist paused for some time before he continued;

"The mind is part of the spacesuit. It disappears with the spacesuit. It cannot go on. But can the mind accept it? Obviously not, as can be seen from the question. Such notions of reincarnation, heaven and hell or of any life hereafter are merely the workings of the mortal mind desperately seeking continuity where there is none. This is how the religions and philosophies of the world grab hold. The mind comes up with a notion. It is the nature of the mind. Rather than facing the truth in the fact it projects itself into a notion, an idea of some imaginary future. You will find it in every religion, every philosophy, in one guise or another; minds have their notional heaven; even the life assurance companies have their notional funds! Check it out! People keep putting their money in, year after year in the promise of a bright, rich future. Then the future arrives with their expectations shattered. But it is too late; their lives have been spent. So it continues, ignorance regurgitating more past. We bury our heads in the sand and pretend to ourselves. But the fact remains the fact, and notional can be nothing other than notional, no matter how hard you might try to convince yourself otherwise. Stay looking at it. See where this question of reincarnation is coming from within you. Look at it bravely. Eventually you might see it more clearly."

Then the alchemist returned his attention to the woman with cancer and he requested that she should stay with him after the seminar had closed. Even though she was dying I could see how fortunate she was to have such a presence to guide her through those final moments.

The train speeded along on the final leg of the journey and I saw myself sitting alone with my mother who had no such knowledge of death. The alchemist had gone; he had departed the body through which I had met him. The woman with cancer must also have gone. But gone where? I silently pondered. As I followed his words in my own experiencing of them I could see they had actually gone nowhere. All they had been was still in the present, at one with the life deep within me.

The train had come to a halt. We had arrived. I'm sure Wakefield can be a beautiful place, but for me on that day it bore the cold finality of death. Everything reflected the heavy dullness that grips the body before the life is finally extinguished. As the taxi pulled up outside the prison gates I was aware of a weird sensation inside me.

On approaching the huge iron doors a porthole opened through which a mouth asked our names and the purpose of our visit. It closed again and we were left standing there in the cold air without a word of explanation for at least five minutes, an eternity in such a situation.

Then we heard some pulling of bolts and releasing of locks. A small trapdoor to the lower corner of the large iron doors opened outwards and we were asked to step through. As we were guided between rolls of barbed wire I noticed soldiers in green camouflage clothing positioned in different places. I though how ridiculous it was to be dressed up like that in a place where there was no other green, no resemblance of nature's colour anywhere. Dull grey would have been a more appropriate uniform in a place where there was nothing but cold, grey concrete and faded bricks as far as the eye could see. It made me realize that mob mentality is so predictable. How easy it is to out-think and out-manoeuvre such minds when one has awakened from this sleep of the living dead.

My mother was clinging tightly to my arm. I could feel how her body was a tightened ball of energy hanging onto the only other form of life that was apparent to her. I knew if she was to lose sight of me, even for a second, she would literally lose her life with the mounting terror that she was just about keeping at bay.

We were taken across a walled, cobblestone yard that led to a single door. As we approached it I noticed the line of barred windows stretching the length of the far wall about five metres up from the ground. Then the heckling started.

"Don't look up, keep your eyes on the ground," my mother said through her teeth.

But I could not help it. I had to look up and my eyes were instantly struck with naked backsides and exposed genitals being squeezed against the bars. The verbal obscenities being hurdled at us were unimaginable as the jail warden led us along. The words from one of Wordsworth's poems "Much it grieves my heart to think what man has made of man," flashed through my mind.

JULIE

In that instance I could clearly see man doing it to himself.
These prisoners were not animals. Indeed, animals have a
courtesy, a specific order about their behaviour and they
live and act in accordance with their nature. But these men
I could see had allowed themselves to sink to a level that
was totally blasphemous to life. I felt if there were such a
system of things as reincarnation then these men who were
reacting that way would have to go through a million
rebirths before they would even reach again the level of
the lowest form of animal.

The warden was fumbling with the keys trying to find the
one to open the door while above our heads the heckling
of obscenities continued. Through the racket I became
aware of the same heavy grunting that had possessed
Roger that night in the car. Just as I looked up I saw a
hand masturbating an erect penis protruding through the
iron bars and suddenly the air was filled with flying
sperm. Instinctually, I grabbed my mother and pulled her
out of the way as the sperm splashed on the ground before
us, some of it catching the back of the warden's coat.

"That's it, we're getting out of here, nothing is worth
this," my mother hissed.

Using all my strength I grabbed her firmly by the arm and
insisted; "We must stand our ground, we have come this
far, now we must see it through."

Eventually he got the door open and by the looks of things
it had not been opened for some time. We were led along a
narrow corridor of ugly grey with chipped walls, then
through a battered doorway into a large room divided by
wire mesh that stretched from wall to wall and floor to
ceiling. He asked us to take a seat by the wire, and then he
returned to the door, locked it and took up a standing
position directly inside it. I found it impossible even to
imagine why anyone would work in such a forsaken place.
To me it was absolute hell. There was nothing about it that

128

reflected the good. My mind had firmly condemned it as a place that had no bearing to life and it should be forgotten as quickly as possible. We sat and waited in silence with the motionless statue standing behind us as the noise outside gradually faded.

Then I began to observe the stillness rising from within me and it seemed to be flowing outwards to permeate the entire surrounds. I felt my body re-connecting again to what I had previously experienced when in the alchemist's presence. I suddenly realized that even in that dungeon the awesome stillness was exactly the same; life was the same good; there was no difference, no separation unlike I had picked up through my first impressions. It amazed me to realize how every moment was showing me a little more about his extraordinary vision. Even my mother broke the silence to acknowledge his unseen presence with the words; "Julie, I am beginning to see there can be such a gentle peace around you. Indeed, I could not be in a place like this with anyone else but you."

I wanted to tell her about the alchemist, but I knew she would not understand. Hers was a different world; as for me, I was still only beginning to know mine and I still had a long way to go.

She reached out and squeezed her hand into mine as the door at the other side creaked open and the light frame of my father appeared between two burly prison officers. He walked slowly towards us trying to recognize who we were. I observed the greying hair, the pale skin and the stubble of beard on his chin all blending into the dullness of the room around us. As he came closer I began to notice the distinct handsomeness of his sharp features behind the greyness. My mother started to shake. First I could feel the trembling in her hands, then in her arms and legs and before he reached us the trembling had consumed her entire body.

"Natalie? Is it... Is it really you?" he asked with a deep frown on his face.

She did not answer. She was speechless and the trembling got worse. I was moved to push my chair closer and I took her in my arms. She broke into deep, convulsing sobs and the trembling entered the chairs causing them to rattle on the uneven floor.

"It's okay, Mum, it's okay, I'm here with you."

Julie ... Julie ... I can't stop," she sobbed.

"Julie!" he remarked with a look of dismay on his face. Then looking straight at me he questioned;

"You're her daughter?"

"Yes, I am her daughter," I answered.

He immediately turned his attention back to my mother with even a greater expression of shock on his face. I had no idea what was going on.

"My God, woman! You called your daughter Julie! You remember the nightmares I used to have and how I used to call out that name in my sleep! You thought I had another woman! And this here is the first Julie I've ever met in my whole life."

"Oh John, whatever happened to us? I don't know ... I just don't know," she tried to respond between her fits of uncontrollable sobbing.

He looked at her blankly for a moment as if she had said something crazy. Then he exclaimed;

"What happened to us? You left me, woman! Don't you remember! You went off and married that yob! Jesus! How could you have done it to me after all we'd been through together?"

Then they started to battle it out with words, each accusing the other for all that went wrong. This was not the intention of our visit and I knew I had to intervene before it got out of hand.

"Tell him, Mum. Please tell him right now."

"Tell me what, woman? How could you possibly have anything to tell me that could be worse than what you've already done?"

"Julie, I am not able ... I just cannot do it. Please tell him yourself."

"Tell me what for Jesus sake? Will one of you tell me what the fuck's goin' on?"

"Julie, must I?"

Yes, Mum! You must. That is why we are here."

"Christ, woman, what have you got to tell me?"

"John ... John ... Julie is your daughter."

"Jesus Christ in heaven! I have a daughter? After all these years in hell, now you tell me I have a daughter!"

"Yes John. Julie here is your daughter."

I could feel the energy rising in my mother's body as she straightened herself in the chair. How amazing it is to see the way one's faltering strength is instantly regained when the barrier against the truth is released.

He fell into the chair at the other side of the wire and looking straight into my eyes he muttered;

"Natalie, this is my daughter! Is it true?"

"John, what other reason could I possibly have for coming into this hell but to tell you this?"

"This is my daughter," he continued as though I were a piece of unclaimed merchandise.

Looking straight at him, his eyes, his nose, his ears, the distinctiveness of his face, I began to recognize myself.

"Yes! I am your daughter and you are my father."

"Jesus, Julie! You know I was having nightmares about you when Natalie and I were together. I can't remember what they were about exactly. I only remember the name. Now I'm rightly confused. But I can see by the very look of you that you must be my daughter. Christ! You're the very spit of my mother. As I look at you I can see her fire in your eyes ..."

"Five more minutes," one of the prison officer interrupted without consideration.

"For fuck sake warden, can't you leave off? I've just met my daughter!"

There was only harshness in his manner as he snapped at the men just doing their miserable jobs and it merely helped to aggravate the situation. The less sympathetic of the two started counting out the remaining minutes. Four more, three more ... two more ... one more ... time up!

In the middle of whatever he was saying they took him by the arms and marched him away.

"Come back to see me, Julie, you and I need to talk much more, do you hear!" he called to me as they forced his body through the narrow doorway.

"Yes, I hear you father, rest assured, I will be back, I will be back," I shouted into the empty space.

"Jesus, I have a daughter, I have a daughter," I heard him repeat as his voice faded into the grey, unconcerned walls.

The warden behind waited for the far door to close before he started his fumbling again with the keys to allow our exit. This time we were both a little more prepared for that walk across the yard. The obscenities started again but at least this time we were walking away from them. As we crossed the open space I was conscious of a nagging pain somewhere within my body. It was heavy and grabbing. As we were ushered to the outer perimeter and the final inner door was banged on our heels it suddenly hit me. Grabbing my mother by the arm I lost control.

"Jesus! My father, my father, my one and only father is locked up for life in this hell."

The sudden reality of it caused my body to freeze as we were about to be ushered through the barbed wire section of the prison. I was going no further without my father and nothing was going to force me. The fire energy had consumed my body and I was not leaving that hell without him. My heels stuck to the ground as I exclaimed;

"Mum! We must get him out of here. We cannot leave him like this. We have to get him out of this place right now."

My mother looked at me with terror in her eyes. She must have thought I had gone completely mad as I stood there shaking her by the shoulders and repeating again and again what I had said.

"This way, Miss, move along please," a warden muttered as he pushed from behind.

I spun around like an enraged tigress and fiercely pushing him away I screamed; "Take your filthy hands off me, you grizzly bastard!"

He lost his balance, fell over and got entangled in the rolls of barbed wire. Within seconds the soldiers in their stupid camouflage clothes surrounded us both. We were grabbed under the armpits, lifted off our feet and literally dumped outside the main gate. My mother gathered herself off the ground and turning to me she swore with words I had never heard her using before;

"Jesus Christ, Julie! Were you trying to get us locked up as well?"

We had to walk from the gates of the prison to the main road. There did not seem to be a bus stop in sight so we continued walking until we eventually spotted a taxi. All the way back to London my mother kept churning it over and over whether or not she had done the right thing. When the fire within me had eased I tried to assure her as convincingly as I could; "Of course you have done the right thing, Mum. Not only have you given me back my real father, but you have also been able to leave your hellish past behind you for good."

"I fail to see what you mean, Julie. Meeting your father again is revisiting my past, is it not? How can this be leaving it behind?"

JULIE

My reply to her question was easy. All I needed to say was exactly what the alchemist would have said under the same conditions, in other words, all I had to do was to speak directly.

"Let me explain. Eighteen years ago you closed the door on the truth. You locked it away and pretended to yourself it did not exist. But the truth cannot be locked away. You might fool the world, but you know in your heart you cannot fool yourself. What you lock away will keep eating at you until finally it has to break through. All that time you guarded your secret, thinking it would never re-surface and you wasted those years trying to live through the pretence. As you can now see, the truth has to re-surface, if not directly through you then through someone else who is very close to you. With my help you faced what you had buried away. So instead of being eventually destroyed by it you have now freed yourself from it completely and no more can it haunt you, no more will you have nights without sleep. For you, it is over, mission complete, now you are as free as the birds of the air. As for me, it is just the beginning!"

I was amazed how easy it is to speak directly relating to a situation at hand when addressing someone who is open to accept it. It was becoming more and more obvious that consciousness has many levels, just like the alchemist had emphasized.

"Julie, you are talking way beyond your years, but I can clearly hear you. Where did I ever get you?" my mother remarked.

"Does it matter where you got me when you are fortunate to have me as your daughter and that is what really matters. You can thank me for that if you wish," I replied through the rising self confidence seeking recognition.

"Julie," she exclaimed, "it is one thing being good, but it is better being good and not taking personal pride in it!"

I noticed the sparkle was back in her eyes and the shine had returned to her face. By the time we reached London we were both very glad with the achievements of the day. She had finally concluded a huge chapter in her life, the cloud hanging over her had disappeared and she was glowing with relief as we hugged goodbye at the station.

It was back to Dublin for her and out to Ealing for me where I knew I would have my peace replenished with that clear energy surrounding Maura's presence.

Oh, how I wish for that clear energy right now. How can I ever again be reunited with it after what I have done this terrible night? But I must not allow the gloom to descend upon me at this critical moment. The alchemist did say one has to drop the burden of the world in order to get the power of liftoff. By the way of things I have arrived at this point in space and time, so no more negativity; I must accept the situation exactly as it is. Yes, acceptance is the only way, like I had to do when leaving that prison and getting on with my life.

The Christmas season was closing in on the fashion world that started in early October. Maura had gone on a buying trip to the continent in preparation for the expected upturn in sales. We were still having problems with the staff in the West End boutique, which meant I had to work extra hours, sometimes from nine in the morning until after eight at night.

The weather had changed and not for the better. Each day I found myself a little more tired than the previous and there was no free time available for me to get back to the prison. But I did write to my father. After thinking things over I considered it better to get to know him a little better before our next meeting would take place.

Then his reply arrived one morning in the early post as I was rushing out the door for work. It had its advantages living as far out as Ealing. Even in the morning rush hour one could still find a seat in the tube, so I settled myself in for the journey and slowly read through the letter.

He was telling me of his passion for life, his stupidity and sadness for losing Natalie and the sudden awakening he got when he saw me. He also expressed his gladness that I decided to write to him rather than returning to the prison again, reminding me it was not a good place for any young woman to visit. Indeed, I did not need to be reminded after that shattering experience of the cold reality.

But the page where he expressed his feelings about the situation in Northern Ireland bothered me a lot. It appeared obvious that he had taken part in bombing campaigns and God knows what else. It made me feel very uncomfortable to have the proof in the letter that my father had been involved in acts of terrorism.

Then towards the end he talked about some agreements relating to the peace process and the possibility of being released as part of a deal to take place some time in the not too distant future. This part really grabbed my attention. It spurred me with the determination to set about freeing his mind from his narrow, nationalist way of reading the situation. I felt this needed to happen before he would be given the opportunity to return again to his confused and mixed-up world, so I took it upon myself that it was my duty as his daughter to liberate him from his conditioning. I felt I had to break down his limited way of seeing things, but little did I know what I was about to take on.

It meant I would have to return to the library and read up on everything I could find relating to Northern Ireland and this I immediately did with enthusiastic vigour. I even attended a nationalist gathering organized by the political wing of the IRA in North London, and I questioned their intentions at the tea break as I talked with the ones who were openly talkative. Then I posed what seemed like a simple question at the second half of the meeting.

"Should the British government decide to fully withdraw from Northern Ireland and leave the way open for a united, nationalist country then what could be done with all the protesting Protestants?"

I could hear the sniggers all around me as if I was some idiot who had just come in from the cold. The question was brushed aside with a vague answer that the Protestants will sooner of later have to accept they are now Irish like everyone else and if they cannot do so then they can go to wherever hell takes them. Christ! I thought, I had been in the presence of an enlightened master, a man whose consciousness was light years ahead of anyone in that gathering before me, there was no way I was going to take their sniggers without a fight. The fire in my veins sparked me to boldly interrupt again.

"Perhaps my question is a little too complicated for your understanding! Allow me to rephrase it more simply at your level of intelligence," I injected with cutting sarcasm.

"Shut up bitch! Who let you in here?" I heard coming from somewhere in the back.

The chairman stood up and called order. As the heckling died down he invited me to rephrase my question. I had nothing in particular to say. Indeed, I had no question, but I had been given the floor. My mouth just opened and I started speaking direct.

"Firstly, I have listened to you saying that we must not rest until all Ireland is a nation united once again. But I beg to remind you that Ireland has never been a nation united in the past. Even before the concept of a nation entered our brains, in the times of the ancient kings it had never been really united, except in mythological fairy tales. This is the fact and I feel we should stay with the fact. So what are you selling here? What are you inciting in the plebs? Let's drop the nonsense! Let's look at it clearly please! You want to drive the British out of Ireland? What then? Is it going to be ethnic cleansing?"

Again a voice bellowed; "Who let this stupid bitch in?"

Obviously there was no one open to hear me and I quickly realized what the alchemist had meant when he said; "You can only speak direct to those who are ready to listen."

"Now order please, we must have order," the chairman pleaded in a south of the border accent.

When the heckling eventually died down the chairman, trying to keep the meeting as balanced as possible, addressed the appointed speakers.

"Now, would one of the panel members like to answer the young lady's question?"

In response a middle aged man stood up and rattled off a full blown speech in the style and fashion of the actor doing the part of Michael Collins in the movie. The crowd broke into jubilant applause when he eventually concluded with the heated words;

"Let us never lose sight of our vision. Let us not fall into a sleep. Let not a stone gather moss on the tombstones of our great martyrs to the cause. Let us fight to the bitter end. Let us not shy away from whatever it takes, until that great day arrives when Ireland is fully united. This is our dream, soon to become the reality. This, and only this, shall be our glory."

There was no way I could rise above them. I could not even shrink myself back into the crowd as the cold alienation gathered around me. But I stood my ground in silence until the end of the meeting. Then I made my way out of there and jumped on the back of a passing bus as it pulled away from traffic lights on Kilburn High Road.

Later I read through all their brochures and whatever I could find relating to Northern Ireland and terrorist groups in general. I needed to know if there might be something important I was failing to see. Then I noticed what seemed like unusual occurrences happening around me, first in the tube station when a man who said he was from Belfast tried to solicit my feelings. Then one evening on the way home from the library a youngish woman with a northern accent sat down in the seat beside me and it was not long before she opened a conversation. I began to realize she already knew more about me than I knew about myself as she touched on the subjects to spark my interest, like the conditions in mental hospitals in Ireland, the Irish government that she referred to as the mafia of Dublin, and finally Wakefield prison. Her mentioning the prison was a little too close for comfort and I could feel the shivers going up my spine.

But she failed to raise me to respond and I was adamant not to be drawn into her world. I excused myself at one of the stops and quickly got off the bus. Needless to say, I was glad to be free of her, but the incident did disturb me and it made me realize there were people out there who were checking me out and watching my movements. I was well aware these were the people of my father's limited world. I began to realize that freeing him from prison and his way of thinking would be one issue, but an issue far greater would be trying to free him from these very people who worked on the pretence of being his good friends.

Out of the blue a few evenings later three plain-clothes police officers called to Maura's house wanting to ask me some questions. Maura made the study room available and insisted on staying herself after having to remind them that she was my guardian. They wanted to know why I had attended an IRA meeting in Kilburn High Road; they mentioned names and showed me photographs to see my response. Then they went on to inform me they were fully aware of my history in Dublin, but, as far as police records were concerned, they told me I was still reasonably clean and they cautioned me to keep it that way before they eventually left. Both Maura and I were very disturbed by their intrusive interrogation in her house. I had been stiff and straight while it was going on but after they left I almost collapsed into pieces. Even Maura had to pour herself a brandy to calm down her nerves.

I had discussed my trip to Wakefield with her, but I had not told her about the extent of my research in my efforts to understand my father's world. She knew how sensitive the situation was and she warned me to be extra careful, particularly in the light of having brought such unwanted attention upon myself. She pointed out the dangers of being caught up in the middle of a conflict situation, especially in relation to the obvious retardation of British Intelligence when trying to understand the Irish. She went on to explain that those working for British Intelligence are not suffering from stupidity, rather it is their insular way of seeing things that causes them to react in an inflexible, programmed manner.

I did not mention any of this in my next letter to my father. I felt it better not to let him know in case he might read wrongly into my reasons. But I did find I was kindling hostility against the British attitudes in relation to Ireland in general. Before any of this interest had been aroused in me I had been completely unaware of being different, of belonging to any particular country or tradition. Luckily, my mind had not been contaminated with such beliefs. The only poison I had been fed related to Judaism and being separate. Now I was starting to feel like an outsider in a foreign country. I was becoming engulfed in the notion of being Irish which was taking on the meaning of being anti-British. In the middle of it all I recalled how the alchemist had answered a question relating to an issue that was somewhat similar to what I was now experiencing.

"You create your world. Whatever you are so also is your world. If you are love then your world is a world of love.

Even those who proclaim to be your enemy and set out to persecute you, you will see their lack of vision and you will find compassion in your heart for them. This is the natural law, the natural order of all things. But should you kindle hate, then your world must be a world of hate. Should you deal in terror then terror must be your worldly payment. Should jealousy be your foray then all that is related to jealousy must be your worldly return. It is as it is, I am not making it up, but I ask you not to believe me. I only ask you to look at it please in your own experience. Then you will know whether or not it is true."

I began to see what I was doing. I was feeding my mind with the poison for the purpose of understanding the nature of the poison without realizing that I was slowly poisoning myself. Quite obviously I needed to broaden my vision on the subject. Now my research was focusing upon the feelings and sentiments of the anti-nationalists, or the Protestant communities in Northern Ireland. But I soon discovered this material was not as readily available.

I needed to find out more about the nature of conflict and this caused me to be on the lookout for anything that might help me in that line. As the year progressed into the cold winter months I came across a course being offered at a college on the subject of Conflict Resolution. It was to run for three evenings per week lasting from early January until mid-June. At the end of the course a diploma was being offered to those who would have submitted the prescribed amount of essays and partook in an oral exam. Those who wished to avail of a post graduate degree could continue the course by doing a lengthy dissertation for two full academic years affiliated to some university.

But I did not have the basic requirements to apply. Apparently, a primary degree was needed and I had not even finished my secondary education. However, places were also being allocated for those outside the normal academic stream, but this meant going for an interview. Again I was presented with barriers because of my age and my lack of experience in any field relating to the subject. But I was not looking for any special favours as I had sufficient saved to pay the fees. On my third visit to the college I was again being met with the robotic response from the secretary when the director of studies happened by on the scene just as I had flown into a rage.

"If I had five years processing behind me through a crap educational system then I would be eligible! You tell me I am being prohibited from doing this course because of my youth and my clear intellect! And you have the nerve to call it Conflict Resolution!"

The director of studies, a man in his late thirties who was passing by intervened.

"Excuse me, I could not help overhearing. I take it you are seeking a place on the Conflict Resolution Programme," he inquired with a bemused look on his face.

"Yes, that is why I am here, but I cannot get through this programmed barrier!" I replied with my hands in the air.

He turned to the secretary and asked for my file only to be told there was none. Then he turned and looked at me with an expression of 'what can I do' on his face. He was about to leave when something caused him to pause, and after frowning in thought he turned again and said; "Come with me to my office."

He offered me a chair and then seating himself at the other side of the desk he asked me my name, my address and the reasons why I was interested in taking the course. I told him exactly how it was and when I had finished I could see he was seriously interested. He went on to explain; "The course is part of a university programme and there are only twenty places allocated to us in this college. We cannot exceed this number. At the moment we have thirty-two suitable applicants and twenty have been selected.

Should any of these decide not to accept then the next in line would be offered that place. I know you do not have the necessary qualifications or previous experience to be accepted by the board. However, I might be able to do something for you, as you have said you are not interested in the diploma. There is a possibility that you might be allowed to take part in the course if I should be able to convince the board of the significance to the others your presence might be, particularly in the workshops that are linked to the programme. Leave it with me and I will get back to you one way or the other."

Three weeks later a letter arrived telling me that the board was prepared to offer me a place on the course which did not include participation leading to a post graduate degree. I was being accepted in exactly the way I desired and it was the most exciting news I received in the heat of the Christmas festivities. Maura arrived at the boutique at five that evening and presented me with a flashy outfit she had found in Paris. Directly after we went out to celebrate and she treated me to a Japanese dinner followed by a trip to a show in Covent Garden, then for special coffee at an exclusive business club close to Trafalgar Square. We ended up at a posh disco where we mingled with film stars and other stepped-up plebs of my own nature. It was the first time I really felt my femininity as the rhythm took over my body and handsome males kept appearing in dance before me.

"Everything is interrelated, interdependent and inter-linked" the alchemist had said. This suddenly hit me again as my mind flashed back to the prison scene that directly led me to that moment of celebration relating to the fore-coming course. In an unseen way my father was deeply entwined in the unfolding events of my life.

Similar to that night of celebration the Christmas was a whirl of activity between the changing fashions at the boutique and the parties taking place in the house. But everyone knew their place and boundaries were always respected, or so it appeared. Little did I realize at the time that I was the one who was about to cross over that line. I now know that nothing is certain, nothing can be secure in this world, no matter how much we try to believe otherwise. It is all but a passing dream playing itself out before these eyes and ears that are looking and listening from some unknown place deep within. While everything is personal, yet nothing can be really personal, since everything I am is not really different to anyone else.

As I stand here alone I can clearly see it at last. Life is merely a play. As little children we know it before we become stuffed with the world. We have to co-exist in this ruthless hell that we seem to continue re-creating for ourselves and I recognize we have to respect each other by respecting our mutual boundaries. If this could be achieved in divided societies then conflict would naturally diminish. But first a maturity has to be present through which the real love necessary for transcending a conflict situation can express itself.

Maura's maturity taught me more than any university course could have done. Little did I know at the time that I was about to be tested in a manner that would appear to many as betraying my best friend when I was later to succumb to Paul's advances. It was a wrongful act and I should be punished, my judgmental self is still selfishly implying. But how can the magnitude of what I have done this night be measured? Even giving up my life does not seem sufficient to make karmic amends, I challenge this judge in myself. Obviously, every mask of the personal must be dissolved before one can truly transcend the human condition.

Mother returned for the January sales. She was now legally separated. The house in Dublin had been sold for an enormous sum and the proceeds were to be split down the middle. Although I loved her dearly yet I felt a little uneasy about her presence. She was the new woman in the house and she feasted on all the attention.

Paul could not do enough for her and Maura was totally engrossed in their shopping binges together. Every night they were out, either visiting friends or to some festivity. I found it difficult to comprehend how much she and I had changed since our first real encounter at the mental asylum in Dublin. Before that time she was a stranger to me and now she was a vivacious and liberated woman competing for the total attention of those most important to me in my life. She was beautiful, exploding with vitality, but still we were in different worlds.

"Julie, you are totally alone," I spoke aloud to my reflection in the main bathroom mirror after they had gone out for another night on the town.

"You'll never be alone while I'm around you, Julie," Paul replied as he was passing the half open door after settling Damian to sleep for the night.

They should not have left us on our own together and then again, perhaps it was right. Who am I to form an opinion! The alchemist advised against judging the situation. I recall how he said; "Let the only mantra in your life be the following words: 'I will not judge the situation'. Do what you do but know you are doing it. Drop the judgment and you will be amazed to see the good will stay while the bad will fall away of its own accord."

I knew I was playing with danger. But something like a tingling anticipation seemed to take over my reason. In the emotional plain I felt quite disturbed by the way Maura had forgotten about me completely when my mother had arrived on the scene. Not alone that but I also felt the pangs of jealousy cutting through me when I saw how my mother openly flirted with Paul. They were the women of the world and I was the discarded child. But Paul did not see me as a child and I was aware of the magnetism sparking between us.

After having a shower I descended the stairs in my nightgown, knowing in my heart I was crossing the boundaries to satisfy my feeling of neglect while at the same time reacting against my mother's intrusiveness. As I entered the sitting room, the lights were dimmed and the log fire was dancing its shadows across the deep red carpet. Paul was preparing a light cocktail and he asked me if I would like to join him.

My God, even now I cannot be true. I seem to be making justification for my actions. Yes, I am still battling myself. Maura and my mother had gone to a show in Piccadilly and they did not consider asking if I would have liked to join them. I know I am making excuses for what I was about to let happen. It is the other side of me talking. Then again it was inevitable that sooner or later it should happen, seeing that Paul is just an ordinary man and such is the nature of ordinary men. Again, I catch the thinking process and it makes me shiver. I now see how evasive I can be when it comes to accepting responsibility for my own actions. Even at this final hour the tendency remains to put the blame onto somebody else. I need to be more firm with my personal self. It was my own doing, rightly or wrongly, and that is it.

The cocktail in itself was not tempting, seeing that I had not developed any real taste for alcohol. But I did have a burning desire to experience proper sex with a man for the first time. The magic was already dancing between us, which led me to say; "Paul, it could be quite dangerous in such a romantic setting."

He looked at me with that adventurous glint in his eyes that would have moved mountains of any resistance that might have possessed me.

"'Tis well you know it, Julie. Being dangerous is the juice of life, is it not?"

But there was no resistance. I had already melted before I had come down the stairs. He handed me the glass and we took the first sip through each other's arms. That was it. The next moment our eyes took over the conversation and before either of us knew what was happening our lips had met in a passionate and lingering kiss. The glasses found their way to the sideboard as he picked me up in his arms and gently laid me on the couch. Gradually, in the most beautiful way, he started kissing me gently all over, first around my ears, then on my neck and shoulders.

As he slowly unfolded my nightgown my nipples eagerly protruded to meet the softness of his lips coming towards them. At this point I could feel my entire body on fire, and unable to harness my impatience, I literally tore off his shirt as he kicked off his slacks. Within seconds we were both completely naked on the carpet and locked in a passionate embrace. I was struck in awe at the sight and touch of his penis while the ache to experience him inside me continued to grow stronger and stronger. I could also feel the urgency growing in him as he positioned himself to enter my body.

"Please Paul, be careful. I don't have protection," I tried to whisper as I opened my legs to receive him.

Protection or not, at this stage all caution had been thrown to the wind. I didn't want to stop, no more than I wanted to continue being a virgin. I felt that I needed to be a full woman like Maura and my mother. Not only that, but the ache in my vagina had by now taken over completely.

Very, very gently he entered me for the first time as my entire body trembled to receive him. The moment of it was the most awesome experience of my life. It seemed as though I had touched the pinnacle of all creation. It was exactly like I heard the alchemist say it would be when a woman in her mid twenties had asked him how to escape from her virginity. His reply was vivid and direct.

"All I can say to you and to any young woman is to find an experienced lover with a kind heart and gentle hand to guide you through that first occasion. I give the very same message to any young man. Go to a woman experienced in love. Believe it or not, the world is a much better place when love comes to you rightly."

Now it had entered my experience in such an incredibly short space of time and in such a beautiful way. I felt it was pure and wholesome, as it was not pre-planned by either of us. It was unintentional and spontaneous, as life always is when we are present enough to be it.

Or was it? Apart from betraying the trust of my best friend, had I willfully orchestrated it to happen?

But is this not the wilful mind again at its work?

Is this not the spoiler of life with its moral codes chewing away on the heart after the action?

When the mind tried to kick in after our first lovemaking, instantly I could see such thoughts were the ugly seeds of guilt. Again I remembered the alchemist's words, as I must remember them now; "Don't judge the situation. Do what you do, but know you are doing it."

I was no longer being ruled by that conscience put there by the religious upholders of a particular virtue. Again I heard myself uttering the words of gratitude, "thank you, thank you, thank you," to the alchemist for this gift I had received through him.

"No need to thank me, Julie," Paul interrupted the thought in a gentle whisper as his kisses continued to flow.

Then we sat on the carpet by the log fire sipping our cocktails. Paul started to say something and my instinct told me what was beginning to play on his mind. I put my finger to his lips and whispered; "Paul! Let it be, let it be; this moment is precious, it is sacred and secret, let us always respect it and let it always be so."

The rising apprehension immediately dissolved from the energy field surrounding his body. Again he was glowing as he replied; "Julie, you are so mature and so full of wisdom. Right now I feel like a boy in your presence."

Once more we embraced and again our bodies moved and made love, equally as gentle but a little more vigorous than before, and afterwards we sat by the fire and continued to sip on our cocktails.

This time there were no words arising to infringe on the moment. We just sat there looking at each other and I became captivated by the golden glow of the fire gently shimmering around his body. His eyes were a radiance of light and then he was moved to speak what I was seeing at that moment in him; "Julie, your eyes are shining so brightly. I can see blue and gold shimmering around you. You seem like a goddess, a real goddess before me."

Again we embraced and made love, but this time we seemed to completely melt into each other. It was as though we both disappeared; there was no Paul, no Julie, just love in its fullness of life's passion entwined by the beautiful rhythm in the natural movement of our bodies.

When it had come to its natural ending we sat by the fire and both of us wept.

"Julie, I love you," he started to say.

Again the words of the alchemist flashed through my mind and I was moved to put my finger to his lips to stop the spoiler from speaking through him.

"Paul, let love in itself be your love, not Julie, not Paul, just love; serve nothing else."

"Yes ... yes, I see what you mean," after a long pause he replied.

We moved together towards the stairs and then to our separate bedrooms after gently kissing good night on the landing. As I lay in my bed I could still feel the sensation of his presence within me. Then the wilful mind started to re-present itself. Am I guilty of betraying my friend? How could I be so callous to do such a thing? My body started to twist and turn as each thought pierced deeper than the previous one. What am I doing? I suddenly questioned. The alchemist had clearly stated; "Do not judge the situation. Do what you do but know you are doing it."

This is exactly how it was. What was done was done. It was beautiful and it had wonderfully enriched my being. The alchemist had said that without judgement the good would remain and what was not good would fall away of its own accord. There and then I could clearly see it would never happen again with Paul. This was not because of moral codes set by man or his mind-perceived gods, it was simply the truth of the matter.

Morning dawned and my body was still glowing with the fullness of love as I entered the kitchen. Maura and mother were in full conversation about something or other and they immediately stopped with stunned looks on their faces. My mother was the first to remark;

"Good heavens, Julie! What have you been doing to yourself? You look absolutely radiant this morning."

"Natalie!" Maura replied with a delightful smile on her face, "your daughter left Dublin as a girl and now she is a full woman."

I could feel myself blushing at how right she was with her comment. They both instinctually knew without even knowing they knew. I heard the alchemist say; "If only you could reconnect with the storehouse of natural intelligence in your body then all things needing to be known would be instantly known. As a matter of fact it is exactly so, but you, as the personal self, are out of tune with the universality of your being. The personal self is the spoiler, thus being cut off by its own doing, and it is naturally so in the greater order of all things. By the very nature of the personal self it can never know love, it can never know truth and therefore it can never receive the elixir of life."

After taking a bowl of cereal for breakfast I excused myself, put on my winter gear and went for an early walk in the park. The sky was clear and there was a white frost on the grass. It seemed as though it was there especially for me as the city continued its sleep on that lazy, Sunday morning. The leaves of golden brown crunched under my feet and I watched the lighter ones dancing away from my boots as I walked through the trees. A red breasted robin hopped through light branches close to the ground as a blackbird fluttered through bushes with its sudden gush of chirping sound. I was in love, completely in love, but not with anyone in particular, thanks to the alchemist. At that moment I was totally in love with life. As I crossed over a stream I noticed the sun of the early morning sparkling on the frosty branches touching the water. I could see stillness in every form of life as though momentarily frozen in a portrait of time. The park was alive with such magic, such wonder and I was fully alive to receive it.

Then Paul appeared with Damian by the hand. I had not expected them to be out so early. Damian came charging when he spotted me and he dived straight into my arms. Such love, such beautiful innocence coming from the child, was awesome at that moment to receive. Paul's voice broke into our bear hug.

"We are on our way back from the pond, we have been feeding the ducks," he explained.

I looked up at him. He was still radiant; amazingly, there was no distance between the magical glow on his face and that of the park. As I gazed at him in awe he remarked;

"I know, Julie. Maura and Natalie have already remarked upon it; you have charged me with love and I can feel it in every bone of my body."

"Paul, it is enough to keep us glowing for the rest of our lives provided we serve it rightly; that means we should never need to repeat it."

"Yes, I understand, Julie, we should never need to repeat it." And then with a boyish glint in his eyes he continued; "Unless we do!"

"Yee...yes; unless we do," I uttered quietly against my better understanding. In truth there is only one first time that cannot be repeated, but I had been given the privilege of seeing it much deeper. Our night of love had brought me to the pinnacle of my experiential being where nothing more needed to be added other than serving the fact that it is here in existence where love is needed. I could see how the very nature of the personal self denies itself access to it; while it thinks it loves someone, yet, in truth, it only loves its own selfish needs, and as soon as the needs are fulfilled it hungers for more, or for somebody else.

Paul returned to the house with Damian and I continued my stroll in the park, allowing the love in my heart to be at one with the beauty of the morning around me. My space was clear to receive it, no more contaminated by guilt.

Right now I can see how personally selfish it is to nurture guilt and how it finds its survival in the base elements of the psyche. Now I realize how important it is to have experienced such love as it opened my heart to receiving man rightly in my life, even though it may never again be received through this body after what has happened this night in Granada.

The following days flew by and I was more than busy with the January sales at the boutique and getting prepared for the course on Conflict Resolution about to commence. My mother was still with us when eventually it started on the

second Monday evening of the month. She insisted on
coming with me, as curiosity, I thought, was beginning to
fill her relating to my private world.

"You'll be okay traveling back in the tube on your own,
Mum," I asked out of concern for her.

"Oh, do not worry, Julie. Paul is meeting me in town. We
are eating out. As you know, Maura is going to a fashion
show tonight with a group from a new fashion line."

"Who is taking care of Damian?" I anxiously inquired.

"Oh! Paul has arranged a babysitter, I'm sure, so there's
no need to be concerned, everyone is being looked after."

Something snapped inside. I had never before experienced
the green-eyes monster of jealousy. I could see how she
had been flirting with Paul. Maura was also aware of it,
but she was too kind-hearted to challenge her friend. I
could tell she was upset by their antics and also I could see
the radiance fading from Paul's countenance each time he
responded to her signals with that look of sex rather than
love in his eyes. I was more than aware of her efforts in
the previous days to re-spark Paul's interest in her when it
had faded after our special night together.

Yes, I was fiercely jealous and I did not even stop to
consider how jealousy was consuming my mind and body.
I could no longer see her as my mother; I could only see a
woman who was obviously dangerous and I flew into
attack immediately. We had entered the college foyer and
I asked the porter to direct us to the coffee room.

"Julie! We don't have time," my mother interrupted.

"Oh yes we do, Mother," I snapped. "What I have to say
to you is very important and I must be sure you hear it."

I pulled out a chair at a table and sat her in it. Then sitting
directly in front of her my jealousy exploded in her face.

"Mother, you have a serious problem. Whether you realize
it or not is another issue. The problem is you have never
matured. As a matter of fact you fucked up all the way.

You fucked up with my real father and then with that 'yob' you married, as my father has called him."

"I do not have to take this from you; I am your mother," she interrupted me in mid- sentence as she raised her body from the seat.

"Oh yes, you do!" I hit back as I rose and pushed her back down. By now the jealous rage had taken me over and I struggled to keep my voice from shaking.

"You are not leaving this seat until I am finished. Do you understand?"

She must have been experiencing the same fire in my eyes that she had previously met in the mental asylum as I clearly perceived her fear. It is amazing where jealousy can lead. I even went as far as threateningly saying;

"There is nothing about you I fail to see. Be aware of that. I can see every thought, every notion in your head. There can be no funny games in my presence, such as using this course as a pretence for meeting up with Paul later. Do you understand me?"

The vulnerability and apparent innocence showing in her reply caused the slimy green consuming my presence to recede a little. I began to feel some compassion taking hold of me as I tried to find words to continue.

"Mother, I am not blaming you for anything. I am trying to show you how it is. You have locked yourself away from the world for eighteen years or more and you would be still locked away if you had not been woken up. You know it is true. Even our visit to Wakefield Prison was part of that awakening. You are back to life and you are still a very beautiful woman. You can have any man you desire. I am not just saying this, it is the way of things, Mum. A beautiful woman like you can have any man she wants. But before you do, you have to be more aware of the difference between love and sex. If you fail to see this, then you are going to bring upon yourself even greater misery than you have ever previously experienced."

She did not respond. I knew she was fully aware of the fact that her intentions with Paul, however innocent they might have appeared to others, were crystal clear to me. True, Paul had been unfaithful to Maura when we made love, but it was not merely sex like in the manner that was gripping my mother. There was a special bond between us, as far as I could see it and he was not up for grabs for any other woman. Again the jealousy started pounding through my veins and I had to fight it for control as I continued.

"I've been closely watching you while you've been here and it's clear that sex is your problem. If you're aching to be fucked then go out to some nightclub or other and find yourself someone to fuck with! But don't fuck with my best friend's man. If you even try it, I will tear you to pieces! Do I make myself clear! I will tear you to pieces!"

She did not respond. She just sat there staring at me blankly. A tear appeared in the corner of her eye and she fumbled in her bag for a tissue. Then she looked at me directly and pierced me open with the remark;

"Julie, you are jealous of me. I can see it!"

I tried to bluster it aside by telling her that jealousy had nothing to do with it. But she would not let go. She knew she had hit the nail on the head. Of course I was jealous, fiercely jealous of anyone coming near Paul, other than Maura. I never realized it had been so obvious. Then she challenged me further with the direct and painful question;

"Have you been sleeping with him?"

I was completely knocked over and I just could not bring myself to answer. But the silence spoke for itself. She had me reeling as she went on to pry;

"Does Maura know about it?"

Her sharpness stunned me and I knew I had walked myself into it. But what had happened between Paul and myself was definitely not up for discussion. I tried to regain my position as I replied;

"We're talking about your intentions, Mother, and this has nothing to do with my life."

"Have it your way, Julie. You seem to have it all. But beware of the serious consequences you may be drawing down on the entire household."

I could feel the tornado going round inside me. One moment it was love I was feeling for her, the next moment it was fury at the point of explosion. But I cannot deny it was all circumvented by the jealousy and it was my first real encounter with it. Looking back on it now I can see how overpowering it can be when one loses one's integrity to such emotional states.

My mother had witnessed this uncontrollable side of me before when I had violently made use of the poker. But that happened in immediate response to an impossible situation. This time jealousy was my immediate problem. But equally, I was again at that edge of losing all control over my actions.

Obviously, she could see how determined I was to protect Paul from falling into the arms of any other woman. She was also fully aware of the extent of my anger and how dangerous I could become when pushed over that edge. She decided to make her retreat with the words;

"I'll phone Paul and tell him I'm not feeling well, that I need to lie down."

But it only enraged me further. Did she think I was stupid, that I could be that naive? Again I grabbed her by the shoulders demanding;

"Get out from between them! Do not phone him. Phone Maura and tell her you will meet her at the show. It is only two blocks from here. Then you can ask Maura to tell her husband you will not be seeing him later."

It was time to go. From the pain on her face it was obvious she had seen more than enough of my darker side. As we made our way out I noticed the total silence in the long narrow room, even though there were people sitting at the far corner; quite obviously some of the ones I was later going to meet in the Conflict Resolution course.

After that we embraced an estranged embrace and she went on her way.

I had no idea who might have been listening to us and it did not bother me. I felt no remorse for what I had said, nor did I feel any guilt, even though I knew I had allowed myself to be consumed by jealousy. My conscience feebly tried to imply that I had been acting wrongly. This made me see how utterly retarded all thinking is in that limited field. There was no shadow of doubt lingering to haunt me. True, jealousy was the major part of it. But I was also clear that I had been acting out of love. I know it may be difficult to understand but the love I had for my mother, Maura and Paul at that moment were exactly the same.

The alchemist had talked from the infinitesimal depths of this state. Indeed, all that he portrayed had come from total impartiality. I was quite sure he had been no angel before his transcendental realization occurred. He made it clear that he was talking directly from his own experience and he continually reminded us not to believe or be carried away with anything he was saying.

"Whenever a belief takes root it cuts off the life line for the seeker of truth," he cautioned.

He always insisted we should apply whatever he said to our own situation by reminding us that the truth can only be realized in the actual moment in one's own direct experiencing of it. I can clearly recall his words;

"As something is occurring in your own experience you are the only one who really knows whether or not it is true. For example, if you say to someone 'I love you' then you are the only one who knows whether it is true or not. The problems arise in your life when the truth is too painful for the personal self to accept. Then you find yourself clinging to your make-believe world by thinking something is what it is not. When life reminds you how foolish you are by flashing the truth in your face you usually cringe in denial and try to bury yourself deeper and deeper. This is the world you create and it is directly related to the personal image of yourself you are trying to protect. Then you set about imposing your self-created world upon the natural wonder of life. You dig yourself into social and religious beliefs in your efforts to create substance for your unacceptable falseness. Deep down it is the source of all conflict within you."

What had just happened between my mother and myself was over and done with for good. There was nothing further to discuss, or to mull over in the wilful mind. The love I felt for her in my heart was all that really mattered and I was confident that this alone would continue as the sacred bond between us.

Now I see it all the more clearly. Love is all that really matters in one's life and this is not through loving anyone or anything more or less than others, rather it is the deeper love we serve when the consciousness does not crash on the particular.

There were twenty-one new students in the lecture theatre including myself. Each of us was handed a folder containing the course outline and a list containing the names and place of origin of every participant. I was amazed at the global representation partaking. There were countries mentioned that I had never heard of before and oddly enough, mine was the only name from the Republic of Ireland.

Then, one by one, the students were asked to face the group, introduce themselves and give their reasons for taking the course. I had absolutely nothing prepared as I had no idea what to expect. Not alone that, but I was still heated from the confrontation with my mother in the coffee room. How would I manage? What could I say? I was trying to figure out in my unexpected panic. I tried to recall what the alchemist had said when asked about public speaking. It took some time for the panic to ease before I could re-connect to his clear reply.

"When one is living the divine life then speaking the truth never needs to be prepared. In such a situation one stands before the people and allows it to happen. The truth takes care of itself. All you, the speaker, have to do is to keep your personal, self-conscious self out of the way."

But it was the first time in my life with the daunting task of having to face an audience and I was instantly struck with the jitters while harboring the thought of doing it. Thankfully, the coordinator called each one up to the rostrum in alphabetical order, so fifteen had to do their bit before my name was eventually called. Ten or more had presented themselves before I finally got on top of the jitters. Then a few more had passed through before I had regained a relative calmness. I did not even see or hear the final ones before my turn arrived as I had focused my attention inwards in order to let my body and mind sink into the stillness behind existence like the alchemist had demonstrated.

"Anything one sets out to do should only be done from the stillness within one's being," he had said. "If everyone were to live by this basic principle then there would be no conflict in the world. Even in the act of lovemaking the couple should first and foremost re-connect with the stillness within by means of some form of meditation if necessary. This would help to eliminate the personal want, or selfishness, being involved and thereby contaminating the natural purity of the act."

The richness of his teaching wrapped itself round me like a warm cloak as I reflected upon it with my full attention. Soon the jitters subsided and I slipped into a relaxed state of deep stillness.

Twice my name had to be called before my eyes reopened. Then my body rose from the seat and calmly walked up to the front without having the slightest idea of what was going to be said. As I placed my hands on the rostrum, paused and viewed the others before me, I felt an extraordinary calm rising from somewhere within. I was amazed to see it also in the faces of the audience even before a word had been spoken. It was exactly how he had said it would be. I just opened my mouth and everything I had previously read relating to the course seemed to spill out. All seemed to go well until I began to realize I didn't know how to stop! My delivery started as such:

"Like all of you present, I am here to explore the nature of conflict in society, starting with the individual, then the individual's relationship with the immediate family and next, with the society. But before I commence on this research I need to understand how the individual comes into being in the first place.

"We all know that the word 'individual' is derived from the verb 'to divide' and division of anything in scientific terms usually causes friction or conflict, even an explosive chain reaction, as humanity has discovered by dividing or splitting the atom. We need to understand the inherent nature of this within the individual before we dare to expand our research into divided societies, such as we have in Ireland, for example."

I seemed to have struck on the right cord, as everyone appeared to be astutely attentive to my delivery, in particular a young German seated near the front who had already given a brilliant introduction of himself at the outset and in perfect, Oxford English. The look of sharp attentiveness on his face indicated to me that he wished to hear more of what I had to say and it filled me with the necessary fire of the moment that enabled me to expand.

"We all seek consistency and continuity in our lives. We do not like change, in the deeper sense of change. We do not like to let go of the relative known. Rigidly we hold on to our positions, our ideas, our beliefs, without realizing that the only consistency, the only continuity in the entire creation is change in itself. Everything is in a state of constant change. This, each of us can see and understand in our own experience.

"If we are real about this course on conflict resolution then we must be true to the fact that the only place we can really develop a better understanding of conflict is in that which occurs directly in our own experience. We must be astutely aware so as not to waste our energy hypothesizing the facts to suit our individual pretentious.

"I see this course as a study of human nature where the micro is also the macro. The micro we know directly in our own experience. But the individual is not the micro as many might falsely think. It is 'you' being the individual that is the micro. Before we commence we need to be very clear on the distinction between the individual and 'you' the individual. The individual is a theoretical concept only, whereas 'you' the individual is the reality.

"If this were not clearly understood before we start out on this course then we would be starting on a false footing, which of course would mean that all our conclusions would have to be equally false. This, I propose, is the problem with most research being conducted by the universities around the globe. All we need do to qualify this is look at the state of our world today. It cannot be denied that conflict is on the increase, even though such courses as the one we are about to commence are also on the increase. Obviously there is something being missed by our great professors and social researchers and we are here not to be led into another dark alley. Rather we are here to discover what is being missed and this is our opportunity. We must not lose sight of the fact that the creation in itself gives us a clear illustration of how conflict arises. The seed in the ground, for example, had to give itself up for the new sprout of life to appear. If it refuses to do so, if it insists on holding on to itself as it is, then it blocks the new coming through. The seed would then be in conflict with the natural law of life.

"How crazy it would be if the seed potatoes formed a union and protested against being put back into the ground. Can you imagine it! Seed potatoes on a protest march down Oxford Street! All different types, fat ones, long skinny ones, funny looking ones with lumps, all carrying big protest banners declaring: 'We demand our civil right to continue our lives as we are!'

"Indeed, what would the poor farmers do? What would the government do? Call out the army in their funny camouflage gear! Then it would look like the spuds had being joined by the cabbage! Spuds and cabbage! Obviously, something would still be missing? The meat, of course! What do rowdy protesters call the police? Pigs, is it not? That's it! The pigs would have to be called out with their truncheons to complete the picture. Now we would have the bacon! The perfect meal, spuds, bacon and cabbage! And these are the ingredients for the perfect society, as far as the individual can see!"

The room exploded with laughter. Even if the college had hired a stand-up comedian to give a performance with the purpose of easing the tension among the new students I felt it could not have been better. The wave of laughter had even got to the coordinator and professor seated at the side waiting to speak at the end. I suddenly realized I had full command of the floor. As I waited for the appreciation and applause to die down a reminder from the alchemist flashed through my mind.

"Initially, you might find it difficult to speak, but when you pass through that barrier you might find yourself facing another, that is being unable to shut up! It is all the play of the personal self, the psychic impostor invading your presence otherwise known as self consciousness, or being overly attached to your personal image. You want to be seen in a particular light and the thought of not being able to portray yourself as you pretend to be to yourself can be very frightening when it becomes over-exposed to the light. The psychic impostor shrivels when faced with the task of speaking the truth in public. But when your true presence takes over and breaks through this barrier of fear the psychic impostor resurrects itself to ride again on your back by taking the credit. This presents itself in the format of not being able to shut up!"

"Thank you, thank you, thank you," again I found myself saying, this time into the microphone. But I was not thanking my audience for their applause after the flash of the alchemist's insight had shown me what was being really applauded. But I found it difficult to pull back from the personal elevation. After that I cautiously continued.

"Each one is here for her or his own reason. But now we are here we have this wonderful opportunity to explore together the subject at hand. We must not allow ourselves to fall into the trap of the ones who have passed through such courses before us. We must not lose our direction by merely striving to become more intellectual, by burdening ourselves with more informational baggage. Rather, we must collectively and individually strive to enlighten ourselves. By this I mean that instead of collecting more of the informational stuff we should consciously endeavor to free ourselves from our current excesses.

"We must be prepared to relinquish the ideas that we tend to cling onto in our resistance to change, such as our political ideologies, our particular beliefs, our particular gods. We must be prepared to transcend all such intellectualized nonsense. Otherwise we are no different to the seed potatoes and camouflaged cabbage protesting against inevitable change on the streets of existence.

"My name is Julie Steinheart from Dublin. I come from a divided country, a divided society and a divided religiosity each claiming to be the true representative of the same mind-perceived god. Potatoes with drums, spuds with crucifixes, camouflaged cabbage trying to keep them apart; such contamination under different disguises is being fed on this plate to the innocent minds of our children. I thank you for your attention."

I could hardly believe what I had done. Seemingly, no one had expected me to say very much because of my age and obvious lack of university or experiential background. I was even more surprised than the audience had been. Perhaps it was the fire of the confrontation with my mother that had initially sparked me. Then the short meditation before I had spoken had set me ablaze. Whatever had caused it to happen, I could hardly believe it when I got a standing ovation as I made my way back to my seat. When the remaining students had finished the professor even commented on my delivery. After thanking us all for our excellent presentations he went on to mention the importance of good preparation, using me as the example saying how obvious it was that I had come fully prepared. There and then the professor was presenting himself to me as another blocked mind, another one unable to see outside the box.

We all retired to the coffee room to become more socially acquainted. The handsome young German seated himself in the circle surrounding my table where I was by this time commanding considerable attention. Of course I was still on a high when I addressed him directly. "You gave me great courage to expand on my presentation when you seemed interested in what I had to say," I opened.

"You must excuse me," he replied, "although I can speak very good English, yet I still find it most difficult to understand. I must confess I did not know what you were talking about and when you introduced some point of view about vegetables I became totally confused."

That certainly busted my bubble on the spot. It was a blow between the eyes for my inflated ego and thankfully I was sufficiently alert to catch life's instant response.

"When you are on the right track all that is necessary will come to you, even sometimes in the most unusual and most unexpected manner," the alchemist had said. "You will know what I mean at that moment it happens in your own experience. But do not claim it. The moment of claim is the moment of contamination. But do not fret! Life is always immediate to wake you up in one way or another! Be sufficiently alert to receive it whenever it does."

Wow! It was all becoming so very clear at last. I was even beginning to understand what he had said about death being another falsity of the mind as I could sense his presence fully alive within every thought entering and leaving my head, within every action arising from within me and outside me. Yes, it was definitely so, for as long as life continued in my body he would not be dead. Nobody else on the course could fully connect with his level of consciousness, nor could they connect with the source within themselves, but it excited them enormously and it won me many new friends.

All my free time was totally absorbed by my new field of study. The weeks that followed dissolved into months. I even completed all the essays required for the diploma. The professor and lecturers were so pleased with my performance that they allowed me to do the oral exam in June, which included a half-hour presentation to the class on a specific topic. The one I chose was based on the psychological imprint on the psyche of the individual living in a divided society.

All my experiences of the past proved immensely valuable. Now I was thankful for all of them, even my years under the tyrant hand of the pretender I had for a father. After enduring him for all that time I had not alone attained to his level of understanding at a very early age but I had long surpassed it, even before I was boosted into what I can only term as cosmic consciousness through my encounter with the alchemist in Temple Bar. It may seem I am again on a high, elevating myself about others, but do not be too concerned. I speak from my heart and life in its goodness is always generous enough to give me a jolt whenever I should need it.

Maura and Paul came to the passing out ceremonies on the last Friday in June. But mother failed to be there. She was holidaying in France with the new man in her life, a friend of the solicitor handling her divorce case.

As I was being presented with my diploma all my friends applauded and, needless to say, I felt on top of the world. Maura found it hard to stop hugging me when the little ceremony was over. Then she was taken over by my closest friends, Frederica from Milan, Mar from Granada, Claus from Hungary and Patrick from Australia.

Paul remained in the background until the excitement around me had sufficiently died down. When he finally approached me I could not hold myself back from flying into his arms. Many months had passed since our magical night of love together and both of us had consciously resisted the urge to repeat it. We instinctually knew that night was sacred and secret and to set about repeating it would violate its sacredness. Such action would only serve the coarser element of lust and what had happened between us was far too precious to be blighted by such. Indeed, I was thankful for my months of intensive study which more than helped to keep both of us out of temptation's way.

But this moment was special and it was our first full embrace since that night. He kissed me on the cheek and then on the side of the neck causing me to melt, and the sudden ache to feel him inside me again almost drove me crazy as my body sensuously wriggled in his arms.

"Paul we mustn't," I whispered.

"Julie, I need you, I need you so much," he urged against my resistance.

"Paul, my need is even greater than yours, but we must not destroy each other," I tried to reason with him.

But Julie, love cannot be destructive," he argued against his better wisdom.

"Paul, it is not possible for us, nor can it ever be possible," I found myself replying. "Maura is my best friend, and Paul, you are also my best friend, this we must protect so we can all continue to be in the state of love together."

"Jesus, Julie, I want you so much I'm prepared to give up everything for you," thus spoke the urgency from the psychic pool of endless want trying to distort his naturalness.

"Paul, I've just finished a course in conflict resolution and I am telling you right now with this diploma in my hand that harbouring such a want is going to bring you nothing but disaster."

"Julie, I'm prepared to suffer any disaster just to be with you again," he interrupted.

"Then Paul, you are obliging me to leave Ealing right now. I can no longer be with you. I must not even go back to collect my things."

"For God sake Julie don't do that. I understand, please forgive me for losing my control. But I want you to know I love you dearly."

"I know that, as I love you Paul, exactly like I love Maura and Damian."

Thankfully, Patrick from Australia arrived on the scene and I introduced them to each other. When they finally struck up a conversation about Australian football I excused myself and returned to the others. Later when Maura got me on my own what she said really startled me.

"Julie, I want to thank you from the bottom of my heart for not destroying my marriage."

I was literally stunned at her directness as she spoke to me calmly without being swayed in any way by emotions. I was suddenly made aware of a maturity of clear understanding she seemed to possess that surpassed anything I had ever met before. At that moment it even surpassed that of the alchemist.

"Don't look so startled, Julie," she continued. "I've been fully aware of the deep bond between you and Paul since Christmas. It clearly shows me what must have happened between you both. But behind the physical attraction I can clearly see how much you love each other and how much you now respect the situation. I do not need to know any more than what I can see myself. At last you are conscious of the boundaries we must respect. Your understanding of love has saved you from what I might otherwise have had to do with you!"

I could feel the blood draining from my face and my legs began to tremble. I knew I was completely helpless in the presence of such an extraordinary woman. All this time she had known and it did not affect the love that possessed her heart. I started to weep in my shame and anguish at the sudden realization of my betrayal to what I can only describe as a goddess before me.

"Julie!" she exclaimed. "Do not weep. What is done is done. I hold on to no illusions. I am fully aware of the world's limitations in matters of real love and I have no misconceptions about Paul. If it had not been with you then it would certainly have been with somebody else. You know exactly what I mean. I admire and love you for the way you have handled the situation. You have shown him his place better than anyone else could have done. Not only that, but I have to admire the way you have excelled in your own right. You have clearly illustrated to me that you are the dearest friend I could have."

Without further words she embraced me and both of us wept. The love between us had surpassed all levels of personal desire, but only through the deep understanding of the greater reality as illustrated to me by Maura.

"When you are on the right track all that is necessary will come to you, even sometimes in the most unusual and most unexpected manner," the alchemist had clearly said. "But do not claim it. The moment of claim is the moment of contamination."

With each event in my life my vision was clearer. It was becoming more and more obvious that my encounter with the alchemist was truly an encounter with an intelligence from another dimension. It had prepared me for these events in my life and through the enlightenment I was capable of receiving the extraordinary wisdom that Maura so clearly possessed. At that moment it seemed as though Maura had ordained all of it from the very beginning.

It humbled me to realize I had not been her greatest friend after she had so fully demonstrated such quality of real friendship. There and then I felt that no man, indeed no other person, would ever again come between us, until I caught sight of the personal self again claiming its part. I could see that the consciousness needs to be sufficiently swift to outpace such subtle contamination replanting its seeds.

But can her friendship still hold after what I have done this night in Granada?

Is it possible for her to be there to help me through the unavoidable consequences I will certainly have to face in the morning?

Time, all of it time; it is merely another dimension of my multi-dimensional essence. But I can no longer see or feel that fullness as a cock crows in the distance. It appears as though the spaceship has gone without me and I am left standing alone to face the truth of myself.

It was a beautiful summer in London and I had just gone through another birthday. When I had first arrived less than a year previous I knew no one other that Maura and Paul. Now I had my international friends. Some were working their way through college in the strangest of jobs, and the privileged ones hung out in the cafés. The boutique, being right in the heart of the city, became the concentric for all.

Catherine, Patrick's younger sister, arrived from Australia and instantly we hit it off together as friends. She proved to be wild and vivacious with breathtaking tales about all her childhood experiences. With a fabulous singing voice, within days she had found a group looking for a female vocalist for their gigs on Saturday nights in Putney and in the Elephant and Castle on Wednesdays.

My social life had really commenced and everything seemed just perfect. Then the letter arrived from my father with his date for release from prison. It came as a bit of a jolt as I had not been expecting it to happen so soon. He had friends in Cricklewood, North London according to the letter, who were organizing a place for him to stay.

When I read it again I realized it was happening that very week. The letter had been a month in transit, twenty-eight days being processed through the prison postal system, then two days by mail once it had hit the outside world. He had not given me a contact address so all I could do was to wait until I would hear from him again. I felt a little unsure of the approaching situation after my brief encounter with the type of people who were likely to be his friends. This made me somewhat uneasy. It felt as though I was about to be sucked into a dark tunnel. On the other hand I would never have ventured to take the course in conflict resolution if it had not been for him and his unending world of conflict. For that I had to thank him.

Two weeks passed and no other letter arrived. Then one early morning in the boutique two dark skinned ladies approached me at the till with some items from the racks they had chosen to purchase. As they were paying I was literally stunned when one of them gave me the message.

"Julie, your father would like to meet you. He suggested the café 'Tea for Two' at three o'clock this afternoon. Can you manage to be there?" she inquired.

For a moment I could hardly reply. How did they know who I was? It was totally unexpected and I was completely startled. But finally I managed to say; "Of course I can be there. But how do you know my father?"

"That's not important," the other lady said. "But you must be careful not to be followed and do not let anyone know where you are going."

"Don't worry; tell him I will be there at three."

They paid for their items and left. I knew exactly where the café was located. I had been there a few times before with some of my friends. But it was by no means a regular haunt. The manageress of the boutique was pleased to oblige me. It meant that she could have extra time for her midday break as she did not have to rush back for two o'clock, which was my usual time for lunch.

I wondered what all the secrecy was about. My father had been released and to me that meant that his past account had been balanced with society. Then it began to dawn on me that his past account with his terrorist connections might have been merely put into abeyance during his period in prison. This could only mean that he was now becoming actively involved again.

I was initially spurted into doing the college course in order to equip myself with sufficient understanding to rehabilitate him. But I had not anticipated this might also mean taking on the IRA and possibly other terrorist groups as well. My initial concern was for his immediate safety so

I did what the women had said. It was less than a fifteen-minute walk to the café. As I made my way through the big department store to the elevators I could see why this particular place had been chosen as the venue. Although I had seldom been down Oxford Street before, plainly this was exactly the type of place I might go if I was on a midday shopping spree. Obviously, it would not arouse undue attention.

When I got to the café he was not to be seen so I ordered a pot of coffee for two and found an empty table where I could sit down. As I was placing the pot and cups on the table he appeared from behind me out of nowhere.

"Julie, my long lost daughter, this is the greatest moment in my life."

I was astounded. It was as if I had not been expecting to meet him and I could hardly find words to respond. I just stood there looking out through my mouth, then I put out my hand to greet him. But ignoring it he embraced me in a bear hug. Next I was crying and I did not know why. My feelings were totally blanked, yet I could not stop the tears from flowing. There was such warmth about him and such energy pouring from his body charging me with all the fatherly assurance I had missed in my childhood that was not his fault. He too had been through great suffering. The realization of this occurred in that moment and then I was hugging him back.

"Father, I have never been lost. My life might have been hell, but I have never been lost, in spite of the fact that I had lost my real father."

"Julie, call me John. It's much too late for the father and daughter bit."

Now we were laughing as I wiped off the tears. I could not get over how handsome he looked. He was dressed in fawn-colored slacks, hushpuppy shoes and a shirt that complemented his deep blue eyes. His hair was thick and dark with natural highlights of grey.

"Okay, I will call you John; but please tell me why all the mystery about our meeting?"

"Julie, you're a beautiful young woman meeting me for the first time in the free world. Don't I need to impress you? We need to wash that first impression clean out of our minds."

"But you could have phoned me instead of sending the message with two strangers."

"Did they bother you, Julie?" he questioned while raising his eyebrows.

"No, not at all; but I could not help but think you might still be caught up with subversive groups when I was hit with the secrecy stuff."

"Julie, there's a lot of things you're not yet fully aware of about my life. You know my situation is anything but ordinary. I'm free, but yet I'm not free. I'm going to be watched day and night for the rest of my life. That's how the police operate. Anyone I make contact with will be thoroughly checked out and possibly harassed."

"But I understand all that and I can easily cope with it," I interrupted.

"Julie! Listen to me, will you! They are using me as a ferret. They feel that anyone I talk to must be in the IRA. That's how they work. That's how they end up arresting innocent people. These people don't give a shit who they arrest as long as they get someone and make a public impression. More often than not the ones arrested and put into jail are the innocent relations or friends of the active members. They do it on purpose. Believe me, there is no integrity in the way they act."

"But I can handle myself. You do not have to worry about me," I tried to assure him.

"It's a dirty business, Julie. Personally, I had nothing to do with the charges they pinned on me. But I'm not going to lie to you. I have been in the IRA since my college years in Cork. I've seen these people lie under oath in the Courts in order to secure a conviction. They are capable of using you as fodder in order to force me to spill on my friends if they thought I had any feelings for you. It's not safe for you, Julie. That's why we must only meet in secret."

I could clearly understand what he meant. As part of my course I had studied the media hype surrounding the convictions and later release of those falsely convicted for the Birmingham and Guildford bombings. But I could also gather from his sentiments that he was still actively involved. This was our first meeting and it was obviously not the right time to open this challenge. My main concern was in getting to know him as my father.

"I find it difficult to call you John," I replied.

"I know you can't help but see me as your long lost father. But we are both adults, Julie. Your childhood is over. 'Tis gone for good. We only have the present and future."

He was right, of course. My childhood was well and truly over. It was selfish of me to even consider the thought that he could take up the father roll. I needed to be honest with myself and be true to the situation.

"John, you need to get out of this environment and start a new life for yourself somewhere else."

He did not even stop to consider as he immediately jumped back in response; "This is my life, Julie. I haven't chosen it. Christ! It was brought upon me by the great injustices still being inflicted on our people back home."

I was not going to be waltzed down this avenue without making my protest.

"Look! You cannot bullshit me, Dad ... John, or whatever. I have had more than my share of injustices. I have just completed a college course in conflict resolution. Before that I had to fight my way out of Dublin with the police on my heels. My entire childhood was suffered under the tyranny of a Jewish psychiatrist who could not come to terms with his fear of reality. He hated me because he could not change the past. Nor could he cope with the fact that my mother had taken him for a ride. I was the culprit. I was the reason for the marriage. Could he acknowledge my presence? Certainly not! He had to punish me without even examining his need to do so. Failing to break me he had me committed to a mental institution."

"Jesus! Julie, I had no idea."

"There is a lot more to me than you could ever possibly know, so do not talk to me about great injustices. I know the world and I am fully aware of your situation. Terrorists are terrorists and I know how you are psychologically caught up in that web. But I can help you. I can show you the way out. If you do not want to get out then there is nothing left for me to do but kill you myself!"

"Bloody hell! You're some woman, Julie. I'm going to enjoy having you in my life."

"In your short life, you mean, if you fail to wake up! I have friends all over the world through my college connections. I can help you get started in another country. But you must be prepared to leave all your past behind you. Now is the time to make that break."

"It's not that easy, Julie. Scores have to be settled. I've obligations to others. I just cannot walk away like that. Neither could you, Julie, if you were in a similar position."

"Then it looks as if I will soon be visiting you in prison again," I reminded him.

"No, not this time, Julie. The next time round they will not take me alive."

A cold chill ran through my veins at the thought of losing him again. I was not having it so I felt I had to attack.

"It is your choice, dear Father. It only takes one from the ignorant mob to be a terrorist. But it takes a real man to rise above it. So which are you? Are you a real man? Or are you a coward like all the others who hide behind their cowardly ways of fighting the world? For God sake, where is the dignity in planting bombs then running and hiding while innocent people are being blown to pieces?"

"Is that how you see it," he interrupted angrily?

"This is your one opportunity to prove your manliness to your only daughter," I replied.

"My only daughter?" he remarked, as his eyebrows raised again with a look of exclamation on his face.

"Are you telling me you have another," I found myself demanding in shock.

"Or others, perhaps! Surely, you haven't thought I've been living a monastic life since your mother left me."

I was momentarily stunned. My entire impression world again had been shattered. I was already loving this intriguing man and relishing the thought of our future relationship together. He was the man of action I had been dreaming about. Now the dream had become a reality, father and daughter, two of a kind about to take on the world in a way it had not been taken on before. But this confrontational suggestion of there possibly being another daughter, or daughters, seriously disturbed me.

Taking on the IRA and the rest of the world was suddenly very trivial compared with that undeniable surge of jealousy then consuming my mind and body. I had not realized I was harbouring such possessive feelings relating to him. I could not find words to respond. His remark had stunned me into silence.

"Julie, we have much to talk about," he broke in.

I was still searching for words when Mar unexpectedly appeared with two of her friends from Granada. Her face lit up as she spotted us and within seconds she had exploded upon us with the words; "Julie! What a surprise! I didn't expect to see you here. Let me introduce you to my friends. This is Cristina and her boyfriend Fernando."

Mar had become one of my closest friends at the college and I was always delighted to see her. But this time she was invading my space and my first reaction was to let it be known. But it would not have been right to snub them. Reluctantly, I put out my hand to her friend and greeted her. In Spanish Cristina replied, "Encantada."

Then Fernando kissed me on both chceks with the greeting "Encantado, Julie."

I introduced my father as John and immediately he broke into a conversation in Spanish with them both. Again he had stunned me. I had been suggesting how I could help to get him set up in another country without even considering he might already have friends all over the world. Mar remarked how handsome he looked and I could see she was flirting with him as she tripped in and out of Spanish while talking to me in English. The simmering jealousy caused me to interrupt.

"Do not allow yourself to be enamored by my father, Mar. He has daughters all over the place and I am sure he has many lady friends all over the world as well."

"You are being a little hard on me Julie," he intervened.

Mar laughed it off and she suggested we should all get together for dinner one evening soon. With that she gave him her mobile phone number that he eagerly noted while apologizing to her for not having one himself.

At the time I looked upon the chance meeting with Mar and her two friends to be purely coincidental. I felt there was no way it could have been orchestrated. Then again, I could not be sure about anything. I had fully confided in Mar about his situation from the very beginning and I knew she was eager to meet him. But I did realize how naive I had been to pigeonhole my father after seeing how skillfully he shattered all my illusions in such a short space of time that we had together. Not alone that, but he had opened up a part of myself that I had not noticed in my character before and I was not too happy with what I could see. The alchemist had made me aware that possessiveness has many destructive relations deep in the psyche.

I noticed he was ready to go as he was saying goodbye to the others in Spanish. He shook Fernando's hand as they continued to speak intensely. Eventually, he turned and kissed Cristina on both cheeks. With Mar it was a little more intimate as they paused for a moment and looked into each other's eyes. Then he turned to me with a warm, fatherly hug.

"When will I meet you again?" I asked.

"Don't worry, Julie. I'll send you a message," he replied.

With that he disappeared out of sight through the clothes section of the busy department store. I fell back into the chair, bewildered, excited and filled with every feeling imaginable spinning around in my body. Mar and her two friends walked me back to the boutique. Maura was eagerly waiting to hear the news. She was the only one I had told when I phoned her from Oxford Street to explain why I had been delayed.

The streets of London were filled with tourists all through that month of July and the boutique was never as busy. When Maura spotted Mar strolling into the shop she immediately engaged her with an offer of work for the rest of the summer. Mar was delighted and so was I with the thought of having one of my best college friends working beside me.

But the intrigue within me relating to my father had been further enflamed. He had more worlds than one and I was determined to know all of them. Secretly, I decided to learn Spanish. I bought a set of teach-yourself tapes and a phrase book to get myself started, and I was amazed at how easy I found it. Perhaps, it was due to my intensity relating to him. Later I was to partake in an intensive course of classes in Spanish at a nearby school for three evenings per week. Again it was happening because of my father. Little did I know it at the time how obsessed I had become about him, nor did I realize the force behind the obsession and where it was going to lead me. I could only see my immediate need to draw him into my life.

I was at Catherine's gig in Putney when the next encounter happened and I did not recognize him. His hair was dyed blond and he was sporting a beard of similar colour with tinted glasses when he unexpectedly appeared. It was Mar who had brought him to me and she introduced him as Don Juan. He muttered a few words of greetings in Spanish. The lights were dim which did not help as he led me by the hand to the dance floor. I was shaping in front of him for at least five minutes before he stopped me dead with the words; "Julie! What do you think of my new disguise?"

"Jesus, Father! Is it you?" I blurted.

"No, Julie, 'tis not father, 'tis John."

"For Christ's sake! What are you trying to do to me, posing like someone about to chat me up?"

"Julie! I'm trying out my new disguise and it seems to have passed the test."

"How did Mar recognize you?" I enquired.

"She didn't. I had to re-introduce myself to her."

"But how did you know I'd be here?"

"Well, Julie, an underground agent has ways of knowing what needs to be known."

"Is that what you are? An underground agent?"

"Not really, Julie. I've taken your advice and I've decided to head abroad."

"Well, that is a relief to hear. Where are you going?"

"It would be better for you not to know. It's possible that you might be interrogated when they realize they've lost my trail and I wouldn't want you to lie."

It all seemed too much to handle. Why was life so cruel to me when it came to my father? Why could we not be given the opportunity to be together? Had I not suffered enough at the hands of the impostor father whom I had all but murdered? Was it my mother's fault? If only she had the courage to have married the right man? My father had just entered my life and now he was telling me he was about to disappear again. How much more could I be expected to endure? The pain and disappointment was noticeable in my voice when I implored him; "Then please tell me at least, when are you going?"

"Well, it's a matter of money, Julie. Whenever it arrives."

"Do you have your own money, Father," I inquired?

"Jesus, Julie, I've been locked up for five and a half years! How could I have any money?"

"Who is supporting you? How are you managing to live?"

"Look Julie. I'm signing up for a job in a few days and I'm expecting an advance."

"What's the job?"

"You know you should be working for the bloody special branch. You're sharper than any of their interrogators I've had the misfortune of meeting!" he blurted.

"Be serious with me, Father. Are you getting yourself mixed up again in your old activities?"

"Julie, I have to do whatever I have to do. We all need to survive, you know!"

"Look, if you need money then I can help you. You only have to promise me you will start out afresh. Then you can have whatever you want."

"What! Are you rich as well, Julie?"

"I have enough to help you escape from your past."

"Julie, I don't know. It doesn't seem right."

"It seems perfectly right to me. You are my father and I am here to help you."

"Hold on a minute, Julie. Let me think about it. I'd better get out of here. They might be watching you."

"But where are you going? When can I see you again?"

"Don't worry, Julie, I'll be in contact again sooner than you think."

It was difficult to hold a conversation with him on the dance floor. It was even more difficult to pin him down long enough to talk some sense into his head. He was excusing himself again as he kissed me on both cheeks and in a flash he was gone. I looked for Mar but she was no where to be found. Then I began to wonder what the hell was going on. I worked my way up to the stage and waited for Catherine to finish her song. Perhaps, she might be able to throw some light on the situation, I thought. She could see more of what was happening from her vantage-point on the stage. As she finished I grabbed the moment to ask if she had seen Mar.

"Yeah, Julie" she replied. "I saw her leaving a little while back with a cool looking blonde guy."

"Did he have glasses," I enquired?

Yeah, I think he had. But I'm not too sure."

Could it be possible, I thought to myself, that Mar had something going with my father? I felt I was participating in a live lesson on conspiracy theory. How did it happen? Well, she did give him her mobile number at the café and he could speak Spanish fluently. She had introduced him to me as Don Juan. Yes, of course, it all fitted perfectly. I could see it then but I was not able to register it. Catherine interrupted my thoughts.

"Julie, I'm nearly finished. The disco will be starting up in fifteen minutes. Can you wait for me and we'll hit the West End together? I feel like a change of venue. It might be good for us both."

"Yes, that's a good idea, Catherine. I'll go to the powder room and get myself ready," I replied through my mental disturbance.

On the way out I tried to get through to Mar on her mobile but all I got was the recorded message. Catherine was not part of the conspiracy so I could not confide in her. There would be far too much explaining to bring her up to speed on the entire situation. We went to the West End as she had suggested and we danced until the early hours. Then we returned to her pad in Notting Hill and slept through Sunday morning. Later in the day when I phoned Ealing to see if Mar had tried to contact me Maura replied; "She called about an hour ago and she sends her apologies for missing you last night."

"Did she say what happened?" I enquired.

"Coming to think of it, yes. She had to leave for an hour or so to help someone with something and by the time she got back you and Catherine had gone. Her mobile was out of credit, she told me to tell you."

I began to think that, perhaps, I was imagining things. It might have all been very innocent. But intuitively I could not deny it. The only way I could know for sure would be to confront her. After all, I could not confront my father. He was the mystery man with no avenues open to reach him so I decided to let it rest until the following morning at the boutique. When I got back to Ealing that evening I had an early night in order to re-settle myself. I was up bright and early the following day and I was first at work, being anxious to clarify things. But Mar was fifteen minutes late. When she eventually appeared in the shop with Fernando and Cristina the three of them were decked out for traveling and I was completely taken off guard. She apologized for missing me on Saturday night and she briefly explained that my father had asked her to accompany him as far as the tube station so as not to arouse suspicion. Before I could tease out any more from her she was apologizing to the manageress for having to leave. She was returning to Spain with her friends and they were in a hurry to the airport as they had managed to get a cheap flight. She hugged me goodbye and she promised she would write to me from her new address in Granada, that is, when she would have found a new place to live. Apparently, she now intended to continue her postgraduate studies at the university there instead of London as previously planned.

"I will accompany you to the airport Mar," I offered.

"No! No, Julie. It's too much of a rush. We've barely enough time as it is. I will write to you and you must come to Granada."

Then they were gone in a flash. I was not at all happy with the way things were being orchestrated by my father. It was not a healthy situation. It seemed as though I was being dangled from the end of a precarious string and in such a way of not having any control whatsoever over the course of events. Not alone that, but Mar and her friends had also become part of the mystery. I was troubled and annoyed with her and Maura was also annoyed at her sudden departure when she later called in to the office. I had not known it at the time, but Maura had lined me up for a buying trip later that week as she wanted to teach me more about the trade. Now this too was in jeopardy. I felt as though I was partly to blame and I suggested Catherine as a replacement.

"If she is interested tell her I will interview her this afternoon at four o'clock. Tell her to bring her CV along and references too if she has them."

Maura was not taking any more chances. She needed reliable staff. Although Mar had been most reliable and trustworthy for the short while she was there, yet leaving the way she did seemed totally out of character for her.

Catherine was over the moon when she got the job. It meant that she could stay on in London while her brother Patrick was completing his studies. It was also a relief for me to have someone steady and reliable to work alongside me. Later that night I told Maura in detail about all the events relating to my father and my failure to get through to him. She carefully listened, accessing the situation as I spoke, but she did not venture to interfere by offering any suggestions as to what I should or should not do. Speaking it out to her was sufficient help at the time for me to see things a little more clearly.

My life was falling into an acceptable routine and I was returning to being my own person when it happened again. This time it was another woman whom I had never seen before. She had dark brown eyes and I could immediately tell from her accent that she was Latin American. As she was paying for some garments she passed me a folded piece of paper with the money and she whispered; "It's a secret message from your father."

Shortly after she had left I went to the bathroom and read it. I could see it was his handwriting and he was asking me to meet him that night at an hotel in Earls Court. He needed money for his escape and he thanked me for my offer. At last I was presented with the opportunity to put that money in the suitcase to good use. It was going to help save my father and this must surely have been the reason it had come my way in the first place, I superstitiously thought.

Meeting him again meant I would have to skip my Spanish class that night. After work I got back to Ealing as quickly as possible. Without stopping I put the two stuffed socks into my bag and headed for our secret rendezvous. He was nowhere to be seen when I entered the bar of the hotel. Yet, it did not surprise me. I was sure he would appear any moment. But it was the woman who had given me the message in the boutique who approached me and asked me to accompany her down the street. She led me to the café where he was waiting and then she excused herself and was gone. Again I hardly recognized him. The café was filled with Australians and, dressed like a backpacker, he was sitting alone at a corner table.

"I'm glad you could make it, Julie. I've taken your advice and I'm making the break," were his words of greeting.

"I am delighted to hear ..." I managed to say before he put his finger on my lips and interrupted; "Julie, before you say any different, my name is John."

"John, I am more than delighted you have decided to do the right thing."

"Julie, don't ask me where I'm going. You know by now it wouldn't be safe for you if I told you."

"I understand that. All I need is your assurance, your word of honor that you are leaving your past behind you."

"Julie, I swear on my life I'm leaving my past behind me. I've got you to thank for it. You've helped me change my direction completely. Believe me, Julie, I'm not telling you a word of a lie. I'm out of this country for good. Meeting you was the luckiest break in my life."

"You need some money?" I questioned.

"Julie, I will give it back to you as soon as I can."

"I do not need it back. Just tell me how much you need?"

"Perhaps, five or, maybe, six hundred pounds. Can you manage that much, Julie?"

I took the two stuffed socks out of my bag and I passed them to him, making sure that nobody noticed. I pointed a finger to his rucksack and taking the hint he immediately packed them away. Then I informed him that he had close to three and a half thousand pounds in his rucksack. I felt the pride in telling him and in letting him know that he had a daughter who was worthy of his full attention.

"This money has come my way for you and I have been holding it for this moment for over a year. Use it wisely and never forget your promise to me."

"Jesus, Julie! Where did you ..?"

Now it was my turn to put my finger on his lips as I said; "Do not ask any awkward questions because you might not understand my answers. The money is now yours, and it has come through me to help you start a new life."

"Julie, I don't know what to say," he replied with a look of joy and wonderment on his face.

"Keeping your promise is more than enough. But I must warn you, if you ever return to your past then I will be obliged to kill you."

"I can see you mean what you say. Woe betides anyone who would dare cross your path, Julie."

Then I challenged him about Mar and he blushed. So my hunches were correct. There had been something going on between them even though he tried to brush it aside. I gave him Catherine's address in Notting Hill as a contact point and I told him to use the name Felicity Andrews. I made him promise that he would only contact me by ordinary post. No more messengers please!

That was it. He paid the waitress, we said our goodbyes at the table and we walked out separately as he suggested. For me it was with a heavy heart. It seemed so strange that I loved him so much. When I glanced down the street in the direction he had gone I noticed his lady had emerged from the shadows and joined him. Side by side I saw them swagger into the distance with their arms entwined.

Was he good? Was he bad? I could not figure him out. Everything about him was impossible to read. Even his energy field was strange and bewildering to me. The only thing I was sure about was the fact that he was my father. Obviously, my emotions had me confused. When I got back to Ealing and made myself a tea in the kitchen Maura noticed the uneasiness in me.

"You have seen him again," she remarked.

"Yes, I have seen him again. Is it that obvious, Maura?"

"Julie, I cannot help but notice. He is the only one who causes you to lose your composure."

I replied: "I do not know what it is about him that causes me so much concern. I cannot even come to terms with the way he attracts me. I am totally confused. There are times when I love him as if he were my own son. Then there are moments I love him as a father. Then I see him as the Don Juan, like Mar introduced him to me, and I want to be his only lover. I even felt betrayed and jealous tonight when I saw him walking away with his arms around another woman. I heard the alchemist say that jealousy is not seeing a relationship as it actually is. If jealousy is present then something is being overlooked. I should not be feeling this way. It is just not right, Maura."

"Well, you never had time enough to build up any kind of relationship with him," she remarked.

Yes, it was true and by the looks of things I could not pretend that a proper relationship would ever be likely to happen between us. I tried to forget about him but I found it impossible to get him out of my mind. Weeks passed without another word from him but the disturbance within me continued.

Then Maura invited me out for dinner one night after I had finished my Spanish class. I could feel she needed to talk to me about something. It was about him.

"Julie, I have been observing you when he is around and I can see you are losing control. I can tell there is something going on that is causing you deep concern. Excuse me for having to say this, Julie, but I think your father is a control freak. He is manipulating you in a dangerous manner, just like he manipulates others. I know I have not met him since your mother left him, nor do I ever need to meet him again. I am only concerned about you. Indeed, you have had enough problems with that man in Dublin posing as your father and you do not need another like him."

"But he is completely different, Maura," I argued.

"Yes, Julie. He might be different, but remember he is only different in the methods he uses to manipulate you. He is much subtler and this can be far more dangerous than your previous experience. Natalie's husband was violent and stupid, but this man is seriously cunning. He thinks everything out. It is his nature. He was like that as a teenager when your mother fell for him. He had her wrapped around his little finger while he carried on doing whatever pleased him."

"But he is my father, Maura. Surely, that makes it different," I pleaded in his defense.

"To you he is your father, but to him you are just another woman to be used. Look Julie, he has never developed as a real father. Being a father is a lifelong process, is it not? They do not come readymade off the supermarket shelves, you know!"

"Yes, I see what you are saying. But then again, he is so innocent, Maura, I feel like protecting him."

"Julie! He is the perfect terrorist. He is good enough to walk into the Houses of Parliament and blow the place to kingdoms come without even being noticed."

Maura was right. She was telling me to be careful simply because she really cared about me. She went on to tease out my inner disturbance and eventually we discovered what it was. He had invaded my privacy by planting the seeds in my psyche. It was very subtle. As well as that I had this feeling that I was being watched and I was losing trust in everyone.

"I can see it, Julie, because I am not so closely involved. I know he is occupying your thoughts most of the time. You may not be aware of it, but he has manipulated it this way. This is how they recruit new members."

"What do you make of this feeling I have that I am being watched wherever I go?" I asked her.

"In all probability you are being watched. The anti-terrorist squad would be well aware of your relationship with him. Do not be surprised if they approach you. They certainly will if they lose his trail. Be prepared. Please call me at once if they do. Promise me, Julie. Do not try to handle them alone. It is far too dangerous."

"That I promise, Maura. I am well aware of the dangers of being caught in the middle. I know I have to watch both sides of the fence."

I was lucky to have such a loyal friend. She was the only person I could fully trust and I felt so safe in her presence. Later we stopped for a drink on the way home and the topic was back to autumn fashions. How refreshing it was to be with her. Maura always had her feet firmly on the ground and she helped me realize I had been walking on quicksand. I made a conscious effort not to entertain any more thoughts concerning my father after seeing how he was playing on my psyche. I was equally resolved not to be sucked in again to any of his manipulative scheming around the emotional play of other women.

Then the call came from Mar inviting me to Granada. She tried to convince me I would love the ancient city and she wanted me to be there for some festival that was about to take place in relation to the new students at the university. When I told her I was not particularly interested she went on to say she had a big surprise for me. I had to implore; "Mar, I just do not have the time. We are very busy restocking with the late autumn fashions. Also I am going on buying trips with Maura and we are already looking into the winter scene. Perhaps, next year I will have some free time for Granada. Thank you for the invite. I will let you know, Mar, whenever I am ready."

She did not sound very pleased. But I was determined not to fall into any manipulative traps with anyone again. It was my life after all, as Maura had reminded me. I was back in control and only then I realized how much out of control I had been taken.

As expected the anti-terrorist squad presented themselves. This time it was a woman and two men who arrived to the house on my day off. I was still sleeping when Maura called me.

"Julie! They are here. Take your time. Come down when you are ready."

Maura had seated them in the kitchen with tea and toast on the table when I entered. To my surprise they were very pleasant. They told me they knew my father had been in contact with me. They also said they had reason to believe he was being pressured against his wishes into partaking in subversive activities and they needed to know of his whereabouts for his own good. After asking me if I knew where he might be I honestly told them I had no idea. I went on to say;

"I have spent six months studying a course in conflict resolution for the sole purpose of being able to sit down with my father with the one intention of freeing him from that world. He has seen me on a few occasions since his release and each time he avoided being drawn into discussion. I would like to know where I could contact him, but he told me he would do the contacting. I am not at all happy at the way I have been treated. If you find him please tell him I would like to be given the opportunity to talk to him."

They accepted Maura's tea and chatted for the greater part of an hour before they eventually left.

I was thankful it worked out the way it did. Maura had helped to clear the rubbish out of my mind with her down-to-earth talk that night in the restaurant. She had also helped me to regain my confidence and sense of control over my life. I felt the police could see my honesty and directness and they were left with no reason to return. But then again, one can never be sure of the programme going on in their minds.

A month passed by and I heard no more from my father. It was as though he had disappeared from the face of the earth. I was glad to have my Spanish classes to keep my mind occupied. But as time went on I could not help but feel the increasing apprehension. I was actually worried. Then, from somewhere far in the back of my mind I remembered the alchemist. What did he have to say about worry? I could hardly recall. It suddenly hit me that he was fading from my memory and I was shocked with myself. A short while previous I had gone through terrible anguish after receiving the unexpected news of his death. Now to my horror, his presence within me was also dying and I myself was causing it to happen. I had not realized how far into the world I had allowed myself to be spun by a force other than my own. Trying to trace back to the place it began to possess me, the most previous thing that swamped out the alchemist's presence would have been the six months of study on the conflict resolution course. But this had attracted many new friends and in itself it was good. Gradually I began to realize it all went back to my father and that first time I had met him in the prison. It was from that moment on that the alchemist started fading within me. Since that time something else had been slowly but surely taking me over in body and spirit. I focused with all the power of my mind and gradually I began to see it as being the same dark force that had taken over my father when he was a student in Cork. I had a feeling this force could have many disguises and in all probability it was even the cause of my confusion about him.

There was something else nagging at me relating to an important point the alchemist had made. I knew intuitively it was very relevant to my situation, but the line of communication had been blocked. Then I began to realize that the force surrounding my father had gradually cut me off from the alchemist's level of consciousness. No wonder Maura had taken me aside to help me back.

But I was not back. I was still out on a limb clinging to air. I needed help from the teacher who was no longer accessible. Who could I turn to? Certainly not to the college, or to my student friends; their knowledge was good but it was merely on the surface of things. They knew little or nothing beyond the realm of cause and effect. The course on conflict resolution had been most beneficial, I had learned much, but my quest had moved into a deeper dimension. If I were to succeed in rescuing my father I would have to learn how to battle and win on the psychic plane. This meant first and foremost I would have to get myself back on line. Again I talked to Maura about it and she did not at all seem surprised.

"Julie," she said, "I think you are ready to meet some of my friends."

That was the start of the process. Necessity was the next step pushing me further into the unknown. Two weeks later it happened. It was my first introduction to yoga with a difference. Maura took me to a weekend workshop in a village in Sussex and there I was introduced to the energy centres in the body.

The event took place in an old manor house being used as a conference centre among other activities. We arrived on the Friday afternoon and after being allocated our rooms we commenced with a vegetarian supper. Maura had been going to yoga for some time and she already knew most of those attending. But this weekend was also new for her. The woman hosting the workshop was French. Her name was Andréa, and her one assistant, Caroline, was from California. This was their first event in England and it was a rather intimate affair with only thirteen people present.

After supper we attended a short talk given by Caroline in the assembly room. Then we did as she had requested and retreated to the gardens of the manor. She had told us to let ourselves completely relax and to avail of the abundance of clear energy coming from the plants. While I was sitting alone by an ornate pond close to two huge oak trees I was joined by a woman who told me she came from Leicester. We chatted for a while about energy fields in particular. She pointed out the difference between morning and evening plants. Then she guided my focus to one particular shrub in autumn flower and she told me to remain absolutely still.

This was not a problem for me. I had ample experience in the psychiatric hospitals that I had been obliged to endure during most of my early teens. I remember how I used to sit on a chair for hours on end just looking blankly into space. But this stillness in the manor garden was totally different. It was filled with joy and Tracy from Leicester was so fine in her energy she appeared to be almost transparent. Her fineness was the opposite end of the spectrum to that heavy coarseness exuding from the medical personnel I had totally lost confidence in during my forced internments.

Tracy gently brought my attention to the glow surrounding the plant. First she helped me see it in one of its flowers. Then she told me to gradually allow my vision to expand without losing my focus. I was absolutely amazed. The longer I held my focus the larger the glow of energy became, until eventually I was completely engulfed in it. Tracy seemed also amazed.

"Julie, you are a natural," she said. "People spend months, sometimes years of practice, before they can even see the initial glow."

Then we spent a half-hour or more just sitting there in total silence. Tracy had closed her eyes and had taken up a yoga position. Her body was erect and her legs were tucked in underneath, with the backs of her hands resting on her knees and the palms facing upwards. I noticed how the tips of her thumbs and forefingers gently met, forming two circles, as she sat there absolutely still with an extraordinary look of serenity on her face. When I focused completely upon her my eyes picked up the energy field surrounding her body. It seemed a golden green in colour tingled with a bluish white, and on holding my attention upon it, it appeared to grow larger. The sensation I felt was amazing. Gradually I could sense myself within it and my eyes automatically closed. I was vaguely aware of being just an observer as everything dissolved into a light that was not a light in the ordinary sense. It can only be described as a sort of nothingness, like the alchemist had previously described. I was emptied, completely emptied in the wonderment of the experience.

It lasted for at least a half-hour before the bell was sounded as a reminder that Andréa was ready to meet us. Slowly I re-emerged to meet my body and my eyes opened just as Tracy's were opening.

She smiled at me softly and said; "Now you can share your vitality with the plant kingdom and you can replenish your body quite naturally whenever it is needed."

We walked back together to the assembly hall and joined the others. When we had all assembled Caroline led us to the meeting room. She took off her shoes before she entered and we all followed suit. I noticed twelve chairs placed in a large circle and Andréa was seated in a meditation posture at the top with a small table holding a vase of white and pink flowers, a small jug half filled with water and an empty glass beside her. A scented perfume exuding from a little burner filled the air. We seated ourselves in the circle around her and the others closed their eyes and slipped into a meditative stillness. But I was already still and my gaze was fixed on the unearthly beauty of Andréa. Her hair was golden. It seemed to be raising from her head and gently falling down to the tops of her shoulders. Her skin was pink in colour and her slender neck resembled that of a swan. Soft white chiffon wrapped her body. Her hands and arms were bare, as were her feet and ankles.

I gazed at her perfectly shaped toes and her long, slender fingers as she sat completely motionless, just like Tracy had been in the garden. But this woman seated before me appeared to be more than human. She was the perfect goddess. My vision was frozen upon her and I am sure I could not have looked away even if I had tried. The type of magnetism that held me I cannot explain. Then she opened her eyes of deep sea blue and smiled directly into mine. The sudden power of it literally blew me away. She poured some water into the glass and the trickling sound seemed to be the cue for the others to open their eyes.

Then she began to speak, first about love, then about life, without referring to them in that order. Instantly, I realized she was coming from the same place as the alchemist I had been with in Ireland. He had continually reminded us that these words were the theme for everything he had to say relating to the truth of our being. But she was speaking much gentler and she did not display the fire energy that he had displayed. It was as though her audience had already arrived. He seemed to have been speaking to the ones outside the gates to the inner paradise, whereas she appeared to be speaking to her special guests within it. But

JULIE

I instantly knew the message from both were one and the same as she opened with the words;
"You are the pure radiance of love, the unending joy of the creative force. You are truth. You are all that is perceived as godliness. You are life and death in oneself. I speak to you from the heart of all that is, and you hear it from the same heart. We are gathered here to remind the one self of its true nature. We are here to reaffirm there is no one better or no one worse, there is no higher or no lower. There is just self, you and I, the one true self of all. Let us join our hands in our sisterhood and let our individual energies be united into the one great refinement."

We joined our outstretched hands and Andréa started the chant to the sound of 'lammm'. First it was very low as she took it through all the musical scales. Gradually the others picked up on the sound. Suddenly I was amazed as I became aware of the vibration of 'lammm' coming through my own vocal cords. As it grew louder and louder the vibration of the note seemed to be coming up from the very core of the earth to the point of almost raising us off the floor.

Andréa's voice was magnificent. It was so sweet and powerful it seemed to be penetrating way beyond our three-dimensional field. When it was at its crescendo the entire building seemed to be dissolving into the deep vibration of sound. She later elucidated that the sound 'lam' represents the root centre of the body. Then she went on to explain;
"This is how the body takes form in what appears to be matter. In the greater reality matter has no relevance. First there is sound or vibration, which acts at phenomenal speed causing matter to appear in sensory existence. The purpose of our weekend here together is to bring our consciousness closer to this speed, or closer to that point where matter is taking form in the here and now."

This seemed a little too much to grasp by some of those present, which I could figure from the expressions of total bewilderment on some of their faces. But for me it tied in perfectly with what the alchemist had said, and hearing it twice from two different sources made me realize its validity. I had no problem following her as she described how the creation takes form.

"In the greater reality there is no past or future; there is only now, which is the eternal point of existence where everything begins and ends simultaneously."

When questions arose from the others Andréa explained it more clearly.

"The human mind cannot be expected to understand this, particularly the current scientific mind that uses the concept of matter as the root, or base from which its enquiries are made."

"Then how can the evolutionary past be explained?" Maura enquired.

To me this was a valid and relevant question. Andréa's reply was almost identical to what the alchemist had said. But this time it was clearly registering as I sat attentively receiving it from a feminine voice.

"The evolutionary past is exactly as it is, but the scientific mind is seeing it back to front. The beginning is not in the distant past as we think. The beginning of time is now, it is forever now. 'Now' is the concentric. The past and future, which is time, projects from the now. The further out the projection we travel the more barren or rock-solid it appears. But it is only a projection. The ancient fossils of the creation are on the outer projection from the point of the now. Should the now disappear then all time, past, present and future, also disappears. I must not take you too fast with this because the mind cannot comprehend it. First you have to open the door to your inner intelligence where all of this is already known."

Her smile was like a sudden blaze of sunshine as she gently brought the meeting to a close. Then she called on Caroline to list out the events for the following day. After doing so Caroline reminded us not to enter discussion among ourselves about what we had already heard. Rather we should let it rest and allow it to work on our subconscious without hindrance. Apart from the scheduled meetings with Andréa it was to be a weekend of silence, and energy should not be wasted.

Saturday started at six in the morning for meditation. This was followed with time to oneself in the manor gardens. Light breakfast was made available between seven and eight. The gym was utilized from half past eight until half past nine for anyone wishing to join in Caroline's class on relaxation postures for the body. The library was open for the others, which I chose and I came upon a book entitled Life by the author J Krishnamurti. Opening a page at random I read something that intrigued me causing the image of my father to flash through my mind.

'Life is a movement in relationship, which is action,' it read. Then it went on to say: 'A real man is a free man; free, not from nationalism, greed, envy and all the rest of it; he is just free.'

The message was powerful and it could not have been said simpler. It helped me to see that I was completely on the wrong track in the way I was trying to rehabilitate my father. As I read further it was illustrated how terrorism, which springs from nationalism, is no different to anti-terrorism when seen more clearly. The entire course I had just completed on conflict resolution completely missed out on this point. Exactly like the alchemist and Andréa there present, I could see that the author was also coming from a place of much higher intelligence.

Obviously, to this higher level of intelligence it is clearly visible that terrorism and anti-terrorism are one and the same. Each is equally dependent upon the other for its co-existence. But the strategists and the political advisers coming from the pool of the intelligentsia available to powerful nations seem to have no real access to this level of vision. They fail to raise their consciousness beyond the basic level from whence they conclude that bombs should be used against bombs, or ways should be explored to counter-manoeuvre the maneuvers of the opposing side. Although the gist of the clearer vision may seem to be applied by the strategists, however, it is only applied from within the limitation of the general mind. But it cannot be seen in the deeper sense when the mind is not consciously refined to understand it. Quite obviously, the world is still in the infancy of its own creation.

That weekend made me even more conscious of the great privilege bestowed upon me, having been in the physical presence of the alchemist. Now I was becoming aware of the fact that such a privilege also must carry a huge responsibility. In other words, I was obliged to be fully responsible for my life and that means being true to the situation, as I have been true this night by doing what had to be done here in Granada.

It was back to the special meeting room at ten that morning for another two hours with Andréa. Again she was seated in a meditative posture and looking exactly the same as the previous night, except she was now wearing light blue instead of white. This time my eyes closed as I fell into a deep stillness without there being any doing involved. Everything seemed to gradually dissolve around me, even the feeling of having a body. After some time the tingling sound of water brought me back to the external. She beamed that blazing smile and commenced.

"This morning we are going to utilize the energy of the genital centre, or the sacral area. This energy is central to the creative force. The sacral is most sacred and it should

200

always be treated with the greatest of reverence. Know that the genital energy is the movement in relationship that is love in action in accord with the natural law of the creation."

I was instantly struck by the coincidence of the words she used relating to love were almost the same as I had just read in the library relating to life. She smiled directly at me and remarked; "Love and life are one and the same."

I was totally stunned. I had not even opened my mouth and she had picked up the thought that had entered my head. This was not a coincidence. I felt it was much more than that. As she continued to smile directly at me I knew she had penetrated to depths within me that I had not yet reached myself. Still looking at me she went on to speak about thoughts.

"The average mind is quite simple. There is a set pattern that involves the thinking process and this pattern is not only reflected in the person's posture, but waves are emitted and they can be easily intercepted by anyone with a little training. As a child I have had the great privilege of being an orphan. I was not encumbered by parents! I was raised in a house of Tibetan monks outside Paris and they taught me a lot. But do not worry. I would never invade anyone's privacy!"

I have to watch what I think, was the next thing flashing through my mind. Again she looked directly at me and smiled. At that moment I completely surrendered and allowed myself to be fully transparent to her. She bowed her head in acceptance and then she continued.

"We are looking at the love energy permeating existence as we focus out attention on the genital centre. Before we continue we must drop every thought that enters the mind relating to love. We have to rise above the world's interpretations. Anything I give you through speech cannot reach the fineness of love. Have you ever really listened to yourself when you spoke the words, 'I love you'? If you have truly listened then you would know their falseness. Deep in your heart you know how any word lessens the quality of love. So I am not going to use any words. All I am asking you to do during our exercise this morning is to be conscious of the love that you are, without a subject, without an object."

This time she asked us to stand and join hands. She introduced the sound 'vammm', very gentle at first, then slowly rising to a crescendo much stronger than the crescendo of the previous night. As the resonance touched the highest point the sensation I experienced in my body was far greater than multiple orgasms simultaneously happening. We were tapping into an incredible source of energy and it seemed to be filling the entire room. Then she gradually brought us back down to the softest note while the energy continued to flood through my body. We sat down again and she continued to speak. Her voice was like silk, as the resonance of the sound seemed to linger in the air around us.

"We are entering a sacred place and we must tread gently. A door is being opened to avail of the energy that is going to bring us closer to the heart centre. We must use it rightly. We must not bring anything with us. We must not carry expectations, not even thoughts. Nor must we take anything from this sacred place."

She asked us to allow our eyes to close as she continued to hum the sound that took me into a stillness and depth in my being that I had never before experienced, not even with the enlightened alchemist who had first awakened my consciousness.

When the meeting concluded we went to sit in the gardens while lunch was being prepared by the staff of the manor. After eating, most of the others retired to their rooms, but I again utilized this time in the library. At three in the afternoon we returned to Andréa and this time the focus was on the navel centre and the sounding of 'rammm'. After supper in the late evening we had our third meeting that was focused on the heart centre and the sounding of 'yammm'. I noticed the chairs had been removed and were replaced by cushions. Andréa had brought us much closer to her and the intensity of our voices had combined into one distinct sound. Elizabeth was directly opposite my eyes and to my amazement her head and upper torso seemed to disappear into a haze of faint light. Strangely, I found nothing unusual about it, even when everyone seemed to gradually fade out of physical sight.

Then something snapped within me. I could sense my body connecting to the beginning of all life and, exactly as Andréa had said, the beginning is now. I could see no past in the subtle reality; neither was I conscious of space or time. There was only nothingness and even that cannot illustrate it, for the word nothing also means something. Nothing cannot stand alone, as it needs something from which to reflect. So I cannot use words to explain it. Like the alchemist had said; "It can only be realized through one's own experience."

I could clearly see the projected reality of the sensory world being real but only in a relative way. Now I was experiencing the subtle reality behind the sensory projection. The consciousness, or the natural intelligence of my body had been speeded up to allow me to see it. But I, the person, was not there, nor was there a mental process to record it. As I dissolved more and more into the subtle, or the nothingness behind all things, I was able to see the reality behind existence being so indescribable that, while seeming to be nothing, yet it is everything in totality. Now I know why it cannot be explained, because the absolute cannot be accessed through the mind.

JULIE

I had the privilege to clearly see that the relative nature of the sensory projection is the continuum of existence as it is known. It is the state of being all that is, yet it is grossly limited and is merely a projection of the reality behind the sensory phenomenon. The human condition arising out of the projected phenomenon is the thinking mind, which is nothing more than the reflection of human ignorance endeavoring to create permanence where there is, nor can be, none. Through this endeavor the existence being perceived by the senses has its formation from which the dichotomy forms as the root of all conflict. Apparently, we are this far removed from our true nature.

Again we commenced at six on the following morning. Andréa introduced us to the throat centre and the sounding was 'hammm'. Elizabeth had difficulty here and Andréa placed her in the centre of the tight circle while she led the rest of us with the sound. She had asked us to focus our energy on Elizabeth to help release her from the emotional blockage holding her back. I could see how the combined focus was working as the obstruction in Elizabeth's energy field was gradually cleared.

The afternoon session was focused on the mental centre and the sounding of 'ommm'. Before Andréa commenced she asked us to lie down in a circle with our feet almost touching and she stood in the middle. The mellowness of her voice was like the gentlest music as she softly spoke. She helped us all to relax and then she explained that we were about to raise the consciousness to a higher plane. She held her outstretched hands high above her head and she instructed us;

"I am going to ask you to stand up in a tight circle around me and to raise your hands above your heads to touch mine. We are going to chant all the chakra sounds, ending in 'ommm'. If the energy gets too fine to bear then please lie down. Do not force yourself to continue. Force can be very dangerous at this level. Not only can it damage you but it can also damage the group."

The chant commenced with 'lammm' and by the time we had reached the heart charka there were only five still standing. Maura gave way at 'yammm' and Caroline lay down as we were passing through the throat charka. Tracy and I were the only ones standing as Andréa led us through the lower scales of 'ommm'. It was a strange sensation as the three of us continued to ascend. Slowly Andréa took us closer to the top and then she stopped, seconds before we reached the climacteric.

She re-commenced, descending the scales back to the base sound of 'ommm' where she motioned for us to sit. Gradually she guided the sound back into the silence and she sat there for some time in a meditative state. Some of the others had fallen into a deep sleep, including Maura and Caroline, to my great surprise. Finally Andréa opened her eyes and with a faint smile she whispered;

"I had to stop where we did. I have not taken it this far before with new initiates."

I felt a little disappointed as I sat there on the cushion eagerly waiting to continue. But Andréa had given us all she had been ready to give at that moment. As she quietly got up to leave the room she put a finger to her lips motioning silence, thus allowing the others to rest where they were, asleep on their cushions. Tracy closed her eyes in meditation, leaving me as the only one awake to the immediate situation. I sat there for a little while longer and then I left the room to walk in the gardens. Gradually the others began to appear just as the bell was sounding for evening tea.

The final meeting was at six-thirty where Andréa spoke for thirty minutes and then she invited questions from all of us present. But I had nothing to ask her. It had been an extraordinary experience and I was more than content with myself. Tracy from Leicester gave me her address and telephone number, as did some of the others. But for me, meeting again in anything less than our experience together did not make any real sense.

I thanked Maura on our way home in the car. She had helped me regain what I had lost to my father. Yes! I had lost my equilibrium through my own attachment to that particular image I held of him. Now my initial awakening by the enlightened alchemist had again been re-sparked by Andréa. But this time it was much stronger. Not only did I have it back, but I also had the additional experience of having it previously and losing it, and that made me determined never to lose it again.

Now I ask myself; am I losing it at this moment?

In its light I can see I was true to the situation and I acted accordingly. I did what I was obliged to do with nothing personal at play, even though I cannot expect the world to understand.

But the alchemist did say; "The world is not life, it is merely a mental imposition reflecting its many levels of ignorance on the screen of existence."

The weekend with Andréa and the others was a clear reaffirmation of these words. Here now it is the life and the love within me, the only reality to be served.

JULIE

Maura's boutique in the West End had really taken off. It was becoming popular for the celebrities and this in turn boosted business enormously. It was obvious that Maura had a natural ability to surf on the front face of fashion. In the short time of its existence the boutique had become a fashion leader. Not alone that, but she had managed to establish her own design logo that featured on a television broadcast.

She was beginning to play with the idea of opening a third boutique in Knightsbridge with me as its new manageress. But Penelope, the manageress in the West End, was eager to hold on to me as her assistant. The West End suited me better and it was convenient for my Spanish classes. Also, I felt I was in the right place to learn more about the business. I had the added opportunity of going on buying trips with Maura, as well as to fashion shows and to schools of art and design.

After discussing the pros and cons of the new idea Maura concluded that we should not move too fast. The boutique in the West End was still very new and it needed delicate handling. We all needed much more experience in the up-market location before we could safely expand to another. Maura could also see that I was developing a good eye for fashion trends on our buying trips together, which, up to that time, were mostly local to the wholesale outlets down the East End of London. I was ready to move further afield and the next buying trip involved a visit to France.

It was my first time to Paris and the three day visit took me through a whirl of leading fashion houses as well as attending a gigantic fashion show and mingling with designers and buyers from all over the world. I was in my element and my age played a major part to the amount of attention I was receiving. Soon I began to see that the majority of producers were eager to see where my focus was being directed. For them it was all about keeping abreast on the volatile world of fashion. They knew that the youth are more often than not the trendsetters for future designs.

Paris expressed itself as the open city of madness. Being mad in this city is being natural, I soon discovered. I also quickly realized that Paris is not just the capital of France, rather it is seen as the fashion and cultural capital of the western world. We spent an afternoon enjoying the shops and the art in the Louvre followed by coffee in a café on the Champs Elysées with two lady designers from New York who had very unusual ideas.

Maura had introduced me to all her acquaintances as her personal assistant and she allowed me a free hand in choosing the colours and designs for our winter stock. It was not at all difficult. I only focused my attention on the designs that I would like to be wearing myself.

Within weeks of our return the new stock arrived at the boutique and Penelope allowed me to do all the window displays. We were quite amazed at the response. Each day the shop filled with a younger age group of new customers who had a lot of money to spend. Maura had to double the initial order and within another week she had to double it again. We could hardly get the stock in quickly enough to keep pace with the swelling demand. It was clear that by the end of the month we should have more than trebled our expected turnover. Much of the credit was given to me, but obviously, it was all due to Maura who had taught me well in the trade.

In the middle of this growing exuberance on the business scene I stayed over with Catherine and Patrick one night at their place in Notting Hill. Patrick mentioned he had just received a short email from Mar's friend, Cristina, telling him in poor English that Mar had been hospitalized undergoing psychiatric treatment.

I asked did he have any more details and he said the email message was short. He could only gather from it that she was in the psychiatric wing of the main hospital in Granada and she expected her to be there for a long time. He said that he had replied to Cristina's email but he got no further response. He also tried to phone Mar several times, but all he got was the recorded message telling him she was not available.

Somehow I knew my father was involved and after my weekend at Andréa's workshop I now fully trusted my instincts. I knew I had to go to her at once, even though it was close to the end of November and the winter scene had been well established in the boutiques. When I later discussed it with Maura she fully understood the situation. But she cautioned me to be extra diligent and careful if my father should have any hand in Mar's condition.

I got a direct flight from London to Malaga and I made my way from there to Granada by bus. It was my first time in Spain and I was glad of the little Spanish I had learned. After getting a taxi from the bus station to the city centre I enjoyed testing what I knew with the driver. It surprised me that I was able to hold a reasonable conversation, even though the man spoke the language something like a cockney half-speaks English. Nonetheless, I did not have difficulty understanding him.

He gave me the address of a good hostel where I managed to get a room for a week. After settling in I bought a detailed map of the city locating the way to the hospital for the following morning. I knew I needed to relax and to have a full night's rest in order to have sufficient energy to meet the situation. I set out to enjoy the rest of the evening exploring the narrow streets and checking out their latest styles in the shops.

Although the weather was similar to what one would expect in an English summer, yet the garments on display were actually heavier than the winter garments in London. It was eight in the evening and the temperature was still over twenty degrees, still people were wearing overcoats and businessmen were wearing suits with neckties. The colours were predominantly dark brown, navy or black. They were not at all adventurous, but I could see they were very fashion conscious. I could sense an insecurity about them, as appearance for them seemed to be very important. It looked as though everybody was trying hard to fit in. I felt that Maura would have no problem being a fashion leader in such a predictable environment.

Later that evening I had a light supper in a café close to the large fountain in Puerta Real. It was well before eleven when I re-entered the street and the night beauty of the city hitting me was almost surreal. Carrera de Genil, a tree-lined walkway, stretched all the way down from the illumined fountain to the clusters of trees by the banks of the river. A full moon was directly in front of me and it appeared as though it was resting on the snow-speckled peaks of Sierra Nevada. To my left I noticed four gigantic trees that were taller than the large buildings surrounding the square. People in elegant attire were strolling in every direction. There was no sense of hurry and little or no movement of traffic. To me it was better than any work of art I had previously seen in the Louvre. This was the real thing, art in motion and I was not separate from it. I could see that these people had their values in order. They appeared to be fully tuned in to life and there was a naturalness about them that allowed them to be in the joy of each moment.

The following morning I enjoyed the typical Andaluz breakfast of freshly squeezed orange juice, followed by toasted bread rolls covered with finely chopped tomatoes and a sprinkling of olive oil. Then I made my way to the hospital, which was about a twenty-minute walk. The staff were most helpful and I found I had no great difficulty understanding them. One friendly nurse went out of her way to guide me to the section where Mar was being kept. I had no disturbing feelings as we came to the psychiatric wing as I had seen it all so many times in my early teens, being at the receiving end. It was not that I had become immune to such feelings, rather it was due to my time with the enlightened alchemist and later with Andréa entering my life. Although I was fully in the world I was seeing there before me, both the good and the bad of it, yet I was no longer of that world in the deeper sense of my being. The door had been opened for me to transcend it all and the only feeling I had left, relating to where I was, seemed to be that of compassion.

When I entered her ward she was sitting on a chair beside the bed and I could instantly see she was in the deepest pit of depression. She looked up at me blankly and there was terrible pain in her heavily ringed, dark brown eyes. I knelt down on one knee in front of her and I just hugged her and hugged her, telling her both in Spanish and English that I truly loved her.

She started to cry, in restrained sobs at first. Then as I squeezed her more tightly, while pumping my energy into her body, she broke into convulsions. I continued to hold her tightly, still telling her I truly loved her and I had come to be with her.

I knew she needed to cry. She needed to release the blocked emotions that had brought on the depression. Then she was saying she was sorry as I expected she would. I was at that moment thankful to my foster father in Dublin for all he had obliged me to learn. I was fully aware of her condition from the inside out. I had been put through it myself and I was therefore in a position to understand it. She needed assurance and I promised her that I was not going to leave her side until she had fully recovered. But she was not even able to listen. I stayed with her for the entire day until well after midnight.

When she was sleeping comfortably I quietly left after telling the night nurse to let her know if she woke that I would be back again at first light. I got a taxi back to the hostel where I grabbed some hours sleep. Then I was up before seven and, after putting the things I considered I would need in a bag, I caught another taxi back to the hospital.

She was awake when I arrived and we shared a bowel of cereal and fresh orange juice together. Very, very slowly she was beginning to come out of herself. We had a pot of tea with lemon at nine when the ward had fully woken to meet the activities of the day. But she was still not saying anything. She needed to be made feel fresh and the nurses were pleased when I managed to entice her into allowing me to wash her hair.

We went to the bathroom together. There was no wash hand basin so I felt there was only one thing for it. I stripped off completely and stepped towards the shower while asking her to do the same. She was reluctant at first so I helped her remove her nightdress. It was then I first noticed the red scars that looked like burn marks on her breasts. But it was not the time to remark on them.

I turned on the shower and gently guided her into the lukewarm water, then shampooed her hair and continued to wash her entire body. Gradually, the colour returned to her skin as I wiped her gently with the towel.

The extraordinary trust mingled with distraught innocence that I saw in her eyes brought me to the point of weeping in anguish. I could see she had been extremely traumatized by whatever it was she had experienced.

I quickly wiped myself and slipped back into my clothes. Then I wrapped a large towel around her and we returned to her ward. I had brought some fresh clothes with me for her to wear, but when I took them out of my bag and laid them on the bed she showed no interest. I had to dress her like I would a child. Then I introduced the hairbrush and she allowed me to brush her hair. When I stopped for a moment to rest my arm she spoke directly for the first time with the simple words; "Thank you, Julie."

I hugged and hugged her and again I told her how much I loved her. Gradually she began to talk, just a little at first with great effort and I allowed her the space to say whatever she wished. When she began to lose control I put my forefinger on her lips and kissed her on both cheeks. She needed to be relieved from any necessity to talk or to explain her condition, so I tried to assure her; "Mar, there is no need to tell me anything. You and I are truly sisters. We can just sit quietly and be together."

That is how the rest of the day passed. We just sat there, holding hands at times, while occasionally I would gently massage her on the shoulders or on the lower back. I would run my fingers through her hair. At times I would caress her face. When she needed to go to the toilet I went with her. Whatever I had to do I was determined not to allow a moment to pass without there being some kind of body contact.

By late evening I could feel her life energy beginning to return. It was very faint, like a light barely flickering on and off. But it was there and that was all that mattered. I knew I had to stay with her throughout that night. The nurse was more than willing and she offered to get me a sleeping chair, but I told her I would not be needing it. Throughout the night as I slipped in and out of sleep I was conscious of the terrible pain flooding in waves through her body. This is how it was in my own experience. When someone is severely traumatized and psychologically damaged the pain can manifest all over, and particularly in the lower centre of the chest as well as the head.

JULIE

Morning arrived and another day passed. I could feel she was slowly healing. The second night together was much the same as the first. But on the third morning I received her first real smile while we were in the shower. It was like the sunshine suddenly breaking through after suffering a month of Irish weather. I hugged her and danced her in and out of the shower cubicle until she finally said; "Jesus, Julie. You're mad."

"Yes, I know it, I know it, and isn't it wonderful," I was singing to her in response.

For the rest of that day we talked on and off about our times together in London. I told her about my experience in Paris and all the places that I was looking forward to sharing with her. I did not try to solicit any information from her relating to her condition. I was very cautious not to even allow such a thought to enter my mind. Having been there myself I was well aware that the intuition can be so astutely sharp under such conditions of pain that the sufferer at times can instantly read what is going on in the minds of those coming close. I had experienced it first hand in those psychiatric hospitals in Dublin as I listened to people telling me one thing while the exact opposite danced in their minds. The state of love is the only real healer and that means being totally honest.

The third night was much better and it pleased me when Mar cuddled me back, particularly when she wrapped her legs around me, which indicated that her genital energy was opening to assist in the healing process.

After breakfast on the following day her parents arrived. Having come all the way from San Sebastian, they were delighted with the improvement they saw, and her mother joined me for a coffee in the canteen while her father stayed with her. She told me they had nearly lost her, that she had almost hemorrhaged to death before someone had found her on the street. After being rushed to hospital, she was a week in intensive care before she was transferred to the psychiatric wing.

I could gather from her that she was finding it hard to accept that her daughter could possibly be in need of psychiatric care. She was doubting the knowledge of the doctors. With my limited Spanish I could not enter the necessary depth of discussion that would be required to help her realize her own condition and how damaging it could be to Mar's recovery. Action speaks louder than words, I thought, so I returned immediately to the ward, lay on the bed beside Mar and put my arm around her for the remaining time of their stay. When they eventually left I could feel the excess tension gradually leaving her body. It was unlikely they would be back for some time as San Sebastian was at least a full day's journey away.

That night I returned to the hostel and after having a long chat on the phone with Maura she gave me the okay to stay on for another week. During the days that followed Mar continued to recover and she began to talk more freely about her family life. She told me she had one brother named Carlos who was working in an engineering plant in Bilbao. She had a long-term boyfriend before she left home and he now had a permanent job in a factory. Her parents were very conservative. Apparently, they would have much preferred to see their daughter settled locally with him, being a housewife and mother rather than wasting her time with universities. But she still did not volunteer any information about her more immediate situation and I was careful not to disturb her by prying.

We were both the same size in clothes and she was beginning to enjoy wearing my louder colours. By the middle of the second week she had allowed me to dress her in four different styles. I had become a familiar face in the hospital and I was being accepted by most of the staff, in particular a young doctor named Ángel who had just recently qualified. Mar was the first to notice his interest in me and she encouraged him to ask me for a date. At last she was starting to come out of herself.

The ward doctor was also pleased with her progress and he indicated that she would soon be well enough to go home. But the possibility of this disturbed her rather than pleased her. When I asked her why, she told me she never again wanted to return to what she had to leave behind her. Again I tried to assure her of being there for her all the way. "Whenever you are ready to talk about it, Mar, you know I am here to listen."

"I know that, Julie and I thank you for not asking, like the others. It's over and I want it to stay over forever."

"Perhaps, you might like to go back to San Sebastian?" I cautiously suggested.

"Julie!" She exclaimed in a voice of disbelief at what I had just said. "You must be joking! Have you any idea what it would be like for me there?"

She paused for a moment and sunk back into herself. Then she cautiously remarked: "It wouldn't be safe."

Having brought her this far in her delicate recovery I was conscious of not allowing her to regress, so I did not try to get her to expand on her last comment. Later that evening as we were strolling in the hospital grounds I suggested she could return to London with me. I reminded her how Maura had engaged her before and there might be the possibility of a job, particularly with the Christmas rush being so close. She did not object to the idea so we left it at that until I would have time to discuss it with Maura.

When I did discuss it with her that night on the phone she sounded a little apprehensive.

"Are you sure she is well enough to travel," was her first concern.

She went on to caution; "Working could be much too stressful for her so soon. I feel she would need at least a month if not more in quiet rehabilitation before she could be expected to face the world again."

She asked me for a contact number so she could call me back the following morning, as she needed to do some checking with her friends. I gave her the hospital's number and the extension number to the ward. She phoned on the following morning as we were having breakfast. She told me she had been speaking with Elizabeth who had been with us at the workshop weekend and she would love to have Mar stay with her for as long as she wished.

Elizabeth's house was in Uxbridge, which was quite close to Maura's. Not alone that, but she was involved in work relating to an organization in Guatemala and she could do with someone who was fluent in both languages. I was over the moon with the news, but when I relayed it to Mar she seemed uneasy. I could see that her confidence had been badly damaged and she needed a lot of assistance to get back to the basics. I tried my best to convince her but she was not really listening.

"Mar, we'll be less that fifteen minutes from each other. Let's give it a chance. If it does not suit you then you can stay with me for as long as you wish."

"But Julie, how can I go? How can I get out of here? Look at me. I have nothing, no clothes, no money, nothing!"

I understood how she felt. I had been in a similar situation when I was only fourteen. I was institutionalized for six weeks, being fed all sorts of drugs and I would probably still be there if it were not for a particular nurse who had managed to talk sense into my mother on that particular occasion. I could easily recall how quickly the institution had become my refuge from him. I sensed that Mar was in a similar position. There was something out there causing her great fear and she was not yet ready to confide in me fully. The most expedient way I could help, I felt, her was to clear her path from the outside.

"If it is too difficult for you to return to your place for your things, allow me to go for you, Mar. I can bring back whatever you need."

"Julie, I couldn't ask you to do that. I don't even have the keys," she replied.

She was not yet ready to take that step so I let the matter rest by changing the subject. The following morning I took her out to a café for breakfast. Ángel had mustered up the courage to ask me for a date and I had gladly accepted on the one condition that it would be a breakfast engagement. This gave me the perfect excuse to ask Mar for assistance. She knew exactly what I was trying to do. She could see I was using the opportunity to entice her back into the outside world and she was having none of it until I pleaded with her:

"Mar! How can I face him alone? You know it would not be proper. And my Spanish isn't near good enough to understand him, so you have to help me. It would be a disaster without you."

After much persuasion she reluctantly agreed. Then I introduced the new clothes I had with me for both of us to wear and it sparked her attention. I grabbed her by the hand and skipped with her to the shower where we splashed and laughed together. When we returned to the ward she suggested that I should wear the dress that I had intended for her and she chose the fawn trousers suit for herself. Then hand in hand, we were on our way back into the world and the feeling was good.

The café was on the Grand Via close to a fish and meat market and it was a good twenty-minute walk from the hospital. Even though the weather was like an English summer's day I soon noticed that my light dress was attracting undue attention. It was not long before I realized that all the women were in trousers and some of the looks I got, especially from the women, made me feel as if I was walking the street in a skimpy bikini. It helped me understand how Mar felt about her family and why she wanted her freedom from them, even though she was just as conservative by choosing the trousers suit instead of the colourful dress.

Ángel was already seated in the café when we arrived and he jumped to his feet to greet us. In a flash he said it all with his eyes. He loved my dress, but not in December! However, his personal image was untarnished because Mar was also present and dressed in appropriate attire. We had a lovely morning together and after breakfast we walked up to a special ice-cream shop in Plaza Nueva. I liked the way he shared his attention equally with both of us and he included Mar when he expressed his wish to see me again.

After saying our goodbyes to Ángel, Mar took a notion to visit a friend when we were making our way back to the hospital, remembering she had left a spare set of keys with her. Fortunately, this friend was in at the time and equally as fortunate she was unaware of Mar being in hospital. After collecting the keys we immediately left after a short exchange of the usual small talk. A little while later when we were crossing through a small square of trees Mar stopped and exclaimed;

"Julie! I'm going back with you to London. Promise me you won't let me change my mind."

I hugged her with joy. She pointed to the street where she had been living and she asked me to later collect the few necessary things for her and to put everything else in the green dustbins that were located directly across the street from the front door.

"Julie, it's the only way I can do it" she said. "If I have to go up that street again I know in my heart it will suck me back in."

JULIE

We talked to the doctor in the hospital later that afternoon and he could see no reason why Mar could not be discharged the following day. After all, she was twenty-one years old, she had been transferred to the psychiatric wing for the care and treatment she needed and she had not been committed there by family or any public authority. The decision was hers to make and her discharge would be at the doctor's discretion.

That evening I made my way alone to her flat. It consisted of one room with a small kitchen and a bathroom. The furniture was sparse and I found her rucksack on top of the wardrobe. I sorted out the things she had listed, her passport, the purse with her identity and credit cards, her personal items and her clothes.

Then I set about packing everything else into plastic bags for the dustbin. That's when I noticed the photos that had been taken and developed in Columbia. I was totally shocked when I came across some with my father and Mar together. It was definitely him. I could clearly recognize him even though his hair was black and he was wearing dark glasses. I checked her passport and sure enough it was stamped showing that she had been there for four weeks during August and September. There were some other photos of them together in Granada and I clearly recognized the Alhambra in the background. Then there was one of him without the glasses and that left me with no doubt. My first reaction was to confront her.

But when I cooled down I soon realized I would only be serving my anger by doing such a thing. I had already known, even before I came to Granada and I was surprised with my initial reaction when I was presented with the hard evidence. I put them aside and continued to clear things away. Then an envelope fell onto the floor with a message inside it. I knew it had something to do with my father even before I had taken it out to see what it said. It was in Spanish but the handwriting was definitely my father's. Translated it would have read: 'This is the money for the job. Get it done right away. Be sensible, Mar. You know it's the only way.'

It was payment for a job he was asking her to do. Suddenly, it all fitted together. Her mother had said that Mar almost hemorrhaged to death before she was found and rushed to hospital. I could only conclude that it must have been money for an abortion.

The money I had given him in Earls Court flashed through my mind. I wondered did it carry such bad energy with it. Was I partly to blame? I was being spun back into the mode of the superstitious mind until I recalled what the alchemist had said about superstition.

"All things are interconnected and interrelated. There may appear to be many parts on the surface of things, but behind it all there can be nothing separate from the whole. Superstition is merely the demonstration of not being able to see this clearly."

I put the note and the envelope into a rubbish bag and I continued to clean up. The photos were the last things I threw out. As I did I noticed a piece of paper with a list of ingredients in the top of the plastic bag. It looked like a recipe for making a cake. Something caused me to read it more closely and then I began to realize it was a list of items needed for making a bomb. I was truly shocked, because the list was in Mar's own handwriting. I was familiar with most of the words, but I had to be absolutely sure, so I put it into my pocket, later to confirm it with the help of the dictionary.

No wonder she needed to make a clean break, I thought to myself. I went through her flat once more and made certain there was nothing left behind. After that I hauled the five plastic bags filled with rubbish down to the dustbins that were lined up like soldiers at the opposite side of the street. Then I returned for her rucksack and dropped it off at the hostel. Before I went back to Mar at the hospital I checked the words in the dictionary and then I was sure. As it was in her own handwriting, therefore, Mar had to be in some way involved in terrorism.

Was it my father who had led her astray? I wondered. That night in Earls Court I remembered how he had promised me he would never return to his past. But, at the same time he had thanked me for giving him a new direction in his life. I wondered if this was what he meant. He might have given up his past with the IRA, but he had not given up his activities as a terrorist. I knew that Columbia was a heated place for acts of terror and violence. What other reason could he have had for being there with Mar other than hiring out his own expertise? When she first met my father and I in the café in Oxford Street it seemed a coincidence at the time. But now I was beginning to feel that she might have been already with him before then.

The alchemist again flashed into my mind with an abrupt reminder to beware of my imagination running wild and to keep my feet on the ground. Like the recipe for the bomb in my hand, I had most of the ingredients to solve the puzzle. Now all that was needed was to put them together. Acting logically with a clear mind means there is no imagination involved.

It was time to return to the hospital. Hurriedly, I changed into my jeans and made tracks. On my way I tore up the list into little pieces dropping bits into street bins along the way. This helped to put all of it out of my mind. When I arrived in the ward with a happy smile on my face I could see the worried tension disappear from hers.

"Mission complete, Mar. I have your rucksack safely in the hostel. No need to worry about anything. The dustbins are full and the flat is as clean as a whistle."

I stayed with her until well after midnight and we talked only about the present and future. On my way back to the hostel that night I purposely walked by her flat and I was glad to see the bin men had been and all evidence of her past should by now have passed through the incinerators.

The following morning I was with her again before nine and at eleven we were ready to leave as soon as Mar had signed all the relevant papers. While she was in the office attending to this Ángel appeared with his phone number. When I told him I was returning to London and we would not have time to meet again, he was most insistent and he said if it meant going to London to take me out to dinner then he would do it. I gave him the phone number of the boutique and I told him I would be looking forward to it. During our little conversation in Spanish his name was being called over the intercom. He kissed me on both cheeks, then looking straight into my eyes, unexpectedly he kissed me full on the lips. It was beautifully innocent and with the suddenness of it, the only thing I could say was, "Wow!"

He laughed with delight as he danced down the corridor, spinning three times while blowing me more kisses. I stood there dazed, as I waved at him and finally blew him one back.

Mar emerged from the office and we were on our way. Our first stop was an Internet café where we managed to organize two seats from Malaga to Luton for the following morning. Mar seemed very anxious to leave Granada as soon as possible, so we collected our gear from the hostel and got a taxi to the bus station. That night we spent quietly together in a hostel in Malaga.

On the plane I assured her that I would be always there for her, no matter what. I told her about the alchemist and how I wished to share with her all that had been given to me. Although most of what I was trying to say was falling on deaf ears, yet I knew she needed a confidant if she were to get through what was still eating at her insides. She nodded quietly as I spoke, but without really allowing any of it to register. I could see she was very closed and no matter how hard I tried to break through her barriers she still was not forthcoming.

I could well understand how difficult it must have been for her to open her heart to me. Although I was her closest friend at the time, yet my father was clearly the cause of her anguish. Obviously, she needed more time, as did the entire situation. I decided to let things rest and I lay back in my seat next to hers to enjoy the rest of the flight. Shortly before noon we had landed to be met with the Christmas spirit of England.

It was a great relief for me to be back at last where I knew Mar would have a real chance to recover with the added help of her neutral friends, and I felt good in myself having been there for her when I was most needed.

I had been her rock of strength at the time, yet how far away now it all seems as I find myself struggling to hold onto my own sanity with my consciousness precariously edging towards crashing again on the particular.

We caught the train from Luton to Euston station. As it was winding its way into the city Mar expressed a wish to visit Catherine and Patrick in Notting Hill.

It was a Saturday and Catherine was busy in the boutique, but Patrick was there to greet us. It was actually good for Mar because it gave her a feeling of home. The three of us had a lot in common, not only the conflict resolution course but also our discoveries of the city together during those months stretching from early January to summer.

We stayed there all afternoon and when Catherine arrived at seven she was so delighted with female company that she invited Mar to live with them. Mar's eyes opened wide with delight and she immediately accepted. In the plane she had expressed how she felt uneasy about staying with people she did not know and I had to agree with her, so I was more than thankful how things seemed to be working out in her favour. It was also a big relief for me. Now I felt my job had been done and I was happy to get home at last to Ealing. Maura and Paul were pleased to see me and they were anxious to hear the news about Mar and my experiences in Granada.

For some days following my return everything seemed a little strange and it took me a while to settle back into my normal routine. Mar hung out at Catherine's for the weeks leading up to Christmas and I saw her as often as I could. She seemed to be doing reasonably okay under the dire circumstances, but she still had some way to go before she would be fully back to herself. One day in the boutique Catherine remarked how Mar seemed to be having problems sleeping. Apparently, she was having regular nightmares and they seemed to be getting worse. It made me decide it would be better to talk with her and help her get everything off her mind. She needed to be freed from the scourge of her conscience. From my own experience I could tell this was her problem and the cause of her nightmares, so I made arrangements to see her when she was on her own. It was my duty as her friend to break her from the mode of torturing herself. I knew she would not open up to me willingly when she had not already done so, therefore, it would have to be in the form of a direct confrontation. Eventually, when I got her alone I sat down in front of her and opened;

"Mar, I am here as your best friend and I am going to help you whether you like it or not. Before I went to Granada I already knew about your relationship with my father. When I was there I found out about the money he gave you to undergo an abortion."

She looked both shocked and relieved without saying a thing as she sat there staring at me with her mouth open. Knowing she needed to get the weight of it all off her shoulders I did not stop there when she still showed no sign of response.

"Mar, I am even aware of your activities in Columbia."

"Columbia? What do you know about Columbia? she anxiously inquired.

"I know you were there with my father and I can only guess what he was up to, but I know it could not be anything good."

"You think you know. But you know nothing, Julie. You have no idea," she opened.

"Mar, he is a terrorist and he got you involved as well."

"It's not true, Julie. I was the one who got him involved. I introduced him to those people."

"What people, Mar?"

"You met them in the café that day. Don't you remember Fernando and Cristina?"

"But they were your college friends from Granada?"

"No, they weren't. Fernando is an activist with ETA and they were here solely to do a deal with your father. At first I thought they had come to see me. But it wasn't the case. They used me, Julie."

"How did you know them, Mar?"

"Jesus, Julie! I was brought up in San Sebastian. Most of the people I know there are Basque separatists."

"What was the deal with my father?"

"He's an expert with explosives. In their circles everyone knows how good he is; they were buying his expertise and that was their real reason for being here."

"And Columbia?" I pried.

"That's when I saw the real thing," she quietly replied.

"What do you mean, Mar?" I asked.

She hesitated. I had to ask her again while telling her that I was there to help her get over whatever it was she needed to get over. I worked hard to convince her that her health was my one and only concern. Still she was not willing to speak any more about her experience in Columbia. I went on to remind her;

"Mar, there is nothing on the face of this earth that could shock me. I want to help you mend, so you must not hold anything back. If you do, it will eat away at your insides until it drives you bonkers. I know what it's like, Mar. I have spent more time than I should have with people who were driven insane by the stuff they had tried to bottle up. I do not want to see it happening to you. I have helped you this far. It is in your own interest, so please tell me now and be finished with it for good."

Her reluctance was beginning to waver. She looked at me directly for a moment as though she was about to continue. Then I could see the distrust and confusion coming back in her eyes. Having further reassured her that I was only concerned for her health and for that reason alone she should get everything off her chest, she gradually opened a little further. But little did I know I was about to be totally stunned by what she was so reluctantly going to tell me.

"We planted a bomb in a restaurant. I carried it in and left it by the toilets. It wasn't supposed to go off so soon. That's what I had understood. But it exploded within minutes after we left. There was no warning."

"People were killed?" I asked.

"It's too much, Julie! Children were killed! Moments before the explosion I was talking to a mother who had two beautiful young children with her. They were going into the toilet. Now they're dead because of me."

"My God, Mar! I am shocked."

"I know, Julie. How can I forgive myself? The explosion had nothing to do with nationalist causes. It was gang warfare and your father and I were hired killers. I had no idea it was like that until I read it in the newspapers the following day."

"But why did you do it, Mar?"

"Why did I do it? I didn't know what I was doing. Maybe it was due to me being a passive supporter of ETA throughout my school years. We were even influenced that way by some of our teachers."

"But Mar, that cannot excuse what you did in Columbia."

"Yes, I know. Jesus! I know. I had no idea what I had allowed myself to become. I'm poison, Julie. I don't even deserve to live."

"No, you are not poison, Mar. We are facing this together and we are going to overcome it. You must not blame yourself. They were many others involved along the way. You are not to blame for them."

It was a very delicate situation for me to handle as I was finding it almost impossible to retain my shock when suddenly faced with the full extent of her activities. Not alone that, but I was equally as shocked with myself for failing to see the evil side of my own father. Not only was he a killer beyond all redemption, but he had callously destroyed the life of my dear friend. I had no grounds to disbelieve her. It had to be true. Mar finally interrupted the heavy silence.

"What I did in Columbia was supposed to be my initiation into active service. I was out of my mind! People were not supposed to be killed. At least that's what I was led to believe by your father who had talked me into it."

"But how could it have been your initiation into ETA when you were with him in Columbia at the time?" I questioned.

"Your father has years of experience and ETA hired him not only for his expertise with explosives but also to train in new recruits. He's still doing it in Spain right now. The last explosion in Malaga was part of his doing. I even know the Columbian woman he was with at the time. She's the one who introduced me to the quack who did the abortion when I fully believed she was my friend. Then I discovered while I was being butchered the two of them were screwing together in his flat just up the street. Jesus, Julie! I walked in on top of them when they were at it! They don't give a shit about anyone! I had stupidly believed him. He'd told me I was the only woman in his life. I planted bombs for him! I had an abortion for him! When I opened the door they didn't even stop! He just looked at me and asked what did I want! I was shocked and I ran blindly down the street. That's how the hemorrhaging started."

My God! This was my father! This was the man who had also become my own obsession, a man I was unable to see because of the fatherly image I was desperately creating to please my wilful self. I could fully understand how Mar had been taken in by him. I could see she was being absolutely truthful and how terrible it must have been for her. But I was even more shocked with myself as a part of me was searching for a flaw in her account so I could give him the benefit of any doubt that might arise in my mind. "Mar, you are free from them now. You never have to go back," I tried to assure her as I fought against my own personal interests.

I knew I was pulling at straws as I tried to accept the horror of her experience. In my heart I could see no way out for her and, being so close, it was not possible for me to hide it. The alchemist had told me that the solution to every problem is within the problem itself. But it can only be seen when one faces the truth of the situation. At that moment I was having difficulty in my own heart when confronted with the truth relating to my father and this was only a personal image being shattered. But Mar was facing the cold reality. Is it possible to face such a terrible truth? Could there possibly be a way back to normal life for her? She clearly picked up my thoughts as she directly replied;

"No, I can never be free. There is no way out for me. I have to be either with them or against them. There can be no middle ground with these people. Now I am much too dangerous. I know too much. They will find me and kill me. I know they will."

I could see she was right. There was no middle ground. She was trapped into being an active terrorist for the rest of her life. She had been induced into it when she did her first job. The results were hard for her to accept and that would have been expected. These people knew the score. Her next job would have less severe effects on her nerves and so it would continue until she would eventually be a cold-blooded killer just like my father. I had to sit down and think it out with her.

"Mar, we can overcome this; there has to be a way out. We have to thread very carefully and surely we will find a way together. The first pact we must make is vow that neither of us talk about this to anyone. It is far too delicate right now, for the most important is your well-being."

She nodded in agreement.

"You are very exposed where you are at the moment. My father has this address; stupidly, I gave it to him as a contact point before I had known the full extent of his character."

"Fernando and Cristina also know it, Julie. Don't you remember they were here with me visiting Patrick last summer?" she had to remind me.

"Come to Ealing with me now and we can meet Elizabeth. She is going to be at Maura's. You can go with her tonight and nobody will be able to find you there," I suggested.

"Julie, I can't. I promised Catherine that I'd be at her gig in Putney. Patrick is coming as well and also Claus who is back in London. I need to get out. I need to escape from my mind. What I've done is unforgivable. I don't know how to live with this terrible guilt. If I stay cooked up my conscience is going to drive me insane."

She had made up her mind to go and there seemed to be no way of changing it. I would have liked to have gone with them but I had to return to Ealing as Elizabeth had planned to call with a videotape of Andréa speaking to a group of women in New York. Tracy from Leicester was staying over with her for the night and I was eager to meet them again. I loved the calmness of Maura's world, but Mar was obviously different. She was more into the speed of the discos and excitement in general. An evening in Maura's house would not have been suitable for her.

If I had that evening back again I would have been more forceful with her. I would have insisted that she escape with me there and then, instead of agreeing with her to do it the following evening. That very night Mar disappeared and two days later the terrible news arrived. We were all devastated. She had been dancing with the same guy for most of that night. He seemed to be a very nice person according to Patrick and Claus and neither of them saw anything sinister in it. Nor did Catherine, not even when Mar announced to them that she was going on to a party with him somewhere near Pimlico.

They were not unduly concerned when Mar failed to show up the following day. When I called at six in the evening to let her know I was on my way to collect her, it was Catherine who answered the phone. She told me Mar had not yet returned from her Saturday night on the town.

Instantly, I knew there was a problem. When I questioned Catherine about the night she told me it was the first time she had seen the guy. But Mar was all over him, she told me. It seemed as if he was someone she had been with before. I was the only person who had knowledge of the entire situation and I knew I had to act. There and then I insisted that we report her as a missing person to the police in Notting Hill. Catherine and her brother Patrick tried to dissuade me, but eventually they relented when they began to see my seriousness after I arrived.

The policewoman at the desk was not too helpful either. She told us there was nothing unusual about a twenty-one year old woman being missing for even a week after meeting a new boyfriend. She was right, of course. I had no way of explaining to them the danger she might be in. Reluctantly, the policewoman fed Mar's details into the computer. She did it more to relieve my anxiety rather than seeing any real need for doing it.

Monday passed and there was still no sign of Mar. Now I was sure and I had fully resigned myself for the worst. It was just after ten on Tuesday morning when the police called to the flat in Notting Hill. Patrick was there working on his dissertation at the time and he was the first to be told. He went with them to identify the body that had been found floating in the Thames close to Lambert Bridge.

Her parents and brother arrived the following day to collect the remains, but it had to be held over for a full post-mortem to establish the cause of death. Contact had to be made with the hospital in Granada. Then I was obliged to make a full statement and to explain my reasons for wanting her to return to England.

Before her body was finally released to her family for burial in Spain the coroner's verdict had to be concluded and his finding was suicide by drowning. But I could not accept it. In spite of the fact that her situation was grave I knew Mar loved life too much. Even though she was depressed she still would not have been driven to end it in such a manner; of this I was absolutely sure, knowing how well she had endured the terrible traumas already imposed upon her. Mar was a fighter, not a defeatist. It was clear to me they had got to her.

Despite what the alchemist had said about guilt, I still could not help but feel partly responsible. I had not realized the gravity of her situation in time and I had unwittingly left all the doors open for them. I was fully convinced that my father had a hand in her death. He was well aware of her movements and he had been to the Putney gig with her in the past. I remembered the words of sarcasm he used that night when I asked him how did he know where to find me. As cool as a breeze he replied;

"An underground agent has ways of knowing what needs to be known."

I realized there and then that I had a duty to conclude. Should he contact me again there was only one thing left to be done and I was fully prepared to do it. It was not a case of vengeance. I was not being caught up in an eye for an eye and a tooth for a tooth. The enlightened alchemist had raised my frequency much higher than that. It was my duty and mine alone. He had clearly said;

"Be true to the situation as I am true to the situation. Should death knock on my door I am ready to die. Should life call on me to make love, I am ready to make love. Without emotion, without conscience, I am ready to do whatever life asks of me. This is total surrender."

He went on to clarify this statement by reminding us that whatever we are moved to do, we should only do it from the state of love and not from the personal self. Obviously, such deep understanding carries enormous responsibility. One must not use it flippantly, nor must one be ruled by the programmed conscience being inflicted upon us by the psychological manipulators of people.

According to my hearing, when the enlightened master clearly stated that one should be without such a thing as conscience, he explained that the conscience arises out of self-judgment when one is trying to live according to some moral code without being aware of its confinement. He further explained how moral codes can widely differ according to one's beliefs.

I could see that terrorists have a moral code, even stronger than the acknowledged moral code of society in general. My friend Mar got caught up in their code and there was no way out for her. Whether she was killed or took her own life is not the issue. The reality is in the fact that she was being persecuted by her conscience. The more she was driven by it the deeper she became ensnared. She could have escaped by changing her life completely, but she was unable, being ruled by the deeper programme that had to serve itself all the way to its end.

One cannot know freedom when one is trapped in any type of moral code. Mar's death has been an illustration of this to me. As the alchemist had said, there is an enormous difference between the one who does no wrong simply because it is wrong and the one who does no wrong because it is the moral code. The former lives in freedom and the latter suffers bondage. Not only that, but the former lives in the state of love, whereas the latter lives in that of ignorance. The former can know God, but the latter is denied God because of the programmed conscience.

Many things had become clear in the deeper sense and it was quite visible to me how religious institutions in general are no different to terrorist organizations. The religious minds that injected the conscience into Mar in the first instance were no different in essence to the terrorist minds that acted from the same programme.

Whether one believes in a particular god or a particular cause, obviously, it is all ignorance acting itself out according to a particular belief.

At a church service conducted by her family in London, one such Irish priest infuriated me further when he said; "We must pray for the repose of her soul." Is there any way possible for him to realize that the only soul needing help is his own? But I am merely a woman from another confinement and I am not expected to know such things!

I was fully aware that such ignorance abounds in Ireland, both North and South, and all things rising within it, such as the educational systems, politics and business have to be similarly bound. I could see that the reason for this lies in the fact that the initial programme has never been seriously challenged.

We have all listened to priests and other clergy condemning acts of terrorism while at the same time upholding division according to their moral codes. It is more than obvious to anyone with real intelligence how they fail to see the programme. In their lack of vision they cannot understand how they are the ones who plant the seeds of terrorism in the minds of their subjects in the first place. They prepare the ground. In their unseen greed for power over the minds of others they have adopted their priestly positions. That is their first concern, which is plain to be seen whenever an enlightened one strips them of their masks. Division is their foray, it starts with them and from there it travels all the way down the line. The hunger for power does the rest. Then the innocent ones, like Mar, become the disposable fodder.

The priests might think they are above it all. But in the eyes of the greater intelligence there is little distinction between them and the less hidden ones who plant the bombs. They are all terrorists, self-alienated from God, while willing only to serve their ignorance. Try telling that to the moralists of society, or the great upholders of conscience, and one is likely to be silenced, just like the fate that Jesus had met when branded a heretic by the minds of his own people.

Then the Jesus being promoted by the Christian world was supposed to be a man who was free from all moral codes. If he had been restricted by a conscience he would not have been able to transcend the incurable state of the masses. Nonetheless, the priests will give you buckets of reasons why one should be ruled by conscience, for their vested interest is sin. This is their foray. They have their gold plated turrets and their discarded numbers of abused left lying in the gutters of existence in their reckless wake to prove it. And all of this is propped up behind the crucifix of a suffering god! Priests! Rabbis! Terrorists! Are they not all the same ilk?

It fills me with rage whenever I see the ceremonial bullshit they use as they dance upon the misfortunes of others. Mar, my dearest friend, had lost her life because of the moral codes of conscience and separatist beliefs imposed upon her innocence.

Right now I know it is not good for me to be enraging myself when it is of the utmost importance to stay focused on the life immediate. Thankfully, the cold wind sweeping down from Sierra Nevada is biting deep into this anger taking root in my body.

JULIE.

It was a bleak Christmas for all of us. Maura was a real friend in the way she helped me through the deep sorrow I was feeling. Even Paul was showing signs of being upset, although he hardly knew Mar. Catherine and her brother Patrick spent Christmas Day in Ealing and the shadow of Mar's presence hung over us all.

I had told no one about Mar's involvement with terrorists. She was gone and I continued to honour the pact we had made together never to speak about it to anyone. As far as I was concerned it had entered the realm of the sacred and secret where it was meant to stay. But after this terrible night all this has been changed. Now it is part of my duty to speak openly about all of it and to fully vindicate my dear lost friend.

Her death had a profound effect upon me. It was far, far greater than I could have envisaged. In relation to death I recall how I heard the alchemist say; "In the deeper reality there is no such thing as death. Bodies die but the essence of all that you are never dies. You will know this as it occurs in your own experience. That is, if you are fully conscious when it is occurring, having already transcended your fear of death. Most people die unconsciously because of their unfaced fear abetted by their beliefs in some life hereafter that can be nothing more than the transference of their miseries back into the turgid pool of the psyche. But do not take on what I am saying as another belief, another crutch to support your denials. I am telling you how it is solely to help you transcend your fear, so you might see it as it is and accept it totally without putting contamination upon it. Then when it comes to physically dying you might be sufficiently conscious to realize the actual wonder of it; you might even see that life, death and God are one and the same. But the person cannot tolerate such wonderment because the person sees itself as separate from God. It sets itself apart; such is the nature of the self. Thus it obliges itself to create some mind-made idea of a god with a particular heaven as a place for the masses attending the masses. It will go on to create institutions and even have the audacity to appoint its saints to sip at the same table as its notional god. What a blasphemy! What an utter blasphemy to Jesus, the man and to all the enlightened walking upon the earth pointing to truth!"

The power of his directness was enough to dissolve all the dross clogging up the mind. It confirmed everything I had seen in the man whom my mother had married; the one who had attempted to act as my father. His fear of death, his utter denial of reality, had all but destroyed the essence of life within me before I broke free from his clutches.

It was the greatest privilege of my life to have happened upon the alchemist. Right now I clearly know it as I stand here alone looking out at the sleeping world. I have no notion what the morning might bring. I am only sure of the fact that my world has now finished. There is no fear harbouring within me of that moment of physically dying, for death has already passed through me this night.

I recall how the alchemist described what actually happens as one enters the moment of death.

"When the body is about to conclude first you will observe your outer world concluding, or fading away from you. Next you will observe those dearest to you fading away and finally you will even observe your own body fading away from your presence. That is death, but all the time you as the observer behind the observer, so to speak, remain present. At that exact moment, should you be consciously in the now, you will know that you never die. The world is constantly dying, but you never die."

After experiencing the shock of Mar's demise I knew what the alchemist had said about death had to be the truth. Everything else he had said proved to be the truth in my own experience long after he had said it. I was fully confident knowing that Mar in her essence was now even more present than she had been before. But still I was grieving for her physical loss. There was still much for me to understand. I knew the alchemist's words would continue to reveal all to me in the ongoing course of my life as long as I remained fully conscious and did not allow myself to become lost again to the world of feelings, emotions and personal attachments.

It snowed on Christmas Day and it was a delight for Damian. Playing with him in the lawn after dinner helped dissolve much of the gloom in my heart. Children are so delightfully spontaneous, immediate to life, being as free as the birds of the air while still not loaded by the thinking mind. Clearly I could see that adults are the adultery, or the mental contamination of life's essence. Perhaps, this is what Shakespeare had meant us to reflect upon in his seven stages of man where he mentions: 'Last stage of all is second childishness and mere oblivion.'

Childhood, I can now see, is the raw innocence minus the experience of living through the adulteration. The final stage is innocence again, but it is innocence having been processed through experience and, perhaps, even purified for those who are fortunate enough to realize the process. Much of these things have been revealed to me in the happenings of my short life, but the revelations occurred solely because they had been mirrored to me through the enlightened teacher. The simplicity of the truth amazed me. The more I knew the more I realized how little I really knew. I can now even see the personal wilfulness behind wanting to know. In fact there is no need to know anything. Once I totally accept everything exactly as it is, then all that is, is my will at one with the divine and there can be no problem related to that.

JULIE

The hype of the New Year sales consumed most of our attention and the whole of January slipped away without being noticed. Then Ángel called. Penelope had answered the phone and she found it difficult to understand his accent so she hung up on him. He called again later that day and we finally made contact. He was coming to London in early February and he wanted to see me. I was amazed with myself at how I had completely forgotten about him. But his voice immediately brought me back to the sensation I had experienced on that delightful moment of impulsiveness when he kissed me in the hospital foyer.

Maura was filled with excitement when I told her about his intended arrival and she insisted that I should invite him to dinner in Ealing. Paul was somewhat aloof about the idea, which I could well understand, but he did not voice any objections. I felt it better to play it by ear and let events take their course naturally rather than planning ahead, for too much planning spoils the spontaneity.

Ángel arrived in London on a Friday morning and he booked into a hotel in South Kensington. He had managed to get four tickets for the 'The Phantom of the Opera' and he had invited me to bring two of my friends along. When I asked Maura and Paul, Maura was delighted but Paul was either unable or not eager to make it, so my friend Catherine came along instead.

We had arranged to meet in a Swiss restaurant close to Leicester Square at six in the evening. When we arrived he was already there and waiting. I would hardly have recognized him again if he had not got up and approached us. Apart from our one breakfast date when he was casually dressed, I had only seen him in his doctor's gown in the hospital. This night he was wearing an elegant suit of light Denham material beneath a fawn overcoat and scarf. As he approached us Maura looked at him and exclaimed: "Wow!"

Yes, he was very handsome. But he had never registered that way with me before, as we had met heart to heart through my deep concern for Mar and that was what had initially attracted me to him. Now I was feeling coy and bashful when he kissed me on both cheeks. I could feel my body tingling all over and I wanted to be instantly passionate with him. But his Spanish blood was more cultivated than the eagerness pumping through mine. He was in no hurry and he shared his attention equally with the three of us present.

Ángel found it a little strange having dinner before the show. He was not aware that the better restaurants do not stay open that late in London. But he fell into the system of things, even to the speed of the meal and the urgency of the staff to get our table cleared for other customers.

The show was a fantastic experience. I was glad I had not seen it before, for it made it all the more magical being able to experience it with Ángel for the first time. After the performance we went to an ice cream and champagne parlour near Piccadilly Circus where we sat and talked for some time. Ángel was doing very well with the language, even though his level of English was poor. Whenever he spoke to me directly he returned to Spanish, but he always apologized to Maura and Catherine for having to do so.

Then Maura, being the romantic she is, suggested I should take Saturday off and spend the day with him enjoying the city. He was delighted with the idea and thanked Maura profusely, as if she had given him the moon and the stars. Needless to say, I was more than thrilled myself. The idea had already flashed through my mind but I did not speak it. The following morning we met in the restaurant at his hotel in South Kensington for our second breakfast date together. Later we explored the city, as tourists would normally do. We visited Buckingham Palace and had our photographs taken with the colourful guards. We went on to the waxworks, to Saint Paul's Cathedral and ended up at the Tower. We held hands, even hugged a few times. I really wanted to be kissed again like the way he had kissed me in Granada, but it just was not happening. The entire day had passed and the moment had failed to present itself. Something had to be done to break it before we parted to prepare for the night. In my eagerness I grabbed him unexpectedly and kissed him passionately in the middle of the street just before I dashed underground to catch the tube to Ealing.

We had arranged to go out to a later dinner that night and then to the nightclub where Maura had previously taken me. When I got back to Ealing to shower and change I was literally exploding with the sensation of it all. In its purity it was the richest feeling in the world. I must say, I was totally enraptured in the magic. It is quite extraordinary when one really looks at it. Such magic can never be bought, even though the world foolishly endeavours to buy it. When it happens it happens, but it can never be forced, or fantasized. I was experiencing the sensation of love as it is between man and woman, just like I had heard the alchemist say, "it is being fully alive to the moment."

I was experiencing the enormous difference between being in the sensation of love in my body and the feelings that arise through the fantasizing taking place in the mind. I had been extremely fortunate to have been shown this important difference. The alchemist had shown me how to stay with the sensation without thinking about it, thought being the spoiler, then Tracy had shown me how to focus and Andréa had introduced me to the fields of energy that are available to us.

The alchemist had shown me how to stop wasting energy, such as thinking about a future event, like fantasizing about a future lover, for example, like I had done on the previous occasion with Roger Crawford and then being insufficiently alert to see the type of man I was actually meeting. If one cannot stop thinking about it, then when the event arrives one will have nothing left to give, or to see what is being met; the available energy having already been selfishly wasted on the fantasizing. The part of me that can only find existence through the fantasizing mind would, of course, have had its fill, while I as the actual life in this body would be reduced to an empty shell. It was all so perfectly clear, but it only became clear to me as it was occurring in my own experience.

We met at nine by the fountain in Trafalgar Square and this time we both were prepared for that passionate kiss before a word was spoken. When Ángel did try to speak I put my forefinger to his lips and instantly he tuned into the magical silence. Then we strolled hand in hand through the gates into the park where we kissed again and again as we walked. The candlelight dinner was another delight as we consciously lingered upon every taste while sharing the experience together. In the nightclub it was quite similar. I felt that practically all who were there were attracted to the love that was happening between us.

When the night drew to a close Ángel insisted upon accompanying me in the taxi all the way to Ealing. He wooed me passionately every inch of the way and then he kissed me goodnight on the doorstep. The following day he arrived as planned for midday lunch and I introduced him to Paul and Damian. It was a hurried affair because he had to return later that evening to Granada. Again he did most of the talking in Spanish, using me as the translator.

Maura drove us to the airport and she tactfully waited in the car park while I went with him to say our intimate goodbye. We promised each other that we'd meet again within a month and the next time was to be in Granada. As we parted I could sense Mar's presence within me. It was as though she was fully alive in the vitality of the love happening between us. She was not in my thoughts, she was in the sensation of the love in my body. There is a notable difference, I must add, between the thought and the sensation. Mar, as I knew her through my mind, was dead, that had gone, but her essence was still right there. The sensation of her presence was full in the love within me. When the alchemist had said there is no such thing as death in the greater reality he also mentioned;

"You merely dissolve back into the state of harmony or the state of turmoil in accordance with your lights, and you ordain which state it is by the way you live your life."

As for me at that moment, Mar was right at the centre of the love between Ángel and myself.

Maura could hardly stop herself talking about Ángel on the journey back home from the airport. Eventually she paused when she realized I was not responding. I was far too filled with the sensation of it all. Talk can only relate to the world of the mind and the mind has no access to the immediacy of the sensation. Having heard the alchemist clearly identify the distinction between mind and sensation now I was truly realizing his extraordinary wisdom in my own direct experience. After a long silence Maura finally interrupted; "Julie, why are you so quiet?"

"Because I am fully with you, Maura. Ángel has gone, but you are here. As you well know it from our time with Andréa, life is only in the here and now."

This is exactly how it is. When you are fully in the sensation of life without it being disturbed by the thinking mind then the immediacy of the sensation and the love surrounding it is available to everyone in your presence. The reverse is equally true. If you are harbouring hate, jealousy or rage, for example, the psychic intonations emanating from your physical presence adds to the contamination of your immediate surroundings. It is so simple to see it, yet most of us seem to miss it completely.

JULIE

Usually after going through such times of contamination
we fall into a state of guilt for what we have done without
even seeing that guilt is more of the contaminative stuff.
Maura had slipped out of the present as she went on about
the wonders of Ángel after he had left. She was still
holding on to the past and she instantly saw it. Time and
again she had corrected me whenever she found me
musing over some thought that had nothing to do with the
immediate moment. Being with the immediate sensation
of life requires a phenomenal speed of consciousness. Any
thought not relating to the immediacy of action is like
putting one foot heavy on the brakes while the other is on
the accelerator. She blushed and smiled in recognition of
her error and returned closer to the moment by remarking
on the exquisite beauty of the trees and the way they
sparkled in the late evening light. We were back in tune as
a team to dance with life immediate.

February was a quiet month in the rag trade so I took
advantage of the time by enrolling in extra Spanish
classes. I found the language to be user friendly and I had
by now progressed to the advanced level. I also kept close
contact with the remaining students who had opted to do
the masters programme. Ángel was in regular contact via
the Internet and phone, so my days and nights were filled
to capacity.

Soon March arrived and the departure date for my long
weekend in Spain. This time I flew direct to Madrid and
took a connecting flight to Granada. Ángel was still on
duty in the hospital when I arrived at the airport, so I made
my own way by taxi to Puerta Real and booked into a
different hostel to the one I had been in before.

I could not help but feel the pain of my previous visit and I
realized I had more grieving to go through for the loss of
my dear friend, Mar. After getting settled into my lodgings
I walked up to the ice cream parlour we had previously

visited together. Then the cold reality quite suddenly hit me. I broke down in tears in Plaza Nueva. Unable to move any further I sat on a concrete bench and inconsolably wept. A gipsy girl came over and sat down on the bench beside me. She reached out to touch my hand, then she put an arm around my shoulders and tried to comfort me. But I had to go through it. I knew it was a natural process and the only way was to cry it out of my system.

"It's okay," she repeated to me in English and Spanish.

She asked me my name but I was unable to answer. Subsequently, she told me that hers was Mar. It was then that I looked directly at her through the tears. Her ice blue eyes were looking unswervingly at me. She had a stud in her nose and her fair hair was platted in ringlets. But the deep compassion in her eyes was incredible and I could see she was speaking to me directly from her heart.

"Would you like some ice cream, Mar?" I asked through my tears.

She nodded with a smile and together we crossed the road to the ice cream shop. Gradually I began to talk. When I told her I was from Ireland she became very excited.

"You'll have to meet my boyfriend. He has spent more than a year in Dublin. He now speaks very good English."

We chatted for some time and we crossed the street again to the café at the corner where we sat outside and had some coffee. She told me she was originally from Romania and she had been in Granada for some years. She explained that she did not have to adopt the Spanish name, she had been called María at birth. Just like what usually happens to every Spanish María, it had been abbreviated to Mar. Then her boyfriend arrived and I could hardly believe my eyes when I saw him. It was José María. He recognized me at once. I could see it in his deep brown eyes as they instantly lit up with amazement.

"Julie! That's your name. You escaped!" he exclaimed.

"Yes, I escaped," I replied. "But I cannot thank you enough for your help at that critical moment in my life."

"I heard you screaming," he said, "and I wondered what they were doing to you. They had me locked up and I couldn't help you. I could hear a lot of commotion."

"I finally escaped from it all. It took me a while, but I eventually made it. And what did they do to you?" I enquired.

"They kept me locked up for another night. Then they threw me out on the street. But I lost my guitar and flute."

"José María. I am sorry."

"No need to be sorry. I found the flute I was carving. It was in the laneway. It only took me a few hours to finish it and I was back on Grafton Street that evening."

His girlfriend Mar interrupted by putting her hand inside his jacket and taking the flute from his inner pocket.

"Look! This is it, 'tis keeping both of us alive!" in glee she exclaimed.

I instantly recognized the piece of wood. It had the same twist in the middle. But all the holes were carved through and it was shining from wear. Without speaking another word he put it to his lips and started to play the Irish ballad, The Fields of Athenry. It was the sweetest sound I had ever heard. People stopped on the street and they started to gather round the coffee table. The waiter came out with a tray of drinks in his hand. He, too, stopped and listened. The tremor of each note filled the air and seemed to echo and re-echo across Plaza Nueva and all the way up to the Alhambra.

I could hardly stop the tears of joy trickling down my cheeks. I could see such incredible beauty, such natural innocence, and such purity of spirit exuding from him as he spoke his heart through the music. It brought the words of the alchemist to life as I had heard them.

JULIE

"When I am no more in this body do not grieve for my loss, for I am always with you. Should you look deeply enough, you will find me in the heart of everyone playing, singing and dancing the eternal dance of life."

They invited me to have supper with them and I immediately accepted. But I needed to phone Ángel to let him know I would not be seeing him that night. Mar called to one of her friends who was seated in a circle with some others under the trees in the open square and instantly she produced a mobile phone. It was as though the entire Plaza Nueva had gathered to serve me. Without leaving my seat I was through to the hospital. Ángel was located and I could hear the anxiety leaving his voice when I told him.

"Julie, I'm snowed under with work. It's incredible. My relief doctor has phoned in sick. Two elderly patients have died and a third one won't last the night. This has never happened before."

I assured him I was fine, that I needed the rest of the evening to be with my friends and we could meet up the following day. My newfound comrades were more than pleased as we paid the waiter and left for the hills behind the Alhambra. With the cool evening breeze on our faces we strolled together up the valley of the Rio Darro. We crossed over the trickling river on the last narrow bridge before the cobbled street turned left for the Albaycin and the caves of Sacramento. I was being led through the heart of Arabian Spain, still in its thousand-year slumber. The haunted ground spoke the voice of past civilizations, past pains and glories steeped with romantic associations.

After going up the first steep incline we arrived at a balcony overlooking the flush river valley decked with tall, narrow evergreens and a profusion of fruit trees breaking into blossom. On the steep hills at the other side the caves of Sacramento appeared as little designs cut into the face of the cliffs. To our left I could see the mouth of the valley opening up to reveal the rooftops of the ancient city now beneath us. We stood there in stillness as the sun slowly descended behind the distant hills laying beyond the rooftops in the general direction of Sevilla. I took my last look at the north tower of the timeless Alhambra before we continued our precarious journey around the curve of hill.

They led me along a tapering footpath that wound its way upwards through dense undergrowth beneath the variety of trees above and below us. At times the path vanished into the brambles and we had to cautiously find our footing as we edged our bodies around evergreens and oaks that seemed to be precariously clinging to the face of the steep incline. Everything seemed to be so delicately balanced, even the apparent looseness of the ground beneath our feet. There was no sense of permanent structure about it. It felt as though it was instantaneously appearing out of the vast nothingness to accommodate our presence. At times we had to step over trickling little streams finding their way down from the hills behind the Alhambra and the gardens of the Generalife high above us.

We edged our way past a few small caves that suddenly appeared out of nowhere through the dense brambles. The solitary inhabitants did not seem too perturbed. Then our journey continued until we reached a fork in the path. From there I took my last look at the valley and then followed my friends as they climbed upwards into the hills. Eventually we reached our destination as night was descending upon us. I had expected a cave but it turned out to be a wooden hut with a door and window built against the face of a cliff. It looked quite small from the outside but when we entered I was utterly amazed. When Mar lit some scented candles the huge room seemed to go on and on into the belly of the mountain. I was absolutely stunned. It was so simple, yet so extraordinary. Mar took me by the hand and exclaimed; "Let me show you, Julie. There's even a bathroom!"

She led me deeper into the cave towards the sound of trickling water. We squeezed through a narrow opening that revealed a small chamber with water dribbling in through the roof and disappearing through loose stones on the floor.

"When it rains it turns into the best power shower in Granada," she laughed.

When we returned José María had emptied the bag he had been carrying and he had laid out the food on the wooden table. It was a feast of watermelons with assorted fruits, cured ham, bread, cheese and milk. The hunger instantly grabbed me. It was the same sensation I had experienced with him when he had returned that evening to the hut in Dublin. My taste buds were ecstatic as we sat down on cushions to savour the food.

I could see how both delighted in my company. This was their private place, their inner chamber of love hidden away from the crazy world and I knew how privileged I was to be there. I could feel the presence of my dear friend Mar dancing through every shadow being created by the flickering candles. After we had eaten, José María sat outside and played soft music into the starry night as Mar and I talked ourselves to sleep on the cushions and rugs.

At daybreak I awakened to the nature sounds of the forest. Mar was sleeping by my side on the left and José María was sleeping on my right. Before he slept he had placed a large rug over the three of us. I lingered there snugly until they eventually woke when the morning sun blazed in through the tiny window. We had apples for breakfast followed by herbal tea before we made our descent back down to the city. The views were equally as stunning as they had been the evening before. By the time we had reached nature's balcony overlooking the green river valley we could hear the contrasting sounds of civilization coming up to greet us. The north tower of the Alhambra came back into view, as did the rooftops of the city. For my companions it was another day on its streets bringing music to the hearts of its people. For me it was meeting again with Ángel, the love in my heart. I was fully alive, fully recharged with the sweet energies of life pulsing through my body.

I insisted on treating them to a full Andaluz breakfast in the café on the Grand Via where I had previously been with Ángel and my dear friend Mar. It seemed as though she was fully alive in my heart and urging me to do so. José María and Romanian Mar snuggled together at the same table where I had sat before with Mar and Ángel. But this time it was I who had to play gooseberry. Later we parted company at Plaza Isabel after embracing and leaving it completely to life to bring us together again.

The receptionist in the hostel gave me a message from Ángel. He had been on duty for most of the night and he was getting some rest. But he would be calling to the hostel at noon. After showering and changing into a dress I decided to call over to his apartment near Plaza Trinidad, seeing that it was yet not eleven o'clock.

When he opened the door in his dressing gown he was momentarily stunned to see me through the sleep in his eyes. We embraced and passionately kissed. To his further amazement I slipped off his gown from his shoulders, while slipping off my shoes and dress. Then I guided his naked body back into the bed and there we remained for the entire day making gentle yet vigorous love. In the late afternoon we showered together and our love-play continued. It was close to midnight when we eventually went out to a restaurant in the Albaycin that overlooked the Alhambra. Ángel had a candlelit dinner pre-booked and, even though we were late, they were still holding the table for us. Our bodies were still in the heat of our lovemaking as we savoured each bite of food and each sip of wine. This has to be absolute paradise, I thought to myself. Nothing could possibly spoil it.

But why did I have such a thought? What was its reason? I knew it was not rising from idle thinking that usually goes on in a mind not under control. I was fully in the moment and not at the mercy of simmering fears kindling an accumulative past.

It must have been two in the morning before we eventually danced, kissed and skipped our way back down the narrow cobbled streets. Then rounding a corner it happened. We crashed into three men and a woman who were walking up the steep incline. Their faces were towards the ground and they did not see us coming. The impact caused one of them to almost fall over. While Ángel was apologizing to them I suddenly found myself face to face with my father. Both of us were shocked by the unexpected encounter. I was literally speechless and he was the first to speak.

"Jesus, Julie! What are you doing here?"

For a moment I could not reply. Then everything flashed through my mind in that instant. Although Mar had said he was living in Granada, yet he was the last person I had expected to see there that night. Knowing his lifestyle he could have been anywhere in the world at that very moment. My strength returned and without the slightest emotion in my voice I heard myself sharply replying;

"I am with my friend and we are going to a disco. Sorry we cannot delay."

"Hang on, Julie! I need to talk to you. Tell me where are you staying?" he queried with urgency in his voice.

"If you want to see me then see me tomorrow," I said while cutting him off abruptly.

"Where, Julie?"

"At Plaza Isabel, six o'clock," I managed to reply through the lingering shock.

"Jesus, Julie. I'll be there. I have to talk to you."

Ángel was still standing there as I grabbed his hand and pulled him away. We resumed our skipping all the way down without stopping again until we had reached the Grand Via. But instead of the previous carefree nature of the skipping it was now an action of fleeing.

"Who is that man?" Ángel inquired when he had finally caught his breath.

"He was Mar's last lover. He is the one who had caused all her problems."

"Why do you think he needs to see you?"

"Not that it matters, but I can only suppose he is anxious to tell me his side of the story."

"Do you think it's wise to see him, Julie?"

"Perhaps not, but I had better see him anyway rather than wondering about him."

We lingered for a while longer around the cathedral where we kissed many times in the nooks and crannies of the narrow little streets. Then we made our way back to our love-nest and allowed our bodies to do the talking for the rest of the night.

At twelve in the morning Ángel had to go back on duty. He had not expected it to be that way; two of the doctors were out sick and there was nothing he could do to avoid it. But it could have been worse, he had been on call since six in the morning but luckily the phone did not ring. At eleven we took a shower and less than five minutes later we were back in bed making love again. At twelve o'clock we were still making love when the phone finally rang and swept him away from my arms.

I lazed there for most of the day allowing my body to savour the warmth and sensuality of his presence still lingering in the bed sheets. At four in the afternoon he rang, telling me he hoped to be back before midnight.

Then I made my way back to the hostel where I changed into a pair of jeans, a sweatshirt and jacket in preparation for the meeting with my father. I had managed not to let any thought of it enter my mind to invade on the intimacy between Ángel and myself during our night and morning together. This had not been difficult for me. After all, I did have the privilege of being shown how to control the mind by the alchemist, and through my previous experience of doing the opposite I had finally learned my lesson. What he had shown me in those four evenings was now faithfully guiding me through each moment, and it is still giving me the strength to hold on as I stand here alone facing the dawn about to explode this coming day of reckoning upon me.

JULIE

He was sitting alone on a street bench by the fountain in Plaza Isabel La Católica when I arrived. The first thing that struck me was the dark glasses. There was no real change, he was still hiding behind them. As I approached I noticed a small shoulder bag on the seat beside him. When he saw me he jumped to his feet. His first reaction was to embrace me, but he felt my coldness and he pulled himself back. He put out his hand, but I put mine in the air, as I demanded what was he doing in Granada.

"I could ask you the same question, Julie!" he replied with a hint of sarcasm in his voice.

"Look, Father! I'm not swallowing your bullshit anymore. I know what you have been up to with Mar. I know of the problems you have caused her."

He did not even appear shocked as he merely brushed it aside with the casual remark;

"Well! Little girls shouldn't play with fire if they can't handle it, should they now?"

It instantly showed me he had no compassion whatsoever in his heart. He had used and abused my friend like a disposable commodity. I had to fight very hard against flying into a rage and losing control of my posture. But try as I did, I could not escape it; the anger had me consumed. I could hardly control the quivering in my voice when I aggressively demanded;

"Tell me about Mar. What is your side of the story? What did you do to her?"

He snapped back in my face; "What about her! She's dead, isn't she? That's all I know about her."

I had to stop and count to ten to let the fury die down. It was almost impossible to restrain. I looked around me and thankfully nothing was in sight that would have sufficed for a weapon. Otherwise I would have killed him there and then on the spot. But I was well aware that losing myself to a rage could only be counterproductive. I was conscious of the alchemist's wisdom in my heart and it, not myself, was still in control of the situation. After all, he was still my father. He may not have been fully to blame and I felt it my duty to give him the benefit of the doubt.

"How do you know she is dead?" I asked.

In exasperation he threw his arms in the air in the manner that I had done when I first approached him.

"Look here, Julie! What's eating you? I came here to see you, not talk about somebody else."

"Why do you want to see me? What reason could you possibly have?"

"Why do I want to see you! Because you're my daughter, for Christ sake!"

"Your daughter!" I exclaimed. "How could you have a bull's notion about what it means to have a daughter! You are a murderer, a brutal, cold-blooded murderer! There is no way a daughter could be part of that!"

"For Christ sake! Will you cool down, Julie. I'm here because I want to see you. I want to get to know you as my daughter. I know I wasn't there for you when you were a child. But it wasn't my fault. It was your mother who locked me out of your life."

Now he was blaming my mother for his brutality. This man was not capable of taking any responsibility for his own shortcomings. Maura had warned me rightly. How much lower could he possibly sink? I knew there was no use wasting any more of my energy on him. He was obviously beyond reach.

"Then tell me about Mar," I asked in a tone that showed I had disengaged from him. "Tell me what really happened between you. I want to hear your side of it."

"There is no my side, Julie. Mar had a fix on me. That's about it. But I didn't encourage her."

"Then what about Columbia? You took her with you, did you not?"

I was astutely conscious of the way he had to suddenly catch his breath at the mention of Columbia, even though he tried to cover it by faking a cough. After regaining his defensive he replied;

"No, I didn't! I was there with a friend and she managed to fix things so she could come along."

"What were you doing there?"

"I don't think that's any of your business, Julie."

Again I lost it and I was back in a rage.

"Of course it's my business. My friend has been murdered and I am certain you did it."

"You think I did it! From what I heard she died in London. That's a fair bit from here, you know! I haven't been back there since I last saw you in Earls Court. So how could I be responsible?"

I walked away from him. Again I had to count to ten in my head. As I regained some of my composure I could hear Maura's words in my ears. She was definitely correct. He had me on the end of a string and he was playing me like a yoyo. Obviously, I was too emotionally involved, both with him and with Mar. It was an impossible situation. But I just had to see it through to the end, wherever it was going to take me.

"Tell me about the restaurant you bombed in Columbia."

"What restaurant? I've no idea what you're on about. I fought for a just cause in the IRA. Now that's all behind me. I know nothing about restaurants being bombed."

"Don't bullshit me! Columbia had nothing to do with your so-called just causes! You were both hired killers. That I know! How much did they pay you?"

He gave me a look of exasperated dismay, as though he had no idea what I was trying to say. My God! He appeared so innocent and the only evidence I had was what Mar had told me. Could I be possibly wrong about him, I wondered, as he voiced his reply;

"What's goin' on, Julie? Who has put all this stuff into your head?"

"Mar told me everything before she died. I even know about your South American woman and how you were involved in the explosions in Malaga."

"Jesus, Julie! What do you want from me? Do you want me to be your father?"

"How dare you even to think of being my father! I have no father. I was foolish to ever think I had. You are a stranger to me. You are a killer and you are going to go on killing until someone stops you for good."

"Is that why you're here? To stop me for good?"

"Yes. That is exactly why I am here. As sure as I am life in this body I am going to kill you when I know for certain you are what I think you are."

"Christ! You're some woman, Julie. Boy! I'm really proud of you! The lads back home could well do with someone like you."

He was getting to me. I began to see he was enjoying the fire in my veins. But what shocked me even more, I could feel there was a part of me responding to his way of recognition, despite the fact that he was only seeing me as a potential recruit. That was number one for him. Mar was right. It came before everything else.

He was so intuitively fast, faster than any woman I had ever met. He was facing my anger and shadow boxing with it until he found the spot. He picked it up in an instant and his face softened into a yielding, innocent smile. Now I could see him as a mischievous boy child who merely relished in doing what boys normally do. I had to look away rather than letting him see the sudden gush of love in my eyes.

"Julie, I'm starving," he remarked with his boyish grin. "Can we go somewhere and eat together?"

I was not going to win, not that I wanted to win, I merely wished to verify what Mar had told me. But he was my father after all, and I had to give him the benefit of any doubt still lingering in my mind. I could perceive he was cunning and my womanly instincts were helpless against him. In less than half an hour he had me totally disarmed, even to the point of wanting to believe anything he had to say. After a long pause I finally replied;

"I will sit with you, but I am not going to eat."

"Well, at least that's a start, Julie. Let's play it by ear and see how things will work out."

He led me down to a restaurant on a narrow street close to Plaza del Carmen where a friend of his happened to be the waiter. He introduced me by my name only and I could see how he enjoyed leaving the waiter wondering as to what type of relationship we had. It was obvious he had a huge ego that needed boosting by every opportunity presented to it. I had entered his world of intrigue and, in spite of my better sense, I was actually enjoying being part of it at that moment.

While he was talking to his friend I suddenly became sharply conscious and I found myself looking at the entire situation as the enlightened teacher would have looked. That meant looking directly at my emotional self being played on the strings of attachment I still held for my father. There and then I endeavoured to let everything go and to allow my body to sink deeper and deeper into the heart of the higher consciousness within me. Gradually, the ease of the rising calmness engulfed me and I could inwardly see the intrigue and confusion clearing out from my mind.

Again I heard the echo of the words 'thank you, thank you, thank you' rising to acknowledge the unseen presence of the alchemist guiding me back to the helm of the immediate situation. I was ready. I knew it. The time had come. From that moment forward I was determined there would be nothing but clarity to guide me through whatever was about to occur.

"Have a look at the menu, Julie. There might be something that'll take your fancy."

The hunger suddenly came upon me as I realized I had not eaten anything since morning. The waiter had mentioned the fish of the day was delicious but I decided on a plain salad while my father ordered a steak. Then I sat back in my chair and took stock of the immediate situation.

At long last, after all this time I was sitting down with my father. I had undertaken a course in conflict resolution to help me reach him. I had even set out to learn the Spanish language because of him. Then he had evaded every effort I had made to pin him down. But now, in the end, it was happening and all I was considering in my mind was how I would kill him if I should have to do so. It all seemed so bizarre, so unreal, yet that was the truth of the situation.

I needed to approach things calmly without any emotions being present. I addressed him further;

"Let us get rid of the emotional stuff. Let us speak logically from now on."

"Julie, I don't entertain any emotions. I look at everything logically and I deal with everything logically."

He was right and it shocked me. I had been at the point of exploding at Plaza Isabel. If there had been a poker nearby I would in all probability have used it to kill him. But he had kept his cool, so much so that he even admired my fiery spirit. This admiration for me he had expressed in his way, in his kind of language from his world and it disarmed me completely.

The waiter arrived with the water for me and the house wine he had ordered for himself. It gave me the moment I

needed to regain myself after his last remark of being always logical. But what was I trying to regain? Just more emotional stuff when I clearly looked at it. I began to feel I was not ready to face the truth of this man. I was not good enough to take him on. Then I heard the alchemist's voice coming from somewhere in the back of my brain, just one word of his in response to my thoughts;
"Bullshit!"
My father was being true to the situation but I was only being true to my feelings and emotions still rising up from the confusion going on in my head. I began to realize that I was not there to administer justice; rather it was still part of my own awakening. The alchemist had said it to me quite logically in Temple Bar with the words;
"Do not glorify me. I am just another form of life rattling my bit before you. Do not look for me or think about me when I am no more. Know that whoever stands before you is your teacher. Life ordains it so. Whatever the situation might be, know it is still the one 'I' speaking directly to you. Know there can be nothing separate from 'I'. It has to be so. You do not have to believe me. Indeed, you do not have to believe anything when logically you know it in your heart. Trust this logic. It is sufficient to get you through."
I sat there in silence pondering the alchemist's words without another thought for my immediate company; that was until I was again jolted back to the moment by his unexpected question that came out of the blue. It stunned me for a moment, as it showed that he was actually taking an interest in my life.
"Tell me, Julie, about your job in London. How's it going? By the appearance of things you seem to be doing all right for yourself."
"Yes, everything is fine. I work with good people and they live normal lives," I awkwardly answered.

"I'm delighted to hear that, Julie. Yes! Indeed, I am. I really like to hear that. 'Tis good to be around people who live normal lives!"

He smiled at me again and it was not helping. There was something about him that would cause any woman to fall for him. I could see how Mar did not have a chance. She was literally swept off her feet and carried away by the tide of his charm. He was fully attuned to this and he used it continuously without even realizing he was doing it. I was his daughter and still he was doing it to me. But I had to give him the benefit of the doubt, seeing that the only relationship we ever truly had with each other was that of man and woman.

For a second time he broke the silence.

"Then again, Julie, being around normal people all the time could become very boring. Perhaps, it's a good thing you have me in your life to add a tingle of excitement!"

Jesus! He was talking right into the centre of my femininity! I needed excitement. It was a fact. I could not stand normality. I could not even wait for Ángel to get through his long, drawn-out courtship rituals. I had to strip him naked and get straight to the point. Just like my father, I relished in the action. He was a man of action in every sense of the word. His life was continuously on the move. Even sitting in a restaurant with his daughter would be an uneasy pause for him if there was not something sparking between us.

"Father, there is excitement and there is real excitement," I remarked.

"What do you mean, Julie?"

"Life is continuously a subtle bubbling, or sensation. You can feel it every moment when you are fully tuned into it. Then you do not need to go chasing around the world looking for places to bomb when you have discovered this real excitement within you."

"Oh! I've discovered it, Julie," he instantly replied. "I live my life right on the edge. I have to be fully alert to everything happening around me each moment. 'Tis like living in the jungle. The thing about me is, I know we are still in the jungle, whereas the so-called normal people have totally forgotten it, they have become so caught up in their illusions. Then they are shocked, they are scared out of their wits when the jungle bites back at them. Look at what's happening around the world. It speaks for itself. Take those American tourists for example, like the three sitting behind me."

I could only see Spanish people sitting behind him and, apart from ourselves, I was only hearing Spanish being spoken. There was no sign of any tourists in the restaurant. I wondered if he was playing another one of his tricks. But no, he actually wasn't, I discovered when he guided my attention to take a closer look.

"Look out the window, Julie. Instead of looking through the glass, try and see what is being reflected in the glass."

I did as he told me and sure enough, I could see them. Whenever people walked past on the street outside the window their bodies formed the necessary background for the reflection to be picked up. I could see five Americans sitting at a table around the corner.

"As I was saying, Julie, these are the normal people. But notice how agitated they are. They're annoyed with the waiter because they've finished eating and now they want to pay. But the waiter is more concerned about serving the food to the other customers. They think their time is more important than the others being served. See how they only care about themselves. That's all that matters to them. But the waiter understands their normality and he doesn't let it affect him. You might have noticed, Julie, how the Spanish are far more intelligent. They are far sharper than these cumbersome yanks."

He was speaking to me by example and it amazed me how he held the conversation totally to the present. I was receiving no indoctrinations from him. He was looking directly at facts and only drawing my attention to facts. The alchemist was the only other person who had spoken to me like this before. I was beginning to see that my father was no ordinary man. He had won my attention.

"You do not like Americans then?" I probed.

"I didn't say that Julie. I'm merely using the three who are seated behind me as an example."

"You mean, the five Americans, Father."

"Look again, Julie. There's only three of them. The other two you're seeing is merely a reflection in the mirror behind their table."

I looked closely and he was right. But I had to focus quite hard to make out the difference between the real and the reflected. He had seen all this in a mere glance and I never even noticed his eyes anywhere else but on me. Phew! This man was something else and he was not even doing this to impress me.

"You know Julie, Americans in general are just the same as the Irish or the Spanish in general."

"What about the British?" I injected.

"I don't see any British in the restaurant, Julie. Do you?"

I felt like a child being the first day at school. He was attentive to the immediate situation exactly in the way the alchemist had illustrated. I was even beginning to wonder could he have been that enlightened man in Temple Bar in another one of his disguises.

"Julie, I'm just pointing out the stupidity of us all when we fail to open our eyes. Like those tourists, for example, they cannot see themselves like the waiter in his clarity sees them. They will go back to wherever they have come from with such stories like Spanish waiters are dumb. They'll continue until they have condemned the whole of Spain, then all of Mexico and Latin America as well."

"I see what you mean." I said.

"But do you really see it, Julie," he wagered.

"These people have completely forgotten the jungle. They try to build up a social system to protect themselves from reality and then they try to live out their illusions in their fairy worlds. Have you noticed how shocked they become when the real world crashes in on top of them? History has illustrated the money disaster of 1929 when Wall Street went to the wall! They had been so carried away with their illusions they were jumping out the top windows of tower blocks rather than face the reality. The same thing has happened again and 'Ground Zero' they've named it! Which only shows they're back to scratch! They'll have to go through it all over again and again and again until they eventually wake up!"

With his last remark his logic fell from its perch as far as I was concerned and I felt I had to intervene.

"The destruction of the twin towers was a terrible disaster. It cannot be condoned. You are aware that thousands of innocent people were killed."

"I agree with you, Julie. The innocent are dying because people in general are unwilling to face up to reality. But we shouldn't take anything out of context. The mental thinking of the world that brought about the crash in the stock markets of 1929 is no different to the mental thinking of today. The effects of it might appear different, but the cause is exactly the same. The ignorance is exactly the same."

Again I was stunned at how close he was to the words of the alchemist. He too had spoken about the ignorance of the world and how we all need to wake up. I was now having a problem trying to find that all-important, fine line between them both. I pressed him further.

"What do you think is the cause of this ignorance, Father?"

"It's not what I think, Julie. I've discovered many moons ago that all thinking is stupid. I used to think that Ireland should be an united country. But the Prods in the North think differently. The world can see how stupid and ignorant they are, how they're stuck in the past. We can see it all on the newsreels, their marches of ignorant aggression and hate. But they can't see it themselves. Why? Simply because they're totally obsessed with the beliefs and opinions that blind them. The others who want a united Ireland are exactly the same. I've discovered at the end of the day that it's nothing to do with nationalism or unionism. Rather it's all to do about ignorance in general and people's unwillingness to face up to reality."

I was amazed at what I was hearing. I had not expected anything like this from him. Before that moment I had been naive enough to imagine that terrorists were uneducated people. I had looked upon them as those who only knew things about bombs and acts of terror and violence. But now I was witnessing my preconceived notions being blown out of the water.

I had listened to highly educated people in the conflict resolution course, some of them were visiting professors from the United States and Canada, but I had never heard anyone before this coming so close to the intelligence of the teacher who had visited Temple Bar.

At that moment my father was touching on it as he spoke about Ireland. He was renouncing all the causes of conflict as being nothing other than ignorance expressing itself through opposing opinions. He illustrated it through the visible stupidity of the Unionists including the Nationalists as well. I knew I had to be careful. He was speaking clearly and all he had said was absolutely true. But I needed to stay focused on the full picture relating to this man sitting before me. Otherwise I too could be sucked into his mercenary world. I tried to break his flow with the simple question;

"Perhaps, that is true for Ireland, but surely not for the rest of the world?"

His response was immediate and accurate, which amazed me even further.

"Look, Julie! Ireland is the microcosm for the rest of the world. It is the perfect case study and I know you've studied it yourself. The problem is with the studiers. They are looking for the wrong thing. Why can't they see it? I'll tell you why! They're acting out of the same stupidity that caused the idiots to jump from the top windows in 1929! Nobody is studying ignorance. Indeed, nobody can until they have fully seen through the ignorance in themselves! Look at the ignorance of the politicians in the White House, instead of looking at their own insularity, instead of facing up to that fact, they are bombing the fuck out of the rest of the world!"

I did not need to interrupt him again. I could hear he was making sense. But I was also bearing in mind what the alchemist had told me. My only duty was to stay looking and listening without being swayed one way or another, particularly when in the presence of someone who likes to hear himself talking.

Then Mar flashed through my mind and the picture of her body floating in the Thames sent a shiver up my spine. Suddenly I realized I was not there for another lesson in conflict resolution and I should not allow myself to be so easily side-tracked. What happened to Mar was by far a more serious issue. I needed to interrupt him and get him back to my questions relating to the trauma and death of my friend. But it was not easy for me to guide the focus of the discussion. Not having his skill of engagement, this caused me to awkwardly intervene in his flow.

"I cannot see how what you are saying links up to the terrorist attacks in New York," I blurted out with the sole intention of breaking his vernacular display.

"Julie! To every action there's an equal and opposite reaction. This is an established scientific fact, is it not? Surely, everybody knows what happened in New York was a direct reaction to their own foreign policies. At least everyone outside of North America knows it."

"Well I do not see it that way."

"Julie! Are you trying to rise me or what? I know you're an intelligent woman!"

"No. I am not trying to rise you. But I refuse to be swayed into thinking that such atrocities can be excused by your theories about ignorance. I experienced these tactics being used by one of the Catholic priests back in my school in Dublin. I could see how his indoctrination had caused such confusion in the minds of my friends."

He raised his eyebrows in a manner of exclamation. He did not even have to ask what I was doing in a Catholic school, as I freely told him.

"Don't look so surprised," I continued, "they could not afford to send me to the Jewish enclosure, or maybe they were ashamed of my apparent madness, so I was packed off to the local ex-convent instead. There I learned much about your Catholic background. You know, dear Father, that priest tried to fuck with my friends. He did not come near me, for he knew I was different. He knew I was free from his indoctrination. One of the girls in the school, she was only fifteen when she killed herself. He was the chaplain of the convent and he had been abusing her since she was twelve. But it never came out because the bishop had him transferred the week after her death."

He threw me a look of bewilderment and, leaning back in his seat, he asked; "Why are you telling me this? What has that to do with our conversation?"

"That priest, he was screwing my friend. Now she is dead. Father, were you screwing my friend?"

"Jesus! Are we back to that again? I thought we had left it behind us at Plaza Isabel!"

"No, we have not left it behind us. Like you said, we are only dealing in facts. Nobody challenged that priest. But I am challenging you now. So, can you answer my question please?"

"Look, Julie! I've already told you that Mar had a fixation on me and she wouldn't give up. That was her problem. Surely you can understand that!"

"Of course I understand it. But that is not what I asked you. I will ask you again and please do not avoid it. Were you screwing my friend?"

"What do you want me to say?"

"Just the simple truth. Now, will you answer me simply please!" I shouted at him in exasperation.

"Mar and I had a thing going for a while. But it was over in a couple of weeks," he replied in a way of closing.

"Look, for Christ sake! Be straight with me. Can you not answer me yes or no?"

"Life is not like that, Julie. For example, can I ask you something? Were you screwing your boyfriend last night and this morning?"

"No I certainly was not."

"Then what were ye doing, Julie? You don't need to tell me. It was more than obvious ye were heading straight for a bed. I haven't heard of any disco joints in Calle de la Duquesa off Plaza Trinidad!"

"You followed us!" I exclaimed in shock.

"I didn't need to follow you. I happened to be going that way, Julie."

No, you were not! You were going up the hill when we were coming down."

"But I was only saying goodnight to my friends. I live just two streets away from where ye went."

He was right. I remembered Mar mentioning that his flat was close to hers. The terrible moment that caused her hemorrhaging flashed through my mind that instant. What a shock it must have been for her, walking in on top of him and his Columbian woman like she did. That must have been the final blow for her. My eyes fell on his steak knife and I had to fight against the urge to grab it. Again I was silently counting to ten while he was refilling his glass. I felt he was aware of my sudden mood-swing, for he kept his eyes turned away.

It suddenly hit me that Mar, Ángel and my father were only streets away from one another. It shocked me to realize what a small world it was that was playing itself out about me. I had to recompose myself.

He had successfully avoided giving me an answer to my question. Then I began to think I might have asked it wrongly, so I decided to rephrase it another way.

"Did you and Mar have an affair?" I broke through the silence.

But again he went into avoidance by playing on the words I was using.

"Julie, affair is a very loose word. You know it can be interpreted in many ways. For example, there's a strong affair between the Americans and the Afghanistan people. You could say there's an affair between the Bushes and the Iraqi oil wells! Bill Clinton had an affair with Monica! Or did he? The media knocked at least a year out of that one trying to figure it out! But are we any the wiser? Obviously not! Now it's all old hat! So tell me, Julie. What exactly do you mean by this word affair?"

Again I lost my composure. He was just playing with me while I was desperately trying to steer clear of my volatile emotions. He was making it impossible for me to keep a lid on my outbursts of rage. It seemed as though he wanted to experience a physical assault. But I was determined not to afford him that satisfaction.

"Fuck you, Father! Do not mess around with me! You have no idea how dangerous I can be!"

"Wow! You're a beautiful woman, Julie; full of fire and vigour. I love what I see in you."

"Do not think you can disarm me so easily. Your tactics will only work once. Now answer the question. Did you have sex with Mar?"

"Oh! That's easy to answer. Of course I had sex with Mar. She had a fixation on me and she wanted me, which I've been trying to tell you. I'm a normal man and who am I to deny a woman her pleasure!"

He was playing between directness and evasiveness and I had failed to see it. Not only was he weakening my determination but also he was undermining my confidence in myself by making me feel I was not being honestly direct in my questions. He was far too skilled and free from emotional encumbrance for me to handle. He had almost succeeded in making me feel that I was the one who was hedging around the issue. Again I had to pause and re-gather myself before I went further.

"Did you give her money to have an abortion?"

"No, I did not! To the best of my knowledge Mar was never pregnant."

"Did you give her money for anything in particular?"

"Julie, that's no concern of yours."

"Yes it is. I know you gave her money and I need to know the reason why you found it necessary to give it to her."

"You gave me money, Julie. You gave me a lot of money in London. What were your reasons for giving it to me?"

Again he was straight to the point and I had to struggle with myself to respond; "I gave it to you because I wanted to help you escape from your past."

JULIE

"Well, that's your answer, Julie. Mar also needed help and you did indicate that I should pass on the good deed rather than returning it to you."

It was true. I had told him that. But I was still feeling very agitated with him. When I examined myself more closely I discovered the reason for my annoyance. I had already put him on trial and convicted him on Mar's account of what was supposed to have happened between them. Now he was not fitting into the picture I had already created in my head. I was beginning to feel a little disgusted with myself. I had the privilege of being with an enlightened teacher, yet my father was the one who was appearing to be true to the situation. Before the confrontation with him I had been convinced that I was true to life and now he was showing me different.

When I thought about it I discovered that Mar had not told me herself that she had had an abortion. I had only assumed it and then she had expanded on my assumption. She did say she almost bled to death after being butchered. But that could have meant a dozen and one things. Now I was not sure about anything anymore. I felt that my father was being open with me and I could see his surprise when I mentioned about the abortion. It seemed as though this was the first time he had heard anything about it. There was only one of two things he could possibly be relating to it. He had to be either extremely honest or extremely cunning and I had to find out.

The waiter returned, gave me the menu and asked what we would like for desert. While they were chatting in Spanish I put my hand in his bag on the chair by the table where he had left it. I could feel there were two books, a packet of cigarettes, a lighter and a wallet of coins inside. I poked a little deeper and I came across a mobile phone. There was another hard object that I managed to get my fingers around and I pulled it out without looking. I could feel it was a gun. I slipped it between my legs on the chair and I put my napkin over it until the chance arose to slip it into my handbag. I had no idea what I could do with it. I knew absolutely nothing about guns. As a matter of fact it was the first one I had ever held in my hand.

Then something caused me to tune myself into their Spanish conversation and I could hardly believe what I was hearing. Quite obviously, my father was totally unaware of the fact that I could understand the language. It made me very nervous because I suddenly realized I had already overheard too much without even paying proper attention to what I was hearing. They were both terrorists and they were openly talking about their future plans while they were under the assumption that I had no real understanding of what they were saying. I realized I was in a very dangerous situation and I needed to protect my vulnerability.

When my father finally looked in my direction I asked him what the waiter was saying relating to the menu, not letting him sense that I understood. Luckily, he was so carried away with his world he did not notice my uneasiness. He explained what deserts were available. I was safe, his astute alertness had let him down. He still had no idea that I had understood everything. They had been talking about a device being prepared to coincide with a meeting of European ministers soon to take place in Madrid. I noticed how the waiter was a little apprehensive of me as they talked. Clearly, he did not want anyone outside the organization to know that he was an activist with ETA. If he had the slightest idea that I had understood then I would be in very serious danger.

Again I interrupted them by asking my father to explain what it said on the menu while I shook my head at the waiter with the innocent words;

"Excuse me, no comprendo."

This seemed to put him at ease and after he noted my order for chocolate cake, which I did not want, never mind not being able to eat any more in such a situation, they resumed their conversation in Spanish. They had one new recruit whom my father felt should be introduced to some action and the waiter thought it might be a little too soon for her. My father disagreed by stressing the point that action was the only way to tie her in to the active unit. Otherwise she could stray and that would be dangerous for everyone else concerned. He went on to say that care was always needed, that this would avoid being later burdened with the extra task of having to clean up loose ends, like had to be so recently done in London.

He was directly referring to Mar. I instantly knew it, even though her name was not mentioned. Now it was definite, she had been murdered by them. I could see that my father was giving all the instructions and I had just eaten from the same table. My stomach went into a knot. He told the waiter to meet him with the others the following night at ten in a place called Gonzo's café. He was obviously in a command position exactly like Mar had said. I was both stunned and sickened. He had ordered her death. I had all the proof I needed but still I felt powerless to act.

A waitress arrived with the cake and the black coffee my father had ordered. Next he reached for his bag and lit himself a cigarette. He offered me one but I shook my hand indicating that I did not smoke. When they resumed their conversation my frustration caused me to write a note on a piece of napkin saying: 'Thanks for the gun, next time we meet I am going to use it'. I thought of putting the note into his bag but my better judgment decided against my anger. They were difficult moments for me. I wanted to explode upon him in a final confrontation but I was also very aware of the burning fire in the centre of my chest. I clearly knew this was being triggered through emotional nervousness and this would impair my actions. It was not the time.

A dragonfly landed on the edge of the table. It seemed to have prematurely come out of its winter hibernation and it appeared quite docile. My gaze fell upon it for some time as I continued to listen to their plans relating to the future action. Then, without thinking my father slowly scorched its wings with his cigarette. When I looked into his face I could see the delight he was having. It was an absolute pleasure for him being able to inflict such agony upon the defenseless little creature. This he did without realizing he was showing me his hidden character as he continued giving orders to the waiter. Slowly he scorched off its tail, while still not killing it outright. At that moment the burn marks on Mar's body flashed through my mind and I could feel my stomach heave. I knew I had to get out of there before I got sick. I excused myself in the middle of their discussion and said I had to go, that I was not feeling too good.

"When will I see you again?" he demanded in English as he broke off from his fluency in the other language. He was so caught up with his conversation that he did not even notice how all my softening towards him had been decimated. I even had to check on myself because I almost replied in Spanish.

"Don't worry. I will be in contact." I told him.

"But how?" He asked with a question mark all over his face.

I realized I was playing his games and I suddenly did not like myself for it.

"The same place at the same time tomorrow?"

"I can't do it tomorrow, Julie. I have something else on," he replied.

Of course I knew that, but I was being overcautious not to let him know that I knew.

"Then Tuesday evening, would that be okay?" I suggested.

"Yeah! That would be fine, Julie. I'll see you then."

With that I left ten Euros on the table to cover the cost of my meal while using my glass to bring a quick death to the suffering insect. I said goodnight to them both and made my exit.

Ángel was waiting for me in his apartment when I phoned. But I was nervous to return there because my father knew exactly where he lived, and I knew he would come looking for me when he would eventually discover I had taken his gun. So I invited Ángel to stay with me in the hostel, telling him that I had booked a double room with both of us in mind, suggesting the change would be good for him and it would help him get his thoughts off his work. He immediately agreed and we arranged to meet at the opposite side of town in Plaza Einstein in half an hour. Granada being a very compact city, I wanted to be absolutely certain my father would not spot us. I got a taxi across after making sure I was not being followed. When Ángel arrived on foot I walked out of the shadows to meet him. We embraced and kissed. Then we linked each other to the taxi rank at the far side of the square and I instructed the driver to take us to the door of the hostel.

Ángel was hungry. He wanted to stop somewhere to eat. But I felt uneasy about being in any place public. I knew he would be searching all over for me once he discovered I had his gun. The situation was far too dangerous. I had taken the first step towards concluding it all and now there was no going back. Perhaps, that is why I took the gun in the first place and almost went as far as placing a note in his bag. Rather than merely wanting him to know how serious the situation really was, more importantly I had wanted to impose the absolute obligation upon my faltering self to conclude the matter for good.

Ángel was innocently unaware of everything and I knew it was not the time for us to be together. Nonetheless, I had come to Granada solely to be with him, until my father had invaded the scene with his unexpected presence. Now everything had changed. Not alone was it my duty to Mar but also to all the others about to be led into his clutches that was now facing me directly. Even my duty to my father, whatever it might entail, also had to be honoured right to its end. This was the fact of the matter and the alchemist had made it clear that being honest to life means facing the fact and being true to the situation. There was no other way, whether he had meant taking it this far or not. Were I to shrink from it like a coward then I would not be true to life, I would be something else, even worse than my father, and that is not putting judgment upon him. He was doing exactly what life had set out for him to do and he was doing it with the utmost efficiency. Thanks to the enlightened teacher I was neither condoning him for his activities nor was I condemning him.

Neither was I relying in any way upon my feelings. I could see how volatile they were; one moment I found myself loving him dearly with all my heart, the next moment I found myself hating him with all my might. I was also conscious not to be swayed by my likes and dislikes. I liked the way he moved, the way he talked, the way he flirted with me, and I really liked how naturally he exploded the mediocre. It would be thrilling to live in his space, to dance through many lives by his side, if only he was not a cold-blooded killer.

The alchemist was the wisest man I had ever met, except for my father. They were both so close in appearance to my eyes that at times I was failing to register which one I was receiving. Then again, I heard the alchemist saying not to be led astray by appearances. According to him there is but one 'I' in all things. It is the same 'I' that is looking out through the crow's eyes as the 'I' who is now writing or reading these words.

Having realized the depth of this I reasoned with myself it was not important whether or not my father and the alchemist were branching from the one and same spirit. It was only important that I did not personify the situation. I can now see the reason for my hesitation, my shrinking away from facing my duty. It was clearly due to my attachment to him.

If I am obliged to kill him, I thought to myself, then that in itself is not my problem. I was clear about that; killing was not my problem, that is, should it have been my duty to kill. The problem was in the personification of the act. This was the source of my despondency and this I was obliged to overcome.

It flashed before me that moment. The greatness of the enlightened teacher and the utter abusiveness of life being displayed by the world had all been condensed in my father's character. Whether he had come to realize it or not, he was actually sacrificing himself for the betterment of my own enlightenment. No wonder he was having those nightmares about my name when he was a child, like he had exclaimed when he first met me through the wire mesh in that prison.

The alchemist had said it most clearly when he reminded those of us present that all things are interconnected, interrelated. Indeed, the relationship between my father and me was so close that I could say he was my masculine half. In the greater reality behind existence it is even closer than that! He is me! We are one and the same! Like the alchemist is me, there can be no distance between us. The deeper we retract from the surface expression of the living forms the closer we become until eventually we dissolve into the one 'I' contracting into the nothingness.

Ángel mentioned the name of a good restaurant. He has been on his feet for most of the day. What was occurring within me did not include him at that moment and there was no way possible for me to bring him up to that speed. It just does not happen like that and I realized I must slow down in order to be with him. I reminded him that the hostel has a good restaurant and they also do room service. He was more than pleased with the opportunity of the added intimacy we could have together.

It worked out a beautiful night for us both. Dinner in the bedroom was most enjoyable and I refrained from taking any wine. I needed to be totally clear and to savour each moment as though it was going to be my last. After eating we came up on this roof terrace to savour the night view of the city and the distant mountains. We talked into the early hours. Then we made the most wonderful love. Ángel later commented that he sensed the strangest feeling coming form me. It seemed to him as though I was making love for the very last time. He spoke through tears of joy and pain in his eyes. I knew he was right. I had been so present I was astutely aware of being in the heart of the divine consciousness simultaneously permeating all forms of life. But still there was a nagging anxiety in the background that kept re-presenting itself. Several times Ángel had to ask if I was all right. Being so close to me he could easily sense the disturbance. I had tried to put everything relating to my father out of my head for the night, but the disturbance remained. Then I remembered something the alchemist had said relating to this;

"Tomorrow is already done. You have even finished your life. It is already over, even as it appears to begin. But right now you can only see yourself in the doing of it from moment to moment. Know that your future is equally the cause of your current situation as is your past. The actual fulfilling of your duty tomorrow already affects today."

Ángel was due back on duty at eight in the morning and my connecting flight was leaving at one in the afternoon for Madrid. But I knew I would not be on it, even though I had planned nothing to the contrary. Being pinned like a butterfly to the web of the spider two worlds were about to collide. The spider still slept, but I knew once he awakes to another day that was to be the end. I was trapped in his lair and there could be no escape from what lay ahead.

We talked about the future. Ángel suggested if I could not bring myself to live in Granada then he would improve on his English and find a position in London. I fully agreed with him that improving his English would be a good thing for his future, particularly in the light of the fact that so much medical research is being carried out in English-speaking countries. But I felt I had to advise him against making any other decisions about coming to work in London until we got to know each other better.

He felt that we knew each other perfectly well and I had to remind him that sexual intimacy is only a small part of getting to know someone. Much more time would be needed and that time he could also spend improving his English. His next break was to be in the middle of May and I hoped to have the same week free to be with him in Paris. But, of course, I was not taking the more immediate situation facing me into account. I could only focus on the assumption that I would get through it, as far as Ángel was concerned. Anything else was far too painful to even consider. Not alone that, but I clearly knew, thanks to the alchemist, that I should not try to pre-empt anything relating to the final outcome of what was immediately ahead. Meeting in Paris was a wonderful suggestion and this is how we left it when we finally parted.

Then I sat there alone in my room facing the greatest crisis in my life. I had to figure it out. I knew I was not going to the airport, I was clear about that. I looked at my flight ticket. It was non-changeable. I would have to forfeit the loss. Could I book another flight for the following day? Would I be alive on the following day? I could not be sure of anything.

I asked myself why I was staying. Was it to kill my father? No, I could not do such a thing. Was it to reason with him? Obviously not, there was no way he would be willing to change. He was a leader and it was now clear that he had been a leader in the IRA. As a result of the political agreements between the opposing factions the commanders had disbanded most of their active members, but without undertaking proper debriefing procedures. My father and others like him, I was pretty sure, were discarded by the peacemakers and left as loose canons rambling the globe looking for any kind of similar action they had become used to doing in their past. This had become their life, their one and only reflection.

The peacemakers seem to be only capable of seeing what is on the surface of things. The necessity for going deeper into the play of the psyche is still being overlooked. I am sure there can never be any real peace while this continues to be ignored. Perhaps, this is why the patchwork keeps ripping apart.

I took out the handgun and decided to examine it carefully. I managed to open the chamber only to discover it was fully loaded. It shocked me. Last night it was just another object, like the mobile phone, the cigarette lighter and the books. But now it suddenly struck me that it was a deadly weapon and I had been carrying it in my bag all night. But I needed to familiarize myself with it. I took out the bullets and then I examined the shooting mechanism. It was very simple. There was a safety catch and a trigger. Everything else was automatic. I reloaded it again, made sure that the safety catch was on, after that I wiped it clean and put it back in my bag.

Would I have to use it? I was not sure. I had no idea what I might have to do. I only knew I was pinned to the task immediately facing me, whatever that might entail, even though I was helplessly feeling like the butterfly pinned to the spider's web. Nonetheless, I had to trust life and I had to trust my response.

Then the despondency re-presented itself once again for its final attack. I pondered, what am I doing here? A voice in my head told me to pack my bags, dispose of the gun and catch my flight back to London as previously planned. My father and his killer friends were none of my concern. The authorities could deal with them in their own way. Why, I could phone the police and tell them about the meeting in Gonzo's café and that would surely let me off the hook.

But would it serve the situation?

No doubt my father would end up in prison again, this time for the rest of his life. I could not help but recall the terrible conditions I saw when I visited him in Wakefield. This made me realize it was not possible for me to escape my duty, whatever that duty might turn out to be in the end. I felt there could be no way out other than a final showdown. This is what the situation demanded and the alchemist had reminded me again and again to be true to the situation and not to myself or my personal feelings. Whatever my father might have done, I felt he did not deserve such dreadful punishment as going back behind bars. No matter how I churned it around in my head I had to finally accept there was no other way, I would have to deal with it all by myself.

The room phone rang. It was the man at reception asking me whether I was leaving that day or staying on longer. That decided it. Without even thinking, I told him I was staying for at least one more night and possibly more. But still the doubts and despondency continued to play on my mind. No matter how much I tried to get hold of myself I still could not stop the mental process from going round in circles. I had tried every way possible to escape from what was laying directly ahead of me. But the more I looked at it the more I could see there was no escape. I had to go through with whatever had to be done. Not only that, but now it was clear to me I would have to face the stark reality that very night. It seemed as though my world was coming to an end and I felt quite cheated.

Had I not endured enough misfortune in my childhood? Had not my early teenage years been hell enough?

Why should the circumstances of other people's lives be drawing into this?

Oh, how I wished at that moment to be free to continue with my new life in London.

Why could I not just leave there and then? After all, Mar was only a recent friend. Not alone that, but this man was only a recent father figure whom I had compulsively attracted into my life. I would have relented if it were not for the alchemist's words echoing behind the torment going round and round in my head.

"You cannot escape from your duty, whatever it may be in the moment. Try if you must, but sooner or later it will re-present itself in the circumstances of your life, in all probability greater and more fearsome than before."

I tried to reason with myself that my duty was to return to London, to my obligations to Maura and to my work at the boutique. But it was not the real truth and I knew it. I was in the centre of this terrible scene being acted out on my stage of existence and my duty was clearly to see it through right to its end.

I walked down to Puerta Real and asked a taxi driver to take me to Gonzo's café. He had never heard of the place. I asked another and he too did not know. Neither did the third or the fourth. I went up to Plaza Nueva and asked a gipsy girl who was begging for money on the street. She knew where it was and she told me that Gonzo's was only a nickname for it. I walked through a maze of narrow streets and sure enough the café she had mentioned was there. I went into a bookshop a few doors down and asked the woman serving if she could direct me to Gonzo's. She confirmed it was the next café just a few doors up. That was it. Now I was sure.

It was the longest day I had ever experienced. Each minute was like an hour as I lay on the bed in the hostel waiting for night. I was not hungry, but I knew the body needed sustenance to be strong enough. At seven in the evening I went down to the restaurant and had a plate of assorted cheese and salad. Then I returned to the room, lay down again and tried to relax. But I fell into a troubled sleep. Suddenly I awakened to the darkness. I looked at the time. It was ten-thirty. Panic set in. It was the same panic I had experienced in Dublin on that night when Jonathan had arrived back home unexpectedly. I had a flash back to that explosive moment when I came so close to killing him with a poker. If it had not been for my mother stopping me on time I would now be surely locked away for murder. But that moment was an explosion of rage. This night was different. Now there was a balance mingled with the panic and a sense of calculation about it that had not been there before. I tried to get a better hold of myself by focusing upon my breathing like the alchemist and Andréa had demonstrated. Gradually I was aware of a relative calm returning to my body and I put all thoughts of being late right out of my mind. I put on my jacket and gloves. I put the gun in my pocket with the safety catch off and placed my bag over my shoulder. Stepping in front of the mirror I viewed myself. Yes, I could see I was ready. Then I left the hostel and walking briskly without being hurried. Within ten minutes I was on the street of the café. This was it, the grand climacteric of my life.

I opened the door and walked inside. The café was long and narrow and it was practically empty, just two men at one table and a middle-aged couple at another. Down at the end I saw them, the waiter of the previous night, the Latin American woman who had met me in Earls Court, another younger woman and my father. A sudden wave of fear gripped my body. My legs started to tremble and I had to internally speak to myself.

"If I am about to die then all I can do is accept it. I must accept it totally."

This is what the enlightened teacher had taught me when he spoke to us about purity in action. I heard him say;

"Complete acceptance without any attachment to the outcome is the only way to go into any action. Do not contaminate it with attachment."

This was the only way I could be totally unhindered. Not being attached to an outcome, I would therefore be ready to do in an instant whatever the situation might demand me to do, this being the purity he mentioned.

They spotted me. The Columbian woman was first to see me, then my father, followed by the younger woman's attention and last the waiter's. The strength returned to my legs and they carried me unswervingly to their table. The four had fallen into a stunned silence. I addressed them only in Spanish. My father's face turned white. The Latin American moved her hand and my father held her arm. Now I was speaking directly to him while keeping my focus fixed equally on all four.

"Sir, this is your doing. You have condemned yourself. I know I cannot redeem you. I could have called the police and have you locked away for good. But you are my father and that I could not do. You have given me no other choice. I am not even asking you to forgive me for what I must now do. I merely want you to see it is the only way."

In a flash the Latin American had a gun in her hand and I heard the shot. But my father had pushed her arm up in the air. I was aware of the shattering glass directly behind me as the bullet ripped through a mirror. In that moment the gun was in my hand. I was not even aware I had taken it out of my pocket never mind pulling the trigger. All I saw was the hole suddenly appear in the centre of her forehead and she slumping onto the table. The waiter moved with a knife and the second shot hit him in the chest just as the knife ripped through my jacket. Then the table was in the air knocking me backwards. The gun fell from my hand and my father grabbed it before it had hit the ground. I felt the pain in my body as I smashed against the marble floor. In an instant I was half on my feet again with the waiter's knife in my left hand and my father was pointing the gun directly at me. But he hesitated for a second as he called my name. In that second the knife pierced through his heart. He crumbled to his knees and fell into my arms. Again he called my name. I saw the shock in his eyes as his body suddenly went limp. Still looking directly at me, my name formed on his lips for a third time. In that instant his body shuddered and I watched him die.

My eyes filled with tears as the finality of death hit me like a thunderbolt. He was gone. He was no more. I hugged him and kissed his forehead. I began to feel the life essence slowly leave his body and somehow I knew it was good. In some strange way I knew it was thanking me for doing what had to be done.

The café filled with an eerie silence. I looked up at the younger woman who still had not moved. She was shaking in terror and I could see she had wet herself. Perhaps, I had just saved her from a similar fate as Mar. It is not for me to know. But somehow I managed to word the warning to her that if she was ever again to get involved with terrorists this is how she would end up. She sat frozen to